A TOWN CALLED HARMONY

Delightful tales that capture the heart of a small Kansas town—and a simple time when love was a gift to cherish . . .

AVAILABLE FROM DIAMOND BOOKS

Dear Reader,

There's a place where life moves a little slower, where a neighborly smile and a friendly hello can still be heard. Where news of a wedding or a baby on the way is a reason to celebrate—and gossip travels faster than a telegraph! Where hope lives in the heart, and love's promises last a lifetime.

The year is 1874, and the place is Harmony, Kansas . . .

A TOWN CALLED HARMONY
COMING HOME

KATHLEEN KANE

Widowed, Libby Taylor came back to Harmony to raise her young son—and to wage a spirited crusade against the evils of alcohol!

He keeps an eye on the local saloon, but Sheriff Travis Miller knows a man likes to kick back and let loose once in a while—and he bends the rules a little when no harm's done . . .

The sheriff remembered Libby as a charming girl who had the whole town wrapped around her finger. Years later, she's as pretty and outspoken as ever—and she's trying to get all of Harmony's women fighting for temperance and storming "The Last Resort." But to the lawman's dismay, that's just the beginning—for soon she comes up with a strategy that turns the town on its ear . . . the women will refuse the men in their beds until they agree to give up their whiskey and beer! But as he gets to know this stubborn beauty, Travis discovers the reason for her fight: she lost her husband to the evils of alcohol. Travis hopes to put an end to this battle of the sexes—and to build a bridge between past sorrows and new desires, as he offers Libby his true and tender love . . .

Welcome to A TOWN CALLED HARMONY . . .

MAISIE HASTINGS & MINNIE PARKER, *proprietors of the boarding house . . . These lively ladies, twins who are both widowed, are competitive to a fault—who bakes the lightest biscuits? Whose husband was worse? Who can say the most eloquent and (to their boarders' chagrin) the longest grace? And who is the better matchmaker? They'll do almost anything to outdo each other—and absolutely everything to bring loving hearts together!*

JAKE SUTHERLAND, *the blacksmith . . . Amidst the workings of his livery stable, he feels right at home. But when it comes to talking to a lady, Jake is awkward, tongue-tied . . . and positively timid!*

JANE CARSON, *the dressmaker . . . She wanted to be a doctor like her grandfather. But the eccentric old man decided that wasn't a ladylike career—and bought her a dress shop. Jane named it in his honor: You Sew and Sew. She can sew anything, but she'd rather stitch a wound than a hem.*

ALEXANDER EVANS, *the newspaperman . . . He runs The Harmony Sentinel with his daughter, Samantha. It took an accident at his press to show Alexander that even a solitary newsman needs love and caring—and he found it in the arms of his lovely bride, Jane Carson.*

JAMES AND LILLIAN TAYLOR, *owners of the mercantile and post office* . . . With their six children, they're Harmony's wealthiest and most prolific family. Now their beautiful daughter Libby has come home again—and she's turned the entire town upside-down!

"LUSCIOUS" LOTTIE McGEE, *owner of "the First Resort"* . . . Lottie's girls sing and dance and even entertain upstairs . . . but Lottie herself is the main attraction at her enticing saloon. And when it comes to taking care of her own cousin, this madam is all maternal instinct.

CORD SPENCER, *owner of "the Last Resort"* . . . Things sometimes get out of hand at Spencer's rowdy tavern, but he's mostly a good-natured scoundrel who doesn't mean any harm. And when push comes to shove, he'd be the first to put his life on the line for a friend.

SHERIFF TRAVIS MILLER, *the lawman* . . . The townsfolk don't always like the way he bends the law a bit when the saloons need a little straightening up. But Travis Miller listens to only one thing when it comes to deciding on the law: his conscience.

ZEKE GALLAGHER, *the barber and the dentist* . . . When he doesn't have his nose in a dime western, the white-whiskered, blue-eyed Zeke is probably making up stories of his own—or flirting with the ladies. But not all his tales are just talk—once he really *was* a notorious gunfighter . . .

Titles by Kathleen Kane

KEEPING FAITH
MOUNTAIN DAWN
SMALL TREASURES

A TOWN CALLED
HARMONY

COMING HOME

Kathleen Kane

DIAMOND BOOKS, NEW YORK

This book is a Diamond original edition,
and has never been previously published.

COMING HOME

A Diamond Book / published by arrangement with
the author

PRINTING HISTORY
Diamond edition / December 1994

All rights reserved.
Copyright © 1994 by Charter Communications, Inc.
This book may not be reproduced in whole or in part,
by mimeograph or any other means, without permission.
For information address: The Berkley Publishing Group,
200 Madison Avenue, New York, NY 10016.

ISBN: 0-7865-0060-3

Diamond Books are published by The Berkley Publishing Group,
200 Madison Avenue, New York, NY 10016.
DIAMOND and the "D" design
are trademarks belonging to Charter Communications, Inc.

PRINTED IN THE UNITED STATES OF AMERICA

10 9 8 7 6 5 4 3 2 1

To my mother, Sallye Carberry,
who taught me everything I know about love.
And through the years, she's been a "Saint"
in more ways than one.
I love you, Mom.

Chapter One

THE EYES OF EVERY MAN IN THE ROOM were on her.

Liberty Taylor Wilder stood perfectly still and let them look their fill. Head high, chin lifted, she waited as a cloud of silence dropped over the smoky barroom. The tinny piano music ceased abruptly. The clink of glass against glass and the solid thump of whiskey bottles slammed down onto tabletops paused. Conversations died in midsentence.

Liberty clenched her hands into fists at her sides. She'd known this wouldn't be easy. But somehow, she hadn't quite expected to feel this . . . conspicuous. Even the blowsy women with trays of drinks held against their generous hips stared at her as if she had two heads.

Slowly, cautiously, she let her gaze move over the shocked faces turned toward her. One by one, the customers whose eyes she met looked away, embarrassed. All, that is, except one man.

When Liberty's gaze locked with Sheriff Travis Miller's, he boldly stared right back at her. In fact, as he lifted his glass of beer in a mock salute, she was certain she saw a hint of amusement in his sharp brown eyes. As an unwanted curl of reaction spiraled through her, a warning bell in the back of her mind rang out loud and clear. Quickly she looked away from him and drew in a long, steadying breath.

No sense in dragging this out any longer than necessary, she told herself firmly. With a determined, if slightly wobbly, step, she started across the wide room. She stopped at the bar and laid her palms flat on the cool, polished surface. Glancing at the bartender, she smiled. "Hello, Charlie. It's good to see you again."

Charlie Thompson looked from her to the uneasy crowd of men behind her and back again. Voice soft, he answered, "Good evening, Liberty. I heard you were back in town—but I certainly didn't expect to see you *here*."

"Life is full of surprises." Even *she* heard the bitter note in her tone and smiled even brighter in an effort to disguise it. But judging from the expression on Charlie's coffee-colored face, she hadn't succeeded. From the corner of her eye she saw the man she'd come to talk to step up to the bar.

With one last, false smile for Charlie, she said, "Please say hello to Cora for me," and turned to face Cord Spencer, proprietor of the Last Resort saloon.

Though she'd never met the man personally— he had, after all, only lived in Harmony a little over a year—Liberty had heard all about him. Her mother's weekly, news-filled letters had kept her up-to-date on everything happening in the little town. Since her return to Harmony, Liberty had learned more than she ever cared to know about the man from Samantha Evans. Samantha Evans *Spencer*, she reminded herself. Liberty's girlhood friend could talk for hours about her brand-new, saloon-keeper husband.

She tilted her head back to look him directly in the eye. And immediately wished she hadn't. Cord's dark brown eyes glittered with humor, and she had the distinct impression that he wasn't the least bit surprised to find her in his saloon. Perhaps, Liberty told herself, she shouldn't have discussed her plans with Samantha after all.

"Mrs. Wilder," he said, dipping his head in a brief nod.

"Mr. Spencer."

Cord leaned one elbow on the bar and looked down at her. "May I get you something to drink?"

She frowned. "I think not. I won't be staying."

"A shame. I'd so looked forward to meeting you. Samantha's told me *so* much about you."

Liberty's eyes narrowed slightly. No doubt about it, she thought. Samantha *had* told her husband about her friend's plans.

"Then you were expecting me?" she asked.

"Eventually. Though I must admit," he added, his lips quirking slightly, "I hadn't expected your visit so soon after your arrival home. I would have thought you'd be busy catching up with old friends."

"There will be plenty of time for that, Mr. Spencer."

"Cord."

"Fine. Cord." She inhaled sharply. "Since Samantha has told you all about me, I presume you know why I'm here now?"

"I think so."

She nodded. A quick glance to her right told her that Charlie hadn't moved an inch. He, along with everyone else in the bar, seemed to be waiting with bated breath to hear the explanation for her visit. Well, then, Liberty told herself, there was no reason to keep them waiting any longer.

"Fine. I'll get right to the point, then." She squared her shoulders and tilted her chin defiantly. "I'd like you to close up your saloon, Cord."

If anything, the silence in the room got even louder. The horrified men sitting within earshot looked from her to Cord, waiting for his response. It wasn't long in coming. His booming laughter filled the room as completely as the blue haze of cigar smoke.

Slowly, hesitantly, his customers joined in until the hearty sounds seemed to shake the walls. As if a signal had been given, the saloon rushed back into life. With a shake of his head, the piano player in the corner once more struck up a tune. The women serving drinks began teasing their customers as they leaned across them, setting bottles and glasses on the tables.

Liberty heard it all. Though her eyes were locked with Cord's, she was well aware of what was going on around her. She'd been brushed aside. Laughingly dismissed. And by tomorrow she knew she would be the subject of conversations all over Harmony. She even knew what they would be saying— *"You remember that oldest Taylor girl? All the scrapes she used to get into and the wild notions she always had? Well, wait till you hear what she's done now. . . ."*

It didn't matter that she had no more in common with the girl she used to be than she had with the women who worked for Cord. The people of her hometown would simply treat her as they had when she was a child. With affectionate patience. They would assume that this "notion" of hers would pass. That she would tire of her latest interest and eventually move on to something else.

Well, she told herself, that might have been true of the *old* Liberty, but it wasn't true anymore. But Harmony would soon find that out. For now, she intended to have her say—whether Cord Spencer cared to hear her or not.

"You're selling these men liquor that will destroy them," she nearly shouted to be heard over the din surrounding her.

Cord stopped laughing and looked down at her through kind but impatient eyes. "Why don't you go on home, Mrs. Wilder? This is no place for you."

"This is no place for *anyone*." She watched his lips clamp firmly together and felt a small thrill of satisfaction that she *had* at least captured his attention. "And I have no intention of going home until I've said what I came to say."

Travis Miller groaned quietly and set his beer back down on the table. Two days. Liberty'd only been back in town *two* days, and already there was trouble.

From the moment she walked into the saloon, Travis had been expecting the worst. Even when she was in her teens, things seemed to *happen* around her. He didn't know why. It wasn't as though she went out of her way to cause trouble. There was just something about her . . . some energy . . . some—hell. He didn't know what to call it.

But whatever it was, apparently its strength hadn't faded any over the years. When the saloon leaped back into full life, Travis let his eyes roam over her leisurely. He'd barely had time to admire the trim figure packed into her tiny frame before he'd heard her tell Cord she wanted him to close the saloon down.

Now he flicked a quick glance at his friend's expression. Thankfully, Cord still seemed to be treating the whole situation as more of a joke than an annoyance. But Travis knew that couldn't last long.

He remembered all too clearly just how determined Liberty Taylor could be when she had her mind set. Unfortunately for him, Cord Spencer didn't know the kind of woman he was up against.

Slowly Travis pushed himself to his feet, straining to keep track of their conversation over the confusion of sounds in the room. As he moved closer to the bar, he didn't have a bit of trouble hearing Liberty.

"I'm afraid I must insist that you stop selling whiskey, Cord."

"Mrs. Wilder . . ."

She shuddered slightly. "Liberty, please."

"Very well. Liberty it is." Cord straightened up, slid his hands into his pants pockets, and looked down at her. "This is my business,

Liberty. And I have no intention of shutting it down. Not for you. Not for anyone."

"But—"

"No. Let me explain. I sell only the best liquor. I don't serve rotgut whiskey, and I don't shanghai men off the streets, forcing them to come inside."

"But your very presence here is detrimental to the town."

"I don't agree."

Travis stepped up behind Liberty and watched his friend struggle for patience before continuing.

"My saloon isn't merely a place to have a drink. Men come here to socialize—"

"Yes," she said wryly and turned her head pointedly toward one of the half-dressed women.

He caught her glance and immediately added, "I do not run a brothel, Liberty. These 'ladies' serve drinks in my saloon. What they do on their own time, in their own rooms, is *their* business. Just as selling whiskey and beer is mine."

"But—"

"Men come here to meet their friends. They play cards, they relax. They do business and listen to rumors of other businesses. In fact, the Last Resort is much more of a social club than a saloon."

"Really."

Travis heard the sarcastic note in her voice and inwardly cringed. He remembered all too clearly what Liberty was like when she had her mind set.

"Then you refuse to stop selling spirits?"

"Yes, ma'am. I do." Cord caught Travis's eye and gave him a barely perceptible nod before locking gazes with Liberty again.

"You realize," Travis heard her say, "that I'll do everything I can to close you down?"

"I do."

"That doesn't concern you?"

"It's been tried before."

"Not by me."

"True enough." Cord held his hand out to the petite woman. "I look forward to our first battle."

She hesitated for a long moment, and Travis could almost feel her indecision before she finally reached out and took Cord's hand in a firm handshake.

"Travis," Cord said as he released Liberty's hand, "I guess you heard that Mrs. Wilder here intends to shut me down."

"Yeah, I heard."

Liberty spun around to face him, and Travis felt the force of her stare shoot right through him. It didn't seem possible, but he'd actually *forgotten* just how green her eyes were. Years ago they'd made him think of the first green grasses of spring after a long, cold winter.

But now there was a wariness in her eyes that had never been there before.

"'Evenin' Libby," he said after a long moment.

"Hello, Travis."

His heartbeat quickened at her whispered greeting. That husky tone of her voice had always affected him far more than he'd ever let on, and it seemed, he thought wryly, that *some* things didn't change.

In the space of an instant his eyes swept over her appreciatively. Her long, curly brown hair, pulled into a loose knot on top of her head, still held the barest hint of red when candlelight fell on it, and her waist still looked as though he could span it easily with his hands. Her small but full breasts rose and fell with her rapid breathing, and the pulse beat in her throat told him she was more upset than she pretended to be.

"C'mon, Libby," he said quietly, "it's time to go."

She blinked, stared at him for another long moment, then shook her head. "I'm not leaving yet, Travis."

Around them interested onlookers once again fell silent, and Travis knew that if he didn't get her out of there soon, somebody just might take exception to her notion of closing down a saloon. He reached out and cupped her elbow. "You've said enough for one night, Libby. We're leavin'."

She pulled free and glared at him. Her green eyes widened and seemed to catch fire.

"I *said* I'm not ready to leave yet."

"Well, Liberty—" Cord interrupted.

She turned around quickly and saw his grin before he continued.

"Since the Last Resort is still *my* place . . . *I* say you're ready." He looked up at the other man. "Thanks, Travis."

A man at the closest table chuckled, and Liberty shot him a withering glare. Travis watched the smile die on the man's face, then he grabbed Liberty's elbow again and began to tug her toward the door.

She turned an icy stare on him next, and it was

all he could do not to shiver from the cold. But he kept a firm hold on her arm and never slowed his step. They'd almost made it to the door when Liberty glanced back at Cord and called out, "I'm not finished with you yet, Cord Spencer!"

Travis pushed the batwing doors wide and pulled her out onto the boardwalk as Cord yelled back, "I never doubted it for a minute, Liberty Wilder!"

More laughter drifted out to them, and Libby finally managed to yank herself free of Travis's grip.

The air around them crackled with the heat and dust of an August night. Moonlight spilled down onto the main street of Harmony, illuminating the features of the two people who stood less than an arm's length away from each other.

Travis waited, knowing full well that any minute Libby was going to explode and launch into one of her well-known tirades. He was, in fact, almost looking forward to it. It had been far too long since he'd heard her voice.

Four years. Four incredibly long years.

How was it, then, that he remembered that last summer she spent in Harmony as if it had just happened? Hell. That was no surprise. He remembered *everything* about Liberty Taylor.

As soon as she hit sixteen, Travis recalled, every male for miles around had rushed to Harmony just for the chance to make a fool of himself with Libby. He'd watched them all, young and old.

And he'd watched Libby.

Travis had been no better than the rest of them. He, too, was caught up by her wide green eyes and smiling lips. His gaze, too, had been drawn to the sway of her hips when she marched down Main Street full of plans and vinegar. And, Travis told himself, he was probably the *only* one who'd even enjoyed her temper.

Lord knew, she had one. But her fury was always short-lived, like a summer storm. It could blow up out of nowhere, crash down on unsuspecting heads, then disappear as quickly as it'd arrived.

Oh, yeah, Travis had wanted her as much as anyone else. But he'd had far too much pride to become one of her admiring throng. He'd had a different plan. He'd thought to wait her out. Wait for her to grow. Mature. He'd wanted her to see that Travis Miller was the only man for her.

And then Robert Wilder passed through town the summer Libby turned nineteen. A wealthy rancher, Wilder hadn't minded in the least joining the crowd vying for Libby's attention. The stranger had courted, complimented, and wooed her with a hasty determination.

Then, almost before he knew it, Travis was sitting in the back of the church, watching Libby Taylor marry another man. When she moved away with her new husband, Travis had done his damndest to put her from his mind. To get on with what was left of his own life. It had taken nearly four years to accept the fact that through his own stubborn pride he'd lost the woman he'd wanted more than life.

But he had finally found peace, if not happiness—then she shows up again. Back home. Where she belonged. And, according to gossip, a widow with a small son.

And it was all starting again. He'd seen the interested gleam in the eyes of the men in the Last Resort. He'd recognized the hungry looks tossed her way.

Even though Libby was changed . . . a bit tougher, less quick to laugh . . . it didn't matter anyway, he told himself. Though he couldn't quite put a finger on what was different about her, he didn't care. He still wanted her.

"Why are you staring at me like that?"

She spoke and his thoughts and memories scattered. "Huh?"

"I asked you why you're staring at me."

"Oh." Travis straightened up, shook his head, and said, "Sorry. My mind was wanderin'." And if she knew exactly *where* it had been . . . he had no doubt she'd turn and leave him standing alone on the walk.

"I see."

He reached for her, saying, "C'mon, Libby, I'll see you home."

Liberty stepped back quickly. "That won't be necessary, Travis. I'm sure I can find my way home alone."

His hand dropped to his side. "I know you can, Libby. I'll see you home anyway."

"You needn't worry, Travis. I won't be going back to the saloon again tonight."

"Damned right you won't."

She crossed her arms over her chest, cocked her head, and glared at him. "You listen to me, Travis Miller. I won't be going back tonight because I don't *want* to," she snapped, "not because you *order* me to stay away!"

He grinned and she continued.

"And while we're talking about the saloon, I have a few things I'd like to say to you, Travis."

"Thought you might." Well, he told himself, he'd been expecting it, hadn't he? By the sound of her, she was just winding up, too.

Her eyes narrowed. "I have no idea how you came to the conclusion that *you* have authority over me . . . but I'll thank you to remember from this night on that you don't."

"I *am* the sheriff, Libby."

"And are you placing me under arrest?"

"No."

"Then I'll thank you not to interfere with me in the future!" She jerked her head to indicate the Last Resort.

Damn, he thought. Libby's not going to give up on this. "I only wanted to get you out of there before you started something you couldn't control."

"I am perfectly capable of taking care of myself, Travis. I've been doing it for some time now."

"Yeah. I heard about your husband, Libby. I'm sorry."

Even in the indistinct moonlight, Travis saw her stiffen. Her mouth tightened just a bit, and she swallowed heavily.

From what gossip he'd heard, it had been almost a year since Robert Wilder died. Was she still so much in love with the man that it hurt to talk about him?

It was a long moment before she managed to say, "Thank you. It was not my intention to garner your sympathy. Merely to point out that I don't *need* a guardian. I'm a grown woman, Travis. I'll take care of myself."

He forced a great gulp of air past the sudden tightness in his chest. "I *know* you're a grown woman, Libby. Believe me, I know. As for takin' care of yourself, I'm sure you can. But for right now . . . I'm going to see you home."

Before she could open her mouth to protest again, Travis grabbed her elbow firmly, spun her about, and guided her down the steps to the street below. After only a few steps she seemed to resign herself to his presence, but he could feel anger as clearly as the hot wind that swept in off the prairie.

When they reached her family's mercantile, he walked around to the back of the building and stopped by the door leading to the family's living quarters.

"I'm not staying with the folks, Travis," she said quietly and turned for the building situated directly behind the mercantile. Harmony's one and only hotel, run by Kincaid and Faith Hutton.

Surprised, Travis caught up to her in three quick steps and walked beside her to the front door. Why would she separate herself from her family? He couldn't imagine Lillie Taylor *asking* her daughter to stay in a hotel. What the *hell* was goin' on here? Determined to find out, he said abruptly, "Why are you stayin' here?"

Her fingers closed around the shining brass knob on the wide oak door. "Because I want to," she answered coolly.

All right, he told himself. Now he knew he wouldn't find out a damn thing by demanding to know. Just the stiff line of her back and the tone of her voice was enough to let him know she was going to be stubborn. Fine. He'd just try a different tactic.

"Libby . . . I'm, uh . . . hell. I'm sorry about makin' you mad. But it's my job to look out for the folks and to keep the peace."

She glanced at him, then looked away again quickly. But not before he saw her features soften. "I know, Travis."

"Well, that is . . ." He inhaled sharply and blew it out in a rush. Best to just say what was on his mind and get it over with. "I was thinkin', Libby."

"Yes?"

"Now that you're back home again . . . maybe you'd let me take you to dinner some night?" He saw her features close up, and he hurried on before she could turn him down. "Right here. At the hotel. Faith's quite a cook, y'know."

"I don't think so, Travis."

Frustrated, he yanked his hat off and crushed the brim in one curled fist. "It's *just* a welcome home kinda thing, Libby."

Her lips curved in a tired smile. "I appreciate it, Travis. Really. But I think it's best if we just let this night end right here."

She opened the door, stepped inside, and closed it again. Alone in the darkness Travis Miller stared at the closed door for a long minute before turning and heading back for the jailhouse.

End? Hell, he'd hardly gotten started!

With every step he took, Travis felt his own determination grow. Not again. He wouldn't let her slip through his fingers like he had the last time.

He settled his hat firmly on his head and smiled grimly to himself. Whether she knew it or not, Libby Taylor Wilder was about to be courted.

Chapter Two

"STAND STILL, BOBBY!" LIBBY THREADED her fingers through her small son's pale blond hair, trying futilely to make it lie flat. She'd given up all hope of being able to pull a comb through it. He'd never stay put long enough for that.

The little boy hopped from foot to foot, excitedly peering around his mother's body. The open door behind her called to him, Libby knew, and a reluctant smile curved her lips as she wished she had *half* the energy Bobby had.

"Gramma's waitin', Mama!" he said in a rush. "She tol' me she's gonna give me a big boy's hat today. I hafta hurry!"

"Your grandmother isn't going anywhere, Bobby. She'll be at the store waiting for you." Libby bent down, straightened the collar of Bobby's shirt, and smiled into the green eyes so much like her own. "May I have a kiss before you go?"

His face scrunched up, nose wrinkled in distaste, Bobby frowned at her briefly as though horrified at the thought. But in a flash his tilted grin appeared. He threw his arms around his mother's neck and planted a slightly damp kiss on her cheek.

Libby's eyes squeezed shut as she wrapped

her arms around the small, sturdy body pressed close to her. Almost four years old, and already his kisses and hugs were granted more sparingly than just a few months ago. He seemed so intent on being a "big boy," when Libby felt as though she would do *anything* to keep him small for as long as she could.

"Mama, you're squeezin' me hard!"

His outraged voice made her loosen her grip, and he stepped back just a bit. Putting his palms on either side of her face, Bobby asked, "Are you comin' with me to Gramma's store?"

Libby laid her hands over her son's and smiled. "In a few minutes, honey. But you go ahead now."

"'Kay—"

The words were barely out of her mouth before the little boy shot past her and ran out the door. She turned to watch him race down the hotel steps and across the wide patch of earth that separated the Harmony Hotel from Taylor's Mercantile. Absently, while watching her son, Libby noted that the black knee pants he was wearing were too short for him.

Sighing, she stood up and leaned against the doorjamb. Bobby was growing, changing almost daily right before her eyes. But then, hadn't *she* changed in the last four years? she asked herself silently. Hadn't *everything* changed during the time she'd been gone from Harmony? From home?

With that thought memories rushed unbidden into her brain, and she closed her eyes, hoping to block them out as easily as she did the morning sun shining down on the bright yellow paint of the mercantile. But it wasn't that easy.

Images of her late husband Robert danced through her mind, taunting her . . . reminding her of how badly she'd failed at her marriage. Libby opened her eyes again quickly, but even staring at the back end of her parents' store didn't end the wild parade of recollections.

She'd hoped that selling the ranch and coming back to Harmony would dispel all of the old hurts. She'd hoped to find peace in the familiar surroundings. But she was beginning to realize that she would never "find" peace. It had to be born somewhere inside her.

And the chances of *that* happening seemed very slim, indeed.

For a moment she wished wildly that she could make time stand still. Make the world stop turning—her son stop growing—her memories disappear.

"Libby?"

She jumped, startled, and spun about, her hand at her throat.

"I'm sorry," Faith Lind Hutton said and hurried toward her. "I didn't mean to frighten you."

Libby shook her head slightly. That should teach her to keep her mind on the present instead of reliving things that couldn't be altered. "It's all right, Faith. I guess I was woolgathering."

"Are you feeling all right?" Faith's frank gaze swept over her friend quickly.

"Of course," Libby countered and reached for her string bag hanging on the nearby hall tree. "Why do you ask?"

"Well . . . you're up and about awfully early."

"It's nearly eight o'clock. Not so early."

"It is for someone who was up half the night pacing in her room."

Libby avoided her old friend's curious stare by opening her bag and unnecessarily checking the contents. She should have known that someone would be able to hear her aimless walking. But she'd tried to be so quiet.

Forcing a nervous laugh, she tried to brush Faith's concern aside. "Oh, strange bed . . . I just couldn't seem to fall asleep last night."

"Hmmm . . ." Faith tilted her head a bit and looked at her friend warily. "The 'strange' bed didn't bother you any the first two nights you stayed here. . . ."

Libby's gaze shot up to meet the other woman's. Those sharp hazel eyes gleamed speculatively, and Libby had only a moment to remember that she'd never been able to hide anything from Faith. Not even when they were children. She was trying desperately to think of *something* to say when Faith spoke again.

"This couldn't have anything to do with the fact that Travis Miller walked you home last night, could it?"

"What?" Good Lord. Had the woman become a mind reader during the time Libby'd been gone? For heaven's sake, she'd hardly admitted to *herself* that it was thoughts of Travis that had made her so restless all night.

Libby felt that odd stirring low in her stomach again. The same feeling that had very nearly swamped her the first time Travis had grasped her elbow the night before. She'd never known such a simple gesture to have such a profound effect. The merest touch of his hand had sent waves of heat coursing through her body.

Nothing like that had ever happened to her before. And, after spending most of the night thinking about it, she'd decided that it wouldn't happen *again*, either.

The very *last* thing she needed in her life was another man! Especially one who turned her knees to butter with a single touch.

She blinked rapidly and tried to concentrate when she realized that Faith was talking to her again.

"You heard me. And don't sound so scandalized, Libby!" She reached out and laid one hand on Liberty's forearm. "You've been a respectable widow for very nearly a year now. There's not a thing unseemly with finding another beau!"

"A *beau*?" Good God, Libby thought frantically, her insides swarming with a sudden nervous energy.

"Certainly a beau. And why not Travis, might I ask? He's got a steady job, he's well thought of in town, and Lord knows he's handsome enough!"

Too handsome by far, Libby told herself grimly.

"Besides," Faith continued, "he's all alone. Just like you."

"Alone?" Libby pulled the strings of her bag closed, slipped them over her right wrist, then clasped her hands in front of her. A bone-deep calm settled over her. "I'm hardly *alone*, Faith. Not only are there more Taylors than you could shake a stick at in this town, but there *is* Bobby, you know."

"Of *course* there's Bobby to be considered." Faith crossed her arms over her chest. "And what better reason to find a decent, upstanding man like Travis? A boy *needs* a father, Libby."

A father. Robert. A bitter shaft of cold stabbed at Libby, and she drew it close, protectively. If she had learned anything in the last four years, it was that the *wrong* father could do much more damage than *no* father at all.

"He has a mother, Faith. That will be enough."

"Oh, Libby," Faith said quickly, apologetically. "I didn't mean to . . . oh, shoot! I'm sorry, Lib. I didn't mean any harm."

"I know."

"It's just that, seeing Travis and you come home together last night . . . I'd hoped that—"

"No." Libby shook her head. She could tell her friend exactly why Travis had been with her the night before. But the way gossip spread in Harmony, Libby had no doubt at all that within the next couple of hours, Faith would hear everything there was to tell about the scene in the saloon. And truthfully, Libby simply didn't feel like talking about it right now. With anyone.

After a quick goodbye, Libby stepped out onto the hotel's wide front porch and paused a moment to relish the early morning sounds of Harmony.

In the distance she could hear the blacksmith's hammer ring with every blow to the anvil. A dog's excited yapping blended with the sound of children's laughter, and the rhythmic creaks and squeaks of wagon wheels rolling down Main

Street told her that the little town was already up and bustling.

She gave a quick glance around her from the shadowed porch. Though she couldn't see all of the town from the hotel, Libby gazed lovingly at the buildings nearest to her.

Though people had laughed at first at her mother's "beautification" idea of painting every building in Harmony a different color, Libby knew that the rainbow-colored town was now a source of pride to most everyone.

Even on the darkest winter day, wild, cheerful color surrounded the townspeople. Smiling, she noted the bright sunshine-yellow mercantile, the green dressmaker's shop, the shining white church and the sky-blue train depot. For a moment, she considered strolling to the depot to have a little visit with her brother William, the stationmaster. They hadn't had much chance to talk yet, and Libby was curious to find out if he was still dreaming of heading off for California.

But even before she could take a step in his direction, she realized exactly what she was doing. Trying to put off having to face her parents. Even at the ripe old age of twenty-four, Libby shuddered to think of the confrontation heading her way once the Taylors found out about what she'd done the night before.

Still . . . she lifted her chin slightly. She wasn't ashamed of what she'd done. Heaven knew, if anyone had the right to lead a temperance movement—*she* did. She had every intention of carrying right on with her challenge to Cord Spencer. And if her parents were going to be angry, she might as well face it now.

Of course, a little voice in the back of her mind told her, if she were honest with them . . . *told* them about Robert and her life with him . . . maybe they'd understand why she felt so strongly about the selling of liquor.

No. She didn't want their pity. And she couldn't bear to see the sadness on their faces. Libby knew that however irrationally, her parents would feel guilty knowing how miserable she'd been all the time they'd been so sure of her happiness. There was nothing they could have done then . . . and *certainly* nothing they could do now to alter the last four years.

Libby drew in a deep breath of the warm morning air and told herself that somehow she would simply have to make her parents accept, if not understand, what she had to do.

Slowly, deliberately, she stepped down from the porch and began the short walk to the mercantile.

The door swung open before she could touch the knob. Overhead, the shop bell clanged as Bobby and his uncle Harry raced through the doorway, crashing into Libby.

Quickly, she grabbed each one of them before they could slip away. Looking from her son's delighted features to her youngest brother's wide grin, Libby felt an answering smile blossom on her face.

"And where are you boys off to in such a rush?"

"Uncle Harry's gonna take me to the river and show me a *frog!*"

Libby saw the adoring look her son threw at

his nine-year-old uncle before Harry added, "It's the biggest dang frog I ever seen, Libby! Ya wanna come with us?"

"No." Frog watching was not high on her list of entertaining activities. Apparently, though, she told herself with one more glance at her son, there was a lot to be said for it. "But," she added to the smallest Taylor, "thanks for asking."

"All right." Harry shrugged, then pulled at Bobby's shirtsleeve. "C'mon, Bobby. Let's go."

Her son squirmed until he'd freed himself from her grip, then ran down the steps and after the other boy as fast as his much shorter legs would carry him. He didn't even look back. Libby squinted into the sun and called out, "Harry! You be careful! Watch him close!"

She couldn't be sure that he'd even heard her since neither of the boys so much as slowed down. Biting at her bottom lip, Libby told herself that she had to give Bobby a *little* freedom, no matter *how* much she worried. At the same time though, she promised herself that she would walk to the river's edge in twenty minutes or so, if they weren't back by then.

Her smile still in place, it slowly faded away as her mother called out from behind her, "Well, good *morning*, missy! And what do *you* have to say for yourself?"

Travis leaned back against the still-cool boulder, rested his forearms on his upraised knees, and looked at the fishing pole cupped in his hands. It had been a long time since he'd felt the urge to go early-morning fishing.

But he'd always done his best thinking while

staring blankly at a pole and line. And Lord knew, he had *plenty* to think about.

After leaving Libby at the hotel the night before, he'd listened to more outraged citizens than he had in all the years he'd lived in Harmony. In fact, he'd even left the jailhouse a couple of hours earlier than usual, just to avoid any more angry men complaining about Libby and her "foolish notions."

But, like most small towns, gossip moved quicker than a prairie fire, and by the time he'd reached Maisie and Minnie's boardinghouse, Libby's escapade was already being discussed. Travis winced slightly in memory. Maybe *discussed* wasn't quite the right word.

Maisie and Minnie, always eager for a good argument, were both trying to outshout the other in an effort to state their opinions. And the only other boarder, a drifting whiskey drummer, was doing his best to get a few words in, too.

Travis sighed and rested his head against the rock behind him. The moment he'd stepped into the boardinghouse, the three people had practically leaped at him, demanding details they were sure only *he* would know.

Though the two sisters agreed wholeheartedly with Libby's opinion of liquor, they were divided on whether or not it had been "proper" for Libby to actually *enter* the Last Resort.

Maisie held that a lady's "place" was anywhere she darn well chose to make it. Minnie, on the other hand, insisted that a "lady" should *never* resort to actually *entering* a den of "sin." The whiskey drummer, naturally, insisted on making his case for the medicinal value of an occasional drink.

It had been another hour or more before Travis had been able to escape to his room. Even then he hadn't found any peace. He couldn't get Libby out of his mind. Hell, he'd hardly slept a wink all night. Every time he closed his eyes, her image flashed into his head. Those green eyes, those luscious breasts. God! he thought and shifted position uncomfortably. If this kept up, he wouldn't be able to walk!

Still, he couldn't make himself stop. Idly now, Travis rubbed the fingers of his right hand together, remembering the sudden jolt of awareness he'd experienced when he'd touched her. A feeling that strong, he knew, couldn't have been felt by him alone. She *had* to have been as affected as he was.

He was near certain he'd seen something promising in her eyes, too, just before she turned down his dinner invitation.

It was almost as if she'd forced herself to say no.

Raising his head again, he looked out across the river, not even noticing how the water level had dropped with the lack of rain. Why? Why in the hell wouldn't she have a meal with him? It wasn't as if he'd declared undying love for her there on the hotel porch. He hadn't been forward. Dammit, he hadn't done a thing wrong.

All right, he'd made her leave the saloon when she clearly hadn't wanted to . . . but surely she could see that was his job. That it was for her own good that he'd gotten her out of there before

Cord's customers took exception to her demands.

Of course she knew that. Her refusal had nothing to do with what had happened in the saloon. Oh, she'd been mad all right. But she hadn't frozen up on him until he'd gotten personal.

The fishing pole hung loose in his hands as he tried to work out exactly what was going on in Libby's mind.

A fine state of affairs, he told himself in disgust. Thirty-five years old and no more idea of what a woman's thinking than some young sprout out on his first buggy ride! His lips curved in a halfhearted smile, Travis reminded himself that no other woman he'd ever known had made any complaints.

Of course, he acknowledged privately, most of the women he'd known were generally the kind who were paid well to tell him what a fine fella he was.

But that didn't matter, he countered quickly, silently. All that mattered now was Libby. Hell, she was all that had mattered to him for years. He'd just been too damn prideful and stubborn to stand in line for her long enough to tell her so!

Well, he had a second chance now, and God help him if he messed it up this time around! Libby wasn't a woman he wanted for a few stolen hours. He wanted much more from her than that. He wanted now what he'd *always* wanted.

To marry her.

Love her.

A tiny seed of an idea took root in his brain

and began to spread. Slowly he sat up straight and examined the notion from all sides. The more he thought about it, the more it made sense.

He'd do it.

By thunder, he'd do it.

That very night.

Before he could talk himself out of it.

Waggling his fishing pole, Travis grinned. He'd just march right up to Liberty Taylor Wilder and announce his intentions. Say it straight out, with no furbelows or fanciness.

"Liberty," he said out loud, practicing what would be the shortest speech he'd ever made, "I love you. Always have. And I wanted you to know right off that I'm plannin' on marryin' you."

"Hey, Travis!" a young voice shouted from somewhere behind him. "You got a fish on the line yonder!"

Startled, Travis closed his fingers around his pole just before the wily fish would have pulled the cane rod into the river and made its escape.

Without taking his eyes off his quarry, Travis yelled back, "You're damned right I do! And *this* time I ain't lettin' her get away!"

Chapter Three

"IT MIGHT INTEREST YOU TO KNOW, young woman"—Lillie Taylor started right in on her daughter—"that every gossip in town is talking about *you*!"

"Good morning to you, too, Mother," Libby said, then turned to give her father a half smile. James Taylor, she noted, did little more than roll his eyes and shrug his shoulders in sympathy.

The shadowed cool of the mercantile enveloped Libby, and she breathed a sigh of pleasure at leaving the already hot outdoors behind her. Even listening to one of her mother's speeches was not too high a price to pay to get out of the sun.

"Don't you 'good morning' me, Liberty Taylor!"

"Wilder," James mumbled in an undertone.

Libby almost chuckled at the glare her mother shot him, but swallowed the impulse when her mother's iron gaze flicked back at her. Somehow the fact that she was a grown woman with a child of her own did nothing to rid her of the instant reaction to her mother's anger.

Just as if she were a child again, Libby lowered her gaze and waited. Absently she wondered how old a person had to be before they stopped being their parents' child.

"How *dare* you go inside that saloon! What in heaven's name were you thinking? No!" Lillie said quickly and held up one hand to silence her daughter. "It is apparent to me and everyone else in Harmony that you *weren't* thinking at all!"

Libby sneaked a glance up. Splotches of scarlet stained Lillian Taylor's high cheekbones. A sure sign that the woman was furious. Even as kids, Libby remembered, the Taylor children had run for the hills when Lillie's cheeks grew apple-red.

Her father, though, Libby noted, didn't look angry. He looked curious. His thoughtful stare almost bothered her more than her mother's strident tones.

"Well? What do you have to say for yourself, missy?" Lillie waited only a heartbeat before adding, "Come on. Let's hear it. By all accounts, you didn't have the slightest *bit* of trouble talking last night!"

"Calm down, Lillie," her husband urged. "Give her a chance to explain."

Libby smiled her thanks, but her mother wasn't in the mood to listen to anyone. She started right in again.

"And another thing!" The older woman smacked her palms down on the wooden counter. "I don't understand why you're staying in the hotel. Why not come home, where you belong?"

Libby knew very well she *really* meant, "Where I can keep my eye on you." As her mother briskly went on, Libby let her eyes move around the familiar store. She inhaled deeply the comfortable scents of coffee, peppermint, and new leather.

Her gaze swept over stacks of fabric, saddle-bags, hand-tooled saddles, books, pots, pans, and the like. Anything anyone would *ever* need could be found in Taylor's Mercantile. And if by some small chance they didn't have what a customer wanted, Lillie would get it.

Letting her gaze slide back to her mother, Libby studied the still-pretty woman behind the counter. Though clearly furious, Lillie managed to maintain her decorum. Without ever raising her voice, the woman let her fury be known with a simple change of tone.

A reluctant smile tugged at Libby's lips as she realized that was the *one* thing her mother'd never been able to get her to accomplish. More often than not, Libby'd shouted her way through girlhood and could still hold her own in an argument. Her smile faded away rapidly as she unwillingly remembered the countless futile arguments with Robert.

"You'd better *not* smile!"

"Hmmm?" Libby blinked and saw her mother wagging one finger at her.

"I said, you'd better not smile when I am *this* mad at you!"

"Mother," she said as she walked across the room to the wide counter that curved around half the store. "I wasn't laughing at you."

Green eyes stared into green eyes for a long moment before Lillie gave her daughter a brief nod. "All right, then. Are you ready to tell me just what in the devil you were doing in a *saloon* last night?"

Unable to resist, Libby asked quietly, "I thought you knew. You *did* say that everyone in town is talking about me."

"Don't get smart with me, Liberty Taylor . . ."

"Wilder," James tossed in again.

Huffing impatiently, Lillie turned on her husband. "If you have something to say, James, say it!"

Libby watched her father's work-worn hands toy with a rawhide bridle as he began to speak quietly.

"I'm only tryin' to remind you, Lillie . . . our Libby's a grown woman. A widow. A mother."

"For heaven's sake! I know that!"

"Then quit callin' her Liberty Taylor. Her name's Wilder now."

Lillie frowned at him, but Libby could have kissed him. In a few short sentences he'd forced his wife to remember that their oldest child was an adult. And didn't *owe* them any explanation for what she did.

"Very well." Lillie tugged at her shirtwaist, smoothed her palms over the front of her black cotton skirt, then clasped her hands together at the waist. "*Mrs. Wilder,*" she said, "would you mind terribly telling us why you felt it necessary to invade a saloon and, while there, engage in a shouting match with the proprietor?"

Libby saw what it had cost her mother to restrain herself. The woman looked as though she could bite through a skillet!

But if she were to explain her reasons for going into a saloon, wouldn't her mother's anger turn to sympathy? What would her parents have to say if they discovered that Robert Wilder hadn't been the dependable, responsible provider Libby'd convinced them he was?

How could she tell them that Robert was weak, irresponsible . . . and a drunkard to boot? Did she really want them to know that most of her married life had been spent in pointless disagreements with a man who was usually so drunk that he had no recollection of them the next morning?

No.

Good Lord. Her marriage was over. Robert was dead and buried, and if she had anything to say about it, the memories would stay that way, too. Libby didn't want her parents' sympathy. She didn't want *anyone*'s pity. And more than that, she certainly didn't want to hear "I told you so."

She could kick herself when she remembered how her mother had tried to talk her out of a too-hasty marriage with a man they knew little about. But a nineteen-year-old Libby couldn't be told anything. All she saw was what she wanted to see.

Robert Wilder. Tall, handsome, well dressed and well spoken. A stranger, not someone she'd known her whole life. A man who promised to take her away from the only piece of the world she'd ever known, Harmony, and show her the rest of the world.

Well, she hadn't seen the world. Only Robert's ranch. And *that* was barely the "estate" he'd described. A ramshackle house whose "glory days" were, more than likely, during the American Revolution . . . a few scraggly cows . . . a chicken or two and three pigs.

But somehow a man with no head for business and no taste for work had managed to acquire the water rights to a wide section of land. So with absolutely no effort on his part, Robert came by a tidy income by leasing his range to the other ranchers in the area.

With easy, steady money coming into the house, Robert couldn't understand Libby's drive to make something of their own ranch.

"Libby?"

She shook her head, pushed the recollections aside, and faced her father's concerned expression.

"Are you all right?"

"Yes, Pa. I'm fine." Taking a deep breath, she looked at her mother. "I'm sorry, Mother. But no. I *don't* want to tell you why I was in the saloon."

Lillie Taylor's jaw dropped and she began to gasp for air like a fish on a riverbank.

"Are you in trouble?" James asked quietly.

"No, Pa. I'm not." Not anymore, she added silently.

"Then I suppose," Lillie finally said when she got her voice to work again, "that you will also refuse to tell me why you insist on staying at that hotel instead of where you belong!"

Libby reached across the counter and touched her mother's hand. She wasn't foolish enough to believe that Lillie'd finished talking about the saloon, but she was more than willing to accept a little delay. "I'm doing that as much for you as for me, Mother."

"What?"

"You're already crowded upstairs as it is. If I were to move back in, bringing Bobby—"

"Have I *ever* given you the impression that you weren't welcome here?" Lillie's faded green eyes filled unexpectedly with tears and the older woman blinked frantically to keep them from falling. "You're our *daughter*. And that sweet boy our only grandchild How could you think that . . ." She stopped suddenly and pulled a white lace hankie from the waistband of her skirt. Dabbing at her eyes, she went on, "It's a treat for us to see the boy, you know. You've been so far away . . ."

"I know, Mother, it's just that—" How to explain? she wondered. How could she tell her mother that if she moved back home with her family, she would be moving backward? Libby told herself that she couldn't pretend that she was simply the oldest Taylor child again. She was much more than that now. A widow. A mother.

But she knew Lillie didn't want to hear that. Instead, Libby said, "It's easier this way, Mother. Besides, it's only for a short time. . . ."

Lillie's face brightened. Quickly she sniffed and tucked her hankie away again. "A short time! Of course! How foolish of me! Certainly you'd want your own home. Why, your father can help you pick out a house kit from the catalog right this minute. We'll order it today, and while we wait for it to arrive, you and I can decide what color to paint it and exactly where you want your house built!"

She reached under the counter for the catalog, already discussing types of curtains, area rugs, and the date Libby should throw her house-warming party.

Stunned, Libby watched her mother as the older woman leaped into action. Good heavens! How had a simple declaration of independence gotten so out of hand? This had to be stopped, she knew. And quickly. Otherwise, Libby knew full well there would be a house with her name on it, sitting out under the cottonwoods. One she'd had no voice in choosing.

On the other hand, her brain chided, why not let Lillie have her fun? At least, Libby told herself, if her mother was busy planning her daughter's house, she wouldn't be fretting over the saloon escapade.

"Come and look, Libby." Lillie hardly glanced up from the catalog as she flipped expertly through the pages.

Leaning over the counter, Libby watched as page after page of new house kits sailed past. One- and two-story homes. Plain and fancy. Brick, tin, and wood. One sketch blended into another until Libby could hardly tell one from the next.

"Oh, I know you'll want to pick out most things yourself, dear," her mother said, sniffing inelegantly. "But you will naturally admit that my advice could hardly be unwelcome." She ran one long finger down a page, mumbling to herself. "Now, where is that *adorable* two-storied place with the sweet gingerbread trim? I know it will be *perfect* for you and Bobby."

The bell over the front door clanged, but Lillie didn't even glance at the new customer.

"Mornin', Maisie," James called, and Libby turned to smile at the older woman headed her way.

"Hello, James, Libby." Maisie nodded at each of them, then looked at Lillie, still bent over the catalog. "What's your mother up to now, Liberty?"

"She's picking out a house for Bobby and me."

"She gonna live in it for ya, too?"

Libby bit back her smile and looked behind her. Her mother had paused long enough to glare at Maisie.

"So, Lil," Maisie went on, setting her empty basket on the countertop and handing her grocery list to James, "what kind of place have you decided on?"

"If it's any of your business, Maisie . . . I believe the nicest one here is this one." She turned the page toward the other woman and laid her fingernail on a particularly gaudy two-story house with gables, shutters at every window, and enough gingerbread trim for *three* houses.

"Lord a mercy, Lillie!" Maisie leaned closer, squinting at the sketch. "That looks like the builder was cross-eyed!"

"Hmmph!" Lillie snatched the book back. "If you'd wear your spectacles, Maisie, you would be able to see clearly that *this* house is absolutely perfect!"

A loud clattering noise filled the air. Libby looked up to see her youngest sister, Sissy, jump down the last three stairs and race into the store, red hair flying.

"Yeah, but for what?" Maisie mumbled and reached for the catalog. "I recall seein' a house in there just the other day that I thought was a nice little place."

Sissy strolled behind the counter, took the lid off the nearest candy jar, and reached inside for a fist full of gumdrops. At sixteen, Sissy's sweet tooth was legendary.

Without even glancing at the girl, Lillie reached back, slapped Sissy's wrist, and slammed the lid back on the jar.

"Little? She doesn't need a little place." Lillie snorted at Maisie. "Libby needs a home with plenty of room for a growing boy."

Libby hid a smile behind her hand as she watched her sister stick out her tongue at their mother's back. Sissy was just a bit too plump for Lillie's tastes, and the woman was determined to help her daughter trim a few pounds.

Whether she wanted to or not.

"Well, yeah," Maisie countered. "But she's only got the one boy, Lil. He ain't gonna be growing into a *herd* of youngsters!"

Libby stood to one side, looking from her mother to Maisie and back again. Clearly, they'd forgotten about *her* presence entirely. She planted her elbows on the counter and propped her chin in her hands. This looked as if it was going to take quite a while.

"Ladies," James said gently, "maybe Libby would like to decide for herself how—"

"But," Lillie cut him off ruthlessly and narrowed her eyes at her interfering customer, "no doubt Libby will marry again soon, and Bobby will have brothers and sisters."

"You gonna pick out her new man for her, too?"

"I don't *want* another man. . . ." Libby straightened up, her eyes wide.

"Who's pickin' out a man?" A younger, very interested female voice interrupted.

Mary Taylor came down the stairs from the family's living quarters above the store. Curly brown hair held back from her heart-shaped face by a yellow ribbon, the eighteen-year-old's face was lit with fascination at the word *man*.

"No one invited you into this conversation, young lady!" Lillie frowned at her daughter. "*Your* opinion of men doesn't go any further than ranch hands and drifters."

"Now, Lillie," James tried, "Danny Vega's not exactly a drifter. . . ."

"He spends all his time on that stagecoach, doesn't he? Moving from one place to the next?"

"He works for them, Lillie."

Mary ignored her parents and looked at Libby. "Is it true, are they picking out a man for you?"

"No," Libby started.

"*I'm* picking out a house for her," Maisie shot back, then sniffed at Lillie. "It's Lillie here who's all het up about gettin' Libby married again!"

"*Married?*" Libby gasped.

"Well, it would be the best thing for her, wouldn't you say, James?" Without giving her husband a chance to answer, she rushed on, "Besides, it wouldn't do to have Bobby grow up a lonely, only child!"

"Lonely!" Libby shouted. "He's got more aunts and uncles than any child has a right to!"

"True," Lillie said, "but it's not the same thing a'tall. And please don't shout at your mother. Why, you children *always* had someone near and dear to you to talk to and share your troubles with. Brothers and sisters are gifts to each other and a treasured reward to their parents," she finished piously.

Mary snorted.

"You hush up, Missy!" Lillie snapped at her daughter and turned back to Maisie. "Now, if you'll get that nose of yours out of my catalog, I'll pick out that house for Libby and see that James orders it right now!"

"Mother," Libby said.

"Can I live with Libby?" Sissy asked no one in particular.

"No," her mother shot back. "You'll stay at home until you marry. As a decent girl should."

"I'm never gonna get married," Sissy declared and reached for a cookie from the tray on the counter.

Lillie snatched the tray from her grasp. "You surely won't if you don't get your head out of the trough once in a while!"

When her mother turned back to the tug of war she was having, trying to pull the catalog out of Maisie's grip, Mary grabbed two cookies. She took a bite out of one and tossed the other to Sissy.

"Mother," Libby tried again, then shrugged helplessly. She might as well admit defeat. Between Lillie and Maisie, she herself would *never* get a peek at those house kits. "I'm walking down to the river to check on the boys, if anyone's interested. . . ."

"That's nice, dear," Maisie muttered and bent double trying to tug the catalog free.

"Maisie Hastings, if you don't let go this minute . . ." Lillie's threat hung in the air, and Libby shook her head.

It would be pointless trying to talk to her mother now. She knew only too well what Lillie was like when she had a full head of steam. But sooner or later the woman was going to have to listen. Because it didn't matter *who* Lillie picked out as a potential husband . . . Libby was *never* going to get married again!

With one last, mighty yank Travis pulled the stubborn fish from the river, and it landed, flopping on the bank. Leaning down, he picked up the wiggling trout and looked it dead in the eye. "Caught you," he muttered and told himself that this was a sign. He was going to land Liberty Taylor Wilder as easily as he had that fish. Carefully he worked the hook from its mouth while at the same time wondering what he could use as bait for Libby.

He frowned and stared at his still wiggling breakfast. Hell, it'd been four years. How the devil did *he* know what to use as bait? Four years was a long time. People changed. Travis knew that Libby used to have a fondness for fresh flowers and chocolate cake . . . but that hardly seemed a worthy enough lure.

No. He'd have to study on this. He'd have to talk to her family. Talk to *her*, if she'd stand still long enough. Lord knows, he didn't have time to waste.

He'd already lost four years with her. He wasn't about to give up any more.

But where to start?

"Say, Travis," the same young voice that had called out a warning to him earlier spoke up again. This time from right behind him. "That's a nice fish y'got there."

Turning slightly, the sheriff saw Harry Taylor and another, younger boy, both watching him with identical grins on their faces. "You're right about that. She ought to fry up real tasty!"

"Can I touch it?" the smaller boy asked.

Harry rolled his eyes as if saying "*You* know how children are!"

Travis swallowed his smile, went down on one knee, and held the fish out toward the small blond boy. As pudgy, tentative fingers stroked the trout, Travis heard Harry say, "This here's my nephew. Libby's boy."

The child looked up and grinned. Travis found himself answering the smile that looked so much like Libby's.

"His name's Bobby," Harry offered.

"Nice to meet ya, Bobby," Travis said thoughtfully.

"Say 'how-do,' Bobby," Harry chided his nephew. "This here's the sheriff."

The little boy's green eyes widened, and he looked from the star on Travis's chest up to the flat-brimmed, dusty brown hat on his head.

"Can I wear your hat?" Bobby asked suddenly.

"Y'don't ask folks things like that, Bobby!" Harry shook his head at Travis, giving the man a silent apology.

"That's all right, Harry. I don't mind a bit." He pulled his hat off and dropped it onto Bobby's much smaller head. The wide brim slipped down past the boy's eyes, but he pushed it up and tilted his head back to keep it in place. "How's that, Bobby?"

"It fits!" The boy nodded, and the brim slipped down again.

"I can see that," Travis agreed and bit the inside of his cheek to keep from chuckling. The boy seemed to take after his mother quite a bit. Not only did he get her green eyes and her smile, he'd also inherited her stubborn streak.

"Give the man back his hat, Bobby. We got to be goin'."

"Where you boys off to?"

"Just downriver a ways," Harry replied. "Want to show this youngster a big ol' frog I found the other day."

"Y'wanna come with us?" Bobby asked, peering out from under the hat brim.

Travis looked at both boys, his brain whirling. This could be just the thing he needed. Who better to talk to about Libby than her brother and her son? Why, if he played his hand right, he could find out everything he needed to know in just an hour or two.

"All right boys, show me that frog!"

"What about your breakfast?" Harry asked, pointing at the trout Travis still held.

Hmmph! He'd forgotten all about the fish. Hell, it was still squirming around. He could just slip it back in the river. Let it go.

But what about its bein' an omen? he asked himself.

Hell, he argued silently, it still is. Proof positive that he could catch her with the right bait. Did it matter if he put the fish back in the river? It would still be there, swimmin' around, waitin' to be caught again.

And just like that fish, Libby wasn't goin' anywhere.

He still had time.

Carefully he slipped the trout back into the river and watched as it swam away. Silently, though, he warned, Don't you get too comfortable, fish. I ain't through with you yet.

Travis stood up, brushed the dirt from his knees, and smiled at the two boys. "All right, fellas. Let's us go see that fish."

Bobby looked up at him, his eyes barely visible. "I'll carry your hat."

Chapter Four

"So your mama doesn't cry over your daddy anymore, huh?" Travis asked the little boy.

"Nah. Mama says Papa is something about water and bridges." He wrinkled his brow. "I don't know what she means."

That's all right, I do, Travis thought. So her marriage was water under the bridge, was it? Well, good. He'd just as soon she wasn't still mourning her husband when he started his courtin'.

He glanced down at the child beside him and told himself that he should be ashamed, the way he'd been peppering the boy with questions for the last hour. But, his brain chided, that was the only way for him to find out about Libby.

Besides, Travis thought, Bobby didn't seem to mind a bit. In fact, the kid had hardly left Travis's side since they'd begun their little "adventure."

And to his surprise, Travis found that he didn't mind all the attention in the least. Of course, he'd always liked children. But there was something about Bobby Wilder that tugged at Travis's heart.

It was something more than the fact that Libby

was the boy's mother. It was more than his bright smile or the green eyes so like Libby's.

Travis turned and looked down at the river's edge, five feet below him. Harry stood, toes in the water, trying to skim stones across the water's racing surface.

Locking his gaze on the swiftly moving water, Travis told himself that maybe it was the admiration shining in Bobby's eyes that drew him to the child. Lord knew, he'd never had *anyone* look at him quite the way Bobby Wilder did.

As if he was Abraham Lincoln, Santa Claus, and an Indian chief all in one.

A grin touched Travis's lips, then faded away again. True, he enjoyed the fact that Bobby obviously thought him some kind of hero . . . but the real reason he was so drawn to the boy was simple. Once he married Libby, Bobby would be *his* son, too.

"Bobby! Harry!"

Travis spun about at the sound of Libby's voice. She stood on the knoll above the riverbank, hands at her hips and one foot tapping dangerously. He squinted in the morning sunlight and had only a moment to admire the pale green dress she wore and how well it fit her before she yelled at the boys again.

"I've been looking all over for you two!"

"I *told* ya we were goin' to look at that frog, Libby!" Harry shot back.

Travis smiled to himself as he watched brother and sister square off.

"You *didn't* say that it was miles downriver!"

"Ah . . . *hell*," Harry muttered, lowering his head. "It ain't *miles*. Durn girl."

"What was that, Harry Taylor?"

"Nothin'."

"I thought not."

"Ya wanna see the frog, Mama?" Bobby asked, pushing Travis's hat out of his eyes.

Her gaze slid away from her brother's, but before she could look at Bobby, her eyes locked with Travis's.

Bobby looked from his mother, to the sheriff, and back again. Mama looked kinda funny, he told himself. Not like she was mad or anything. More like she was surprised.

He glanced back at the big man beside him. Travis was fun. He liked to do stuff. Why, he'd even waded right into the river with his boots on to grab hold of that big frog just so's Bobby could see it better.

Besides, the big man told good stories and he smiled a lot and he even smelled good. Like peppermint. And Bobby thought it would be real exciting having a *sheriff* for a papa. Why, if any big boy ever picked on him, he could ask his papa to lock him up in jail!

Slowly the little boy nodded. For months he'd been lookin' for a father. Somebody who'd play with him and not yell much. Maybe even somebody who'd like his mama, too. Course, *everybody* knew that a papa and a mama have to be married, so Bobby figured that'd be much nicer for his mama if his new father liked her, too.

He tilted his head to stare at the man he'd picked out to be his papa. Travis was tall and he looked strong and the way he was smilin' at Libby, Bobby figured that it wouldn't be too hard to make his parents like each other.

"Bobby?"

He turned and looked at his mother. She was still starin' at Travis with a funny look on her face.

"Yes, ma'am?"

"Let's go, son. It's time to get back to town."

"Can Travis come, too?"

"What?"

Bobby shook his head. He wished that grown-ups would listen, sometimes. "This is Travis. He's my friend, Mama. And he put a fish in the river, and it swimmed away."

"Swam."

"Swam," he corrected. "Can he come and have breakfast with us, Mama?"

"I'm sure Travis has work to do, Bobby. . . ."

"Nothin' that can't wait, Libby," Travis answered quickly.

"Well, I . . ."

"You goin' to have breakfast at the hotel, Libby?" Harry asked.

"Yes, I suppose so. . . ."

"Well, then, I'll just come along, too. Mrs. Hutton makes the best blueberry muffins in the world!"

Harry climbed the small hill to his sister's side, but Libby didn't notice him. She couldn't seem to tear her eyes away from Travis.

"Well, Libby? Am I invited?" he asked, his voice low, dangerous.

Libby felt something inside her stir, and she desperately fought to tamp it down. She couldn't allow the youthful feelings she'd had for Travis to bob to the surface every time she saw the man.

That was all a long time ago. She'd grown. Changed.

Besides, she wasn't interested in men anymore. Hadn't she made a solemn vow *not* to let her emotions rule her head a second time? If she made a mistake again, she wouldn't be the only person to suffer. There was Bobby to think about now.

And he had to come first.

Deliberately she inhaled slowly, deeply. She forced herself to smile at Travis, but when he smiled back, she felt her resolve weaken. And even though staring into those too-dark eyes of his was disconcerting, she managed to hide that fact from him.

After all, she was home again. She planned to live in Harmony. Raise her son there. Since she'd be seeing Travis Miller every day, she'd just have to train her heart not to do somersaults every time she saw him.

And the best way to do that was simply to be friendly. That way she could prove to him and to herself that that was all there was between them. Friendship.

"All right, Travis," she said and wished her voice sounded stronger. "I'm sure Bobby would love it if you joined us."

"And you, Libby?" he asked.

"Me?"

"Would you *love* my company, too?"

She looked away from him and tossed anxious glances between her little brother and her son. Her blood raced unexpectedly, and she felt a flush of color creep into her cheeks. He wasn't going to make this easy.

Finally she answered stiffly. "We've been friends a long time, Travis. I'm sure it would be very . . . 'nice' to have breakfast with you."

He nodded slowly and Libby thought she heard a rumbling chuckle, but she couldn't be sure. All she knew for certain was that everyone seemed to be pleased with the situation except her.

Kincaid Hutton leaned over his wife's shoulder and planted a kiss on her neck. Faith sighed and leaned back into him, the bowl of bread dough before her temporarily forgotten.

"Breakfast about ready, Mrs. Hutton?" he whispered in her ear.

She grinned and nudged him with her elbow. "I thought you were being romantic, and all you're interested in is your stomach!"

"First things first!" Kincaid wiggled his eyebrows at her. "A man needs his strength, y'know."

"Then," she replied and turned into his embrace, "by *all* means, keep up your strength." Faith tilted her face up to his and sighed when his lips came down on hers. After much too brief a time, Kincaid pulled away again reluctantly.

"If you need me to chop some kindling for you, you'd better stop toying with my affections, ma'am. . . ."

"Mmmmm . . ." Faith ran her fingertip across her husband's bottom lip. "Do you think the guests would notice if there was no breakfast this morning?"

"Maybe we should risk it," he replied and gave her another quick peck.

"Mama?" a voice called from the parlor.

"And maybe not," Faith said, shaking her head.

Kincaid kept his arm around his wife and looked at the door as his daughter, Amanda, stepped into the kitchen. In her arms she held a squirming puppy who would soon be too big for her to carry.

"Boom's hungry," the little girl said.

"Go get him his breakfast, then," Faith told her and turned back to the waiting bread dough. As her fingers worked the sticky mass through the flour, she asked, "And where have you been already this morning?"

"I went for a walk. Boom wanted to."

"Uh-huh," Kincaid said. "Where exactly did Boom want to go?"

"He wanted to see Mr. Thompson."

Charlie? Faith thought. Why on earth would the child be going to see the bartender at the Last Resort?

"What on earth for?" she asked.

"Mr. Thompson went hunting the other day, and he promised Boom he could have a bone today." The girl sighed heavily and sat down on a kitchen chair to watch her puppy gobble up the table scraps she'd fed him. "But he forgot it."

"Oh. Well, I'm sure he didn't mean to," Kincaid said as he sat down opposite his daughter.

"No, him and Mr. Spencer was talkin' about Harry Taylor's sister, and Mr. Thompson says he just"—she shrugged—"forgot."

"Libby?" Faith turned a quizzical eye on her

husband. "Why would Cord and Charlie be talking about Libby?"

Kincaid shrugged.

"Mr. Spencer says she's gonna cause trouble."

"Libby?"

"Uh-huh." Amanda reached for a cookie, but her father took it from her.

"After breakfast," he warned, then asked, "What else did Mr. Spencer say?"

"He told Mr. Thompson that if Libby didn't stay out of the saloon from now on, he wasn't sure what might happen."

"The saloon? Libby?"

Faith forgot about the bread dough.

"Uh-huh." Amanda's heels began pounding on the legs of her chair. "He says she's got a bee in her bonnet." She looked up at her father. "How did Libby get a bee in her hat?"

When no one answered, Amanda shrugged again, climbed down off the chair, and lay down on the floor beside Boom.

"What on earth?" Faith mumbled.

"Maybe I'll just slip down to the Last Resort and find out what's goin' on," Kincaid offered.

Faith nodded thoughtfully, and as her husband left, she tried to understand exactly what it was her old friend was up to. But for the life of her, she couldn't think of a thing. Maybe it was time the two of them sat down for a long, heart-to-heart chat.

"Do you mean to say that Lillie is picking out Libby's new house?"

"I do." Maisie sat down across the table from

her sister and accepted a cup of tea. "And you should see the one she picked!"

"Is it dreadful?"

Maisie slapped her open palm down on the scrubbed white pine kitchen table. "It's the biggest durn thing I've ever seen. And it's got enough curlicues and doodads tacked on every which way, Libby probably won't know if she's comin' or goin'."

"A shame," her sister agreed.

"And do ya think the woman would listen to a word I said? Nosir!" Maisie lifted her right arm gingerly. "About tore my arm clean off tryin' to get that catalog away from me, too!"

"And what color is she thinkin' of painting it?" Minnie reached for the china creamer and poured some of the thick white liquid into her too-hot tea.

"Oh," Maisie snorted and leaned back in her chair, "she's already decided that! It's gonna be green. With pink trim."

"Good heavens! Are you sure?"

"Sure I'm sure, Sister. I stood right there while the woman wrote out the order. Then James hightailed it to the telegraph office and sent it off." Maisie shook her head. "Lillie put a rush on it, and I expect it'll be here within the next week or so. Lord help us."

"Why, Sister?"

"She's decided to put Libby's house under the cottonwoods, as you come into town?"

"Yes?"

"Now anytime we want to come or go, we're gonna have to traipse by that godawful place Lillie's picked out."

After a long moment Minnie pushed a plate of lemon cookies closer to her sister. "That's enough about the house now, Mae. There'll be plenty of time to talk about that while it's being built. What *I* want to know is, what did you find out about the saloon?"

Maisie glanced at her younger sister by five minutes. The woman's perpetually smiling face was shining with curiosity. It was a shame to disappoint her.

"Nothing."

"Nothing?"

"That's what I said."

"But you went to the store precisely to find out why—"

"I *know* why I went. Is it my fault that no one was talkin' about the durned saloon? Lillie was so fired up over that house and such . . . and Libby wasn't sayin' much of anything. And hell, *you* know James. Just stood there while Lillie's mouth ran roughshod over all of us."

"But what about the saloon?"

"I tell ya, they weren't talkin' about it. Either Lillie don't know yet, or she's gonna pretend it didn't happen."

"Hmmm." Minnie poured a bit more tea in their china cups. "Perhaps we should invite Libby over to tea this afternoon."

"We could try, Sister. We could try," Maisie agreed and took another long sip of tea.

Libby sneaked a glance at the tall man walking on the other side of the two boys. He looked completely at ease. Almost pleased with himself.

And why shouldn't he? she asked herself.

He'd managed to get himself invited to breakfast, hadn't he? She sneaked another glance at
him and felt her heart quicken in response. What
was it about this one particular man that was
so . . . disturbing?

Libby looked away again quickly and told
herself that it was nothing. That the agitation he
caused her meant nothing. It was probably just a
case of nerves brought on by her parents and
Maisie and Sissy and Mary!

And even as she thought it, she didn't believe
it.

Maybe coming home was a mistake, she told
herself. Maybe she should have taken Bobby and
gone someplace new. Someplace different. Where
no one knew or cared to know anything about
them.

But she'd wanted Bobby to grow up in Harmony. Her features softened. It was a lovely little
town. And a perfect place for children. With the
river close by and the wide-open prairie to
explore, a child could have as much or as little of
the world as he wanted. All in one little corner of
Kansas.

Besides, her family was here. And now the
Taylors were all the family Bobby had. She
wanted him to know them. Especially now that
he had no father. Libby knew that her son would
need a man in his life. Someone who could teach
him what he would need to know to become a
good man himself.

And since she had no intention of remarrying,
she wanted Bobby to have her father and Billy
and even little Harry to count on, to watch. She

wanted him to see that not *all* men spent every waking moment in a saloon!

Yes, she told herself firmly. She'd done the right thing. Coming home was the right decision. It would be wonderful for Bobby. And good for her, too.

It didn't even matter that her mother was once again taking over. Libby didn't much care *what* her new house looked like. As long as she and Bobby would be living there *alone*.

She inhaled deeply, enjoying the hot summer air for the first time that morning. Everything was going to be fine. She just *knew* it!

"I'll race you to the edge of town!" Harry yelled and started running.

"I'll win, I'll win!" Bobby took off after him, his short, chubby legs no match for his faster, skinnier uncle.

A long moment passed, then Travis spoke, and a tingle of warning shot up her spine.

"Alone at last!"

Chapter Five

JUST WALKING BESIDE HIM WAS DANGER-
ous, Libby decided after only a few feet. With the
boys running ahead, it was just the two of them
left together. And Travis had moved in unusually
close to her. There wasn't more than an inch of
space between them.

The sleeves of their shirts brushed together
with every step, and it was all she could do to
keep from jumping away and insisting he keep
his distance. But she didn't want him to know
how his very closeness affected her, so she kept
quiet.

Libby found herself hurrying to match her
much shorter strides to the pace he set with those
long legs of his. Reluctantly she looked down
from the corner of her eye and noted how well
the faded, threadbare jeans he wore clung to his
muscled thighs.

She swallowed and raised her gaze quickly.
For heaven's sake! She had no business entertaining such thoughts! And yet, something warm
and pleasant settled low in her abdomen, and
she was hard-pressed to ignore it. Staring
blankly ahead, she tried desperately not to think
at all.

But Travis's presence was too powerful a distraction.

It seemed that those few, small stirrings she'd felt when she'd seen him for the first time in four years had been only a warning of what was to come. She risked a glance up at his profile and told herself dismally that he'd gotten even *more* handsome than she'd remembered him to be.

Her gaze followed the line of his strong jaw, across his freshly shaved tanned cheeks, to the collar of his pale blue shirt, where wavy, dark hair hung just a bit too long over the back. Closing her eyes briefly, she shook her head. It made no difference, she told herself.

She'd let her feelings rule her mind once before—she wouldn't do it again.

Then the slight breeze shifted, and she caught the barest whiff of peppermint in the air. A half smile curved her lips as she let herself recall that Travis always *did* have a fondness for peppermint candy.

"What's funny?"

She jumped at the rumbling deep voice cutting into her thoughts. "Oh . . . nothing."

"That's a fine boy, Libby."

"Yes, he is. Thank you."

"Seems to be real partial to hats, though."

Libby looked at her son and brother, some thirty yards ahead of them, and laughed shortly. Bobby was continually having to shove Travis's hat out of his eyes, but he gave no indication of giving it up anytime soon.

"I promise I'll get it back for you," she said softly.

"Doesn't matter," Travis answered. "Give me an excuse to buy a new one."

"No, Travis."

"Let the boy have the hat, Libby."

She looked up then and found his deep brown eyes watching her. Waiting. Slowly she nodded. "All right."

"Good." He grinned suddenly and asked, "What'd your mother have to say about your doin's last night?"

"Not too much, actually." Libby looked back at the rambling trail ahead of them. Of course, the only reason for that was that Libby had successfully distracted her mother with the search for the perfect house. But she didn't need to explain all that to Travis. Instead, she pretended to study the gnarled cottonwood branches that stretched out overhead.

She didn't want to discuss what had happened in the saloon with anyone. Let alone a man who would no doubt have all too much to say on the subject!

After a few long moments of silence, Travis said, "Are you really planning on doing that again, Libby?"

"What?" she asked, tilting her head up at him. "Go back to the saloon?"

"Well, yeah."

"I certainly am, Travis. I've already told you that."

"What in hell are you tryin' to accomplish, Libby?"

"Just what I said last night. I want Cord Spencer to close down that saloon." She watched his full lips tighten into a grim line and told herself it was better this way. All of the warm feelings she'd felt toward him only a moment ago began to slide away, and Libby breathed easier.

"What d'you care if Harmony has a saloon or not?" Travis asked in a dangerously calm voice. "Hell, *most* towns our size have two or three!"

Why *shouldn't* she care what happened to the place she grew up in? The place where she wanted to raise her son? And who was Travis Miller to decide what she should or shouldn't do?

Libby wanted to shout her questions at him. In fact, it took nearly every ounce of willpower she possessed to hold her tongue and curb her temper. But she managed. Somehow. Instead, she said only, "I want to do everything I can to make sure my hometown is safe."

He snorted. "Safe? From what?"

"Drunks and the people who cater to them."

"It won't happen, Libby. You know that."

"No, I don't know that, Travis," she said flatly. "And neither do you."

"Oh, yes, I do," he argued.

Grabbing her elbow, he pulled her to a stop and swung her around to face him. Not more than twenty feet away lay the edge of town. But there, beneath the concealing shadows of the cottonwoods, it was as if they were the only two people for miles.

"I know that Cord ain't about to be told what to do by *anybody*. That saloon is his business."

"A nasty business, if you ask me," she shot back and tried to yank free of his grip.

"Well, no one asked you, Libby. You can't just

sail into town and start tellin' folks how to run their lives."

"I'm not—"

"That's *exactly* what you're tryin' to do!"

She glared up at him. If he only knew how much right she had to speak up for the wives of men who spent all their time and money in saloons! Who better than she would know about dealing with a man who came home falling down drunk every night? Or about hiding candles and matches from a full-grown man so he wouldn't burn the damn house down?

Did he think this was some silly *whim* of hers? That it was something she'd come up with as a way to pass the time? Lord! It was on the tip of her tongue to shout at him—to tell him everything and then to tell him to mind his own business and leave her alone!

But she didn't. Mainly because she still didn't want anyone to know about Robert. Not that she cared about preserving the man's memory . . . but there really wasn't any point at all in dredging the past up daily to look at and cry over. And that's *just* what would happen if people found out the truth.

Libby deliberately bit back what she really wanted to say and instead said calmly, "Perhaps the people who frequent *saloons* need to be told."

"By you?"

"If necessary."

"Dammit, Libby . . ." His hands moved to her upper arms, and she felt the warmth of his touch right down to her bones. His thumbs moved, rubbing over the fabric of her sleeves, and she had to steel herself against the wandering curls of delight snaking through her body.

What *was* it about his touch? Why was it she felt so . . . disoriented when he was too near? And why couldn't she find the strength to pull away?

"Don't you see there'll be trouble if you keep this up?" He bent his head closer, and Libby tried to concentrate on her righteous indignation. But all she could think of was his mouth, inches from her own. The clean, sharp scent of peppermint surrounding her and his strong hands on her arms.

She knew even before he dipped his head to hers that he was going to kiss her. It was in his eyes. And despite her better judgment, Libby tilted her head back and leaned forward to welcome him.

It was not as he'd imagined it would be. Their first kiss, he'd thought, would be in the moonlight. After a long leisurely supper and a walk through town. He'd envisioned them walking together, laughing together, then sharing a soft, gentle kiss that would affirm what should always have been understood.

That they belonged together.

Instead, he thought wildly as his mouth covered hers, they stood in broad daylight, in the middle of an argument, with her son too close by for comfort.

And then it didn't matter. Nothing mattered except the wild, pulsing need that snaked through him with all the power of a river too full for its banks.

He drew her closer and felt her surrender. Her hands moved up his arms to his shoulders. She pressed her full, luscious breasts against his chest and opened her lips for his questing tongue.

When he tasted her warmth, Travis sighed and gave himself up to the sheer pleasure of it. He'd waited so long for this moment. This kiss. Slowly his tongue swept the inside of her mouth, stroking, teasing. His left hand moved up and down the length of her back while his right slipped around to caress her breast.

Her breath caught, and as his thumb moved over her fabric-covered nipple, Libby's tongue darted into his mouth and he groaned. She moved against him, silently consenting to his touch.

Travis covered her breast with his palm and felt the small peak hidden beneath her dress harden with his attentions. He shifted position slightly, his body suddenly uncomfortably tight. Pulling her hips close, he let her feel how her kiss affected him.

Reluctantly he drew his mouth from hers and began to plant small, nibbling kisses down the length of her slender throat. Under his lips the pulsebeat at the base of her neck thudded erratically.

"Mama?"

A young voice called out from a distance.

"Mama!"

Bobby called again, and this time Libby heard him. Abruptly she straightened and pushed Travis from her. Breathing raggedly, she stared at the man opposite her and saw the haze of passion still clouding his eyes. She didn't need a mirror to tell her that a matching look could be found in her own.

Good God! Libby trembled slightly and forced herself to draw in one shaky breath after another until she felt the fire inside her flicker and die. If Bobby hadn't called when he did . . . dear Lord. How had this happened?

"Libby?"

She shook her head and took one step back.

"Libby, I, uh . . ."

Her gaze snapped up to his. "Don't, Travis," she finally said. "Don't make apologies. We're both adults. It just—happened, that's all."

He took two quick steps that brought him to within a breath of touching her again. Libby held her ground stubbornly, but silently she prayed that he wouldn't reach for her. She didn't know if she'd have the strength to pull away a second time.

"I didn't apologize, Libby," Travis said firmly, "and I ain't about to. I've been wanting to do that for more years than I care to think about."

"What?"

He couldn't be serious! But one quick glance at him told her different. She'd never seen that flash of hunger in his eyes before.

"You heard me . . ."

"I prefer to pretend that I didn't." Libby knew her voice sounded stiff, cold. But it was better than giving in to the rampaging fires coursing through her body.

"Libby, you can't just wish me away. I won't go."

"Travis . . ." What on earth was happening to her? How had this morning turned into such a jumble? "You don't have to 'go' anywhere. Harmony is your home as well as mine. We'll just have to somehow ensure that we don't spend much time together. I'm sure this . . . well . . . this *foolishness* will stop if we spend enough time apart."

"You think so?"

"I'm sure of it."

"Well, I'm not." He lifted her chin with his fingertips. "Y'see, you've been gone four long years, Lib. And none of the 'foolishness' I felt for you then has gone away. Not one damn bit."

She swallowed heavily and moved back a pace. This was a Travis she'd never known. A strong, determined, altogether *disturbing* Travis. A self-satisfied smile on his face, he was watching her like a fox would a well-stocked chicken coop.

And a little voice in the back of her mind asked, why shouldn't he? You all but melted in his arms a moment ago! You allowed him to touch you in a way that your own husband never did!

She shuddered slightly. Just the memory of his fingers at her breast sent trickles of warmth twisting through her. She'd had no idea. She'd never have guessed that a kiss—a touch—could be so . . . shattering.

In three years of marriage Robert had never . . .

"Are you comin', Mama?"

She flinched at Bobby's voice but couldn't seem to drag her gaze away from Travis's. She forced herself to shout back, "Coming, Bobby. You and Harry go on ahead to the hotel!"

"Okay, Mama!" he yelled back. "But don't get lost!"

Lost. If she wasn't careful, that's exactly what she *would* do. Only not the way her son thought. If she spent too much more time with Travis, there was every danger of getting lost in his eyes.

His voice.

His touch.

"Libby?" He spoke and she shook her head, trying to rid herself of the ridiculous notions swamping her.

"What?"

"Why don't we go on to breakfast?" He smiled and Libby felt her traitorous heart race in response.

She stared at him blankly for a moment, caught off guard by his sudden change of subjects. Then what he'd just said sank in. "Surely you're not still planning on all of us having breakfast together?"

Good heavens! He didn't really expect to sit across a table from her as if nothing had happened?

"Of course." Travis leaned forward and traced one finger down her jawline.

Libby jumped.

"In fact," he added with a wink, "I plan on us sharing quite a few meals. And more."

Libby swallowed heavily. She didn't remember Travis being this bold in the past. In fact, she didn't remember him ever giving her a second look.

This Travis was going to be much harder to ignore.

"You know what they say about 'the best-laid

plans, don't you?" she asked, backing up a pace or two.

"Yeah. I know." He stepped up close again. "But there's another old saying, too. 'He who hesitates is lost.'"

Once more she put a little distance between them. But she could still feel the warmth in his eyes. Quickly she countered, "And what about 'Haste makes waste'?"

He grinned.

There was something in that smile of his that set warning bells clanging in every corner of her brain.

"How about that breakfast?" he asked and grabbed her hand. Linking it through the crook of his elbow, he looked down and added, "There'll be time enough later for us to finish this little 'conversation.'"

He started walking with those long strides of his, and she gave up trying to pull her hand free after only a second or two. Still, she took a deep breath and told him firmly, "No, Travis. This 'conversation' is finished now."

The tall man beside her looked down and winked.

As they entered town, Libby cast one look at the Last Resort across the street, then turned her head away. No point in doing anything now, she told herself. It would be night soon enough. Then she would go right back and face down Cord Spencer, even if she had to do it every night.

"Mornin', Travis!"

A deep, throaty voice with a trace of hidden

laughter called out from the purple building on the right.

Luscious Lottie's First Resort.

Travis came to a stop, and Libby looked up to the second-floor balcony. A woman, one of Lottie's girls obviously, lay draped across the wooden railing.

Her long black hair trailed down over her scantily clothed body, and even from a distance Libby saw the makeup enhancing the girl's eyes.

"Been a while, Travis honey," the woman said, pouting prettily.

Libby looked at the man beside her and lifted one eyebrow. He appeared to be decidedly uncomfortable.

"Mornin', Cilla," Travis answered.

"Who's that with ya?" Cilla asked.

"Liberty Wilder," Libby answered before Travis could.

Cilla clapped her hands delightedly and leaned even farther over the railing. Her full breasts pushed and strained against the flimsy barrier of her pale pink wrapper. "I heard all about you, Mrs. Wilder. You mean what you said? You really want to close up Cord's place?"

Libby's lips twisted slightly. Glancing up at Travis, she said, "Didn't take long, did it?"

"Huh?"

"Harmony," Libby said. "I'd almost forgotten how quickly news spreads."

"This is just the beginning, y'know."

"So!" Cilla called out, louder this time. "Liberty Wilder! You comin' after us next?"

Libby looked up at the woman and idly noted how strange it was that she should be standing in the middle of a street, having a shouted chat with a . . . "soiled dove." But then again, she told herself, after the morning she'd had already, maybe it wasn't so strange after all.

"No," she finally answered, mentally banishing all of the gossips who would no doubt run to report to Lillie her daughter's latest indiscretion. "I have no complaint with you or Lottie."

The look of surprise on the girl's face was almost laughable.

Libby supposed that most women would consider shutting down a bordello as the proper thing to do. But, she told herself, Cilla and the others who worked for Lottie were only trying to survive.

They didn't stagger home at two in the morning shouting and carrying on. *They* didn't darn near burn the house down because they fell asleep with a lit cigar in their hands.

Libby took a longer look at Cilla and mentally judged that she and the other woman looked to be about the same age. Strange, she thought, how completely different two women's lives could be. But were they really all that different? she asked herself a half moment later. Weren't she and Cilla and most other women just trying to get by?

"No," Libby finally said. "It's the whiskey sellers I'd like to shut down."

Cilla nodded sagely. Tilting her head to one side, she shouted, "Your man a drunkard, hon?"

Libby's jaw dropped, and she sucked in a gulp of air. There it was. A direct question about the one thing she'd dreaded talking about. And why was it that Cilla could guess her reasons and no one else had?

The old familiar rush of shame spread through her. Recollections of Robert's flushed face and sloppy grin flooded her. Images of herself, declining invitations and refusing to have people in her home for fear of how her husband would behave, swam before her eyes.

Libby forced herself to breathe deeply, evenly. Her mind worked with a frantic haste. Now that the question had been asked, what should she say? Deny it? Go on pretending that her marriage had been perfect? Let everyone in town think that she was simply a sharp-tongued woman with nothing better to do than drive an honest man out of business?

She flicked a quick glance at Travis and saw that he was watching her through newly curious eyes. Looking away again, Libby told herself that maybe it was good Cilla'd broached the subject.

Maybe it was best if Travis knew. Then he would realize that she had the best of reasons for not giving up on her campaign to close down the saloon.

Straightening her spine, Libby threw her head back, met Cilla's direct stare, and answered in a stronger voice than she'd thought herself capable of. "That's right, Cilla. He was."

"Shame, that." Cilla nodded and pushed her long hair out of her eyes. "My pa was, too."

They stared at each other with sudden and complete understanding. After a long moment Libby nodded, and Cilla lifted one hand in silent goodbye.

Without another word Libby began walking toward the hotel again.

She wondered idly how many people had heard Cilla's shouted question. Of course, Libby had nothing to be ashamed of. Logically, she knew that. She'd been the best wife she knew how to be. It wasn't her fault that Robert . . .

"Libby, wait a minute!"

Travis caught up with her in just a few quick strides. Absently he nodded to Jake as the big man stepped outside the smithy. As he passed the barbershop, he waved to Zeke, the barber, perched on his favorite chair on the boardwalk.

Then Travis grabbed Libby's arm and pulled her around to face him. The calmness in her eyes stopped him dead for a moment, but he pushed past it, determined that she talk to him. And he was past caring *who* heard them, or who was watching from behind their curtains.

Oh, he could've cheerfully wrung Cilla's neck for her when she first spoke up. But now . . . maybe it was best that it had happened. The young prostitute had obviously struck a nerve with Libby. And maybe now that the cat was out of the bag, Travis could find a way to get closer to the hardheaded woman.

"Libby . . ."

"Leave me alone, Travis."

"No. Not until you talk to me."

"About what?" She laughed shortly, but it was a flat, harsh sound, without a hint of a smile.

"Dammit, Libby!"

"Maybe you didn't hear me, Travis. My husband *was* a drunkard." She pulled free of his grip and stared up at him. "And maybe *now* you'll understand why I'm going to close up Cord Spencer's saloon."

"Nope, I sure don't."

"What?"

"One has nothin' to do with the other, Libby." Lord, the woman had a hard head. But now that he knew what the trouble was, maybe he could sort it out before she caused herself any more trouble. "Gettin' rid of saloons won't cure a drunk."

"I didn't say that."

"Sure you did."

"All I'm saying is by getting rid of saloons, there'll be no place for a drunk to *find* a drink."

"Don't kid yourself, Lib. A man who wants a drink bad enough will find one."

"We don't have to make it easy for them!"

"You can't make people live the way you want them to!"

"I know."

"Yeah," he admitted with a nod. "I suppose you do."

"And don't start giving me 'poor little Libby' looks, either, Travis Miller! I don't want them, and I don't *need* them!"

"Never said you did." He reached for her again, but she stepped back out of his grasp.

"And while we're at it, Travis . . . there's one other thing you should know." She lifted her chin slightly and squared her shoulders. "I have no intention of allowing another man into my life. So you'd better rid yourself of *that* notion, here and now."

That may be what she thinks, Travis told himself silently, but the way she responded to his kiss told him something else entirely. Libby wasn't the kind of woman to live her life alone. And even if she was—he'd find a way to change her mind.

Suddenly he decided that arguing with her wasn't the answer. He'd *show* her just what he thought of her ridiculous statement.

Travis moved in closer and pulled her into his arms. Lowering his head, he claimed her mouth with a kiss designed to steal her breath away.

Standing in the middle of Main Street, he held on to her as if she were the last handhold on earth. He put every ounce of passion, desire, and longing he'd felt for the last four years into his kiss, and when she sagged against him, he knew he'd succeeded.

His own breath ragged, his heart pounding, he slowly raised his head and looked down into her cloudy green eyes. The morning sun danced on her shining deep brown hair, filling it with tiny dazzles of red. He noticed a faint tracing of freckles across her nose that he'd never seen before and told himself that he wanted to spend the rest of his life discovering new things about her.

"You might as well hear this right off, Libby," he whispered, just a breath away from her lips. "*This* man is already in your life. And that's just where I'm gonna stay."

She pushed against his chest ineffectually. She wouldn't get away from him *this* time, until he was ready to let her go. "You get used to it, Libby. I ain't goin' away. And neither are you."

Chapter Six

IT WAS THE LONGEST MEAL OF HER LIFE.

Libby stood uncertainly in the dusty street outside the hotel. She still wasn't quite sure how she'd managed to sit through breakfast without screaming. Or, she thought with a wistful smile, punching Travis Miller dead in the face.

He'd sat directly across from her at the long community table in the hotel dining room. His deep brown gaze hadn't drifted from her for a moment. Even though she'd kept her own eyes on her almost untouched plate, Libby was as sure of his stare as she was of the sun coming up tomorrow.

It didn't matter that there were other people around. Her own *son*, in fact! No, nothing seemed to get in Travis's way if his mind was made up.

And he'd obviously decided to drive Libby Wilder insane.

She groaned quietly and tried to forget the curious looks the other diners had given her. Why, even *Faith*, Libby's *friend*, had found one excuse after another to reenter the dining room just to watch Travis mooning at her.

Then, to make matters worse, when he left for the jailhouse, he'd actually stooped down beside her and kissed her on the cheek! In front of everyone!

Libby clenched her jaw and ground her teeth together in frustration. She would never forget the pleased-as-punch smile on Faith's face or her brother Harry's disgusted expression. But as she recalled that moment now, she realized that the one person whose reaction had surprised her the most was Bobby.

Her own son had ducked his head briefly, in embarrassment, but when he looked up and met his mother's gaze, he'd looked downright delighted. In a way, she could hardly blame him for looking at every man he admired as a potential father. Lord knew, his *own* father had been a disappointment.

But for heaven's sake! *Travis?*

She inhaled slowly and laid the flat of her hand against her abdomen. Despite Harry's glowing compliments, Faith's blueberry muffins lay like lead shot in the pit of Libby's stomach.

That infuriating man had absolutely *ruined* a perfectly good breakfast.

Lifting her chin, Libby squared her shoulders and told herself to stop fretting over spilt milk. She couldn't undo the morning's events, so it would be better to simply go on from there. She started walking. At least with Travis safely in his office, she could get on with her plan. All she had to do was stop thinking about him.

That shouldn't be too hard. Should it?

Walking quickly across the dusty road, Libby ran one finger under the collar of her pale green dress. The already hot August sun shone from a cloudless deep blue sky, and she could feel small drops of perspiration roll down her back. What she wouldn't give to be able to roll her long sleeves back and undo the top couple of buttons at her throat.

But she could just imagine people's reaction to *that*. And she'd already given the citizens of Harmony plenty to gossip about. Although, once her plan was set in motion, how much more harm could a few loose buttons do?

She shook her head. First things first.

Cautiously she skirted the edge of the mercantile. Libby wasn't in any mood to deal with her mother again quite so soon after their last go-around. Even as she slipped past the yellow building, though, she told herself that caution was probably unnecessary. Lillie was so wrapped up in choosing houses, paints, and furnishings that keeping track of her eldest child was undoubtedly the *last* thing on her mind.

Still, it paid to be careful.

A farmer on the bench seat of a rickety hay wagon waved as he passed directly in front of her. Libby raised one hand in greeting, then fanned at the rising cloud of fine dust that settled over her like a feather-weight gray blanket.

Coughing quietly, she lifted the hem of her skirt and stepped onto the walk outside the Harmony *Sentinel*. From inside the newspaper office came the distinct sounds of someone hard at work.

Libby found herself hoping that it was Alexander Evans she heard and not his daughter, Samantha. Ordinarily she would have looked forward to visiting with her old friend. But since

Samantha was now married to Cord Spencer, Libby was less certain of her welcome.

But there was nothing to be done about it now.

Quickly, before she could change her mind, she grabbed the doorknob and turned. The heavy odors of ink, paper, and sweat greeted her, but Libby ignored it, stepped inside, and closed the door behind her.

At the printing press, her back to the door, stood Samantha. One quick glance around the building confirmed that Alexander was nowhere in sight. Libby pursed her lips thoughtfully. Well, there was no other choice. She would have to deal with Samantha Evans Spencer and hope for the best.

The woman behind the counter turned, looked at her customer, and grinned. Dusting her palms together, Samantha walked to the whitewashed plank countertop and held out both hands.

"Libby!" she crowed. "It's so good to see you again!"

Two quick steps and Liberty grasped her friend's hands in hers. Samantha's long blond hair was pulled back into a braid that hung halfway down her back. Her sharp blue eyes moved over Libby in a lightning flash of movement, and there was a streak of black ink across her nose and cheeks that looked very much like war paint.

Appropriate, Libby told herself. When Sam took hold of a story, she had the tenacity and courage of *any* bunch of Apache.

Covered with sweat-soaked grime and dust, Libby also felt at a slight disadvantage as she looked at her friend's clothes. Even working on a newspaper wasn't enough to cause Sam Evans to look anything but fashionable. Her plain white shirt was tucked into the waistband of an apple-red skirt, and even the black over-sleeves she wore to protect her cuffs from newsprint didn't detract from the elegant image she presented.

"I was hoping to get to the hotel this afternoon to visit for a while," Samantha said, squeezing Libby's hands before releasing her. "But I'm so glad you came in now!"

"It's good to see you, too." Libby leaned on the counter and went on, "And I'm glad that you're still pleased to see me. I was a little afraid that I might not be so welcome."

Sam frowned, then slowly grinned. "Oh! You mean that little 'business' at Cord's place last night?"

"Yes."

"He told me all about it," Sam conceded.

"I rather imagined he might."

"But that has nothing to do with us, Lib. You should know that."

"Thanks, Sam. I *do* appreciate it." She hesitated, unsure of quite how to go on. Her indecision must have been plain, she told herself when Samantha spoke again.

"Is this visit purely pleasure?" She tilted her head to one side and watched her friend. "Or is there some other reason?"

"Well . . ."

"I have to warn you, Libby. Cord doesn't tell me how to write a newspaper, and I don't tell him how to run a saloon."

"Oh," Libby cut in quickly, "it's nothing like

that. Honestly. Sam, I would never want to pit you against your husband."

"Good. Because I wouldn't go." She smiled then and pushed a stray lock of hair off her forehead, leaving yet another streak of ink in its place. "So, what can I do for you?"

"I'd like to place an advertisement in your paper."

"Advertisement?"

"Yes."

"What kind?"

Libby's fingertips toyed with a sliver of wood that had poked up from the rough plank counter. "It's more of an announcement, really. About a meeting I'm going to hold."

"All right." Samantha rummaged around on the desk behind her and came back with a sheet of paper and a pencil. "Just tell me what you want it to say."

Libby took a deep breath and prepared herself for what could be a gasp of outrage from her old friend. "Women of Harmony—Defend your families—protect your right to a harmonious life—make our town safe for our children. Come to a meeting at the schoolhouse—Tuesday, three-thirty."

Samantha finished writing, read what she'd put down again, then glanced at Libby warily. "Interesting notice. And how do you want it signed?"

Meeting the other woman's gaze steadily, she answered, "Liberty Taylor Wilder—Chairman, Harmony Temperance League."

"*Temperance* League?" Sam echoed. "I wasn't aware there *was* one in town."

"There is now."

"I see."

"Is there a problem with running my advertisement, Sam?"

"My husband *is* the saloonkeeper in town, Lib."

"Well, yes. But *you* run the paper, don't you?"

"Yes . . ."

"And I *am* a paying customer. . . ." She laid her money on the counter.

"Libby . . ."

"Sam, if you really don't want to run it, I'll post a notice in my folks' store window."

The short, blond woman was silent for several minutes. Her blue eyes locked on the paper in front of her, Libby knew that Samantha was weighing both sides of the problem carefully. She only hoped that in this case, at least, the newspaperwoman in her was stronger than the wife.

"Okay. I'll run it."

"Wonderful!"

"But I won't be joining your league, Lib."

"I understand, believe me," Liberty assured her. "But you *could* attend the meeting as a reporter. Couldn't you?"

Chewing on the end of her pencil, Samantha thought about it briefly before agreeing. "All right. I'll cover your meeting. But the men in town aren't going to like this one little bit!"

"When has *that* ever stopped *you?*"

Samantha grinned and bent to check the wording of the announcement one more time.

The saloon was even *more* crowded than the night before.

Libby stood uncertainly, just outside, on the boardwalk. Peeking over the top of the batwing doors, she chewed at her bottom lip nervously.

Between the piano music, laughter, and men shouting at or to each other, she could hardly hear herself think. And maybe, she told herself, it was just as well. If she had too much time to think about what she was about to do, she just might change her mind.

Her visit the night before had been more or less a whim. Somewhat along the lines of delivering a direct challenge *inside* the lion's den. But tonight . . . she *had* to show up.

She'd heard the whispers all day. Even Maisie and Minnie had invited her to "tea," though Libby knew that they were just trying to get information from her. She'd felt the stares of people she'd known her whole life looking at her as though she'd lost her mind. Oh, they were used to her antics as a girl. In fact, almost nothing she could do then had surprised anyone.

But it seemed that folks generally expected that when a person became a certain age, they should naturally acquire some sense of what was "proper." Apparently, everyone in Harmony was completely satisfied that Libby hadn't.

Countless numbers of people, men and women alike, had managed to say in her hearing that a "decent" woman would remove herself from a man's domain. That a respectable "widow woman" should know better than to flaunt herself in a saloon, or—worse yet—actually *speak* to one of Lottie's girls. In broad daylight, no less!

Frowning, Libby's foot began to tap against the wooden planks. Her fingers curled over the tops of the doors and tightened until her knuckles were white.

Libby'd never liked being told what to do or how to act. That was, in fact, the main bone of contention between her and her mother during her growing-up years. There'd always been a stubborn streak in Libby that grew and deepened any time someone tried to foist his or her ideas on her. And she was no different now.

She was even willing to admit to herself that everyone's "opinions" were a large part of her decision to return to the saloon. Libby wasn't about to be told by *anyone* that she couldn't set foot anywhere she had a mind to.

Though she *had* expected Travis to try.

But she hadn't seen him since breakfast, though she'd heard plenty about him. Besides her visit to a saloon and her chat with Cilla, the main topic of conversation in town appeared to be that kiss Travis had branded her with in the middle of Main Street.

She ground her teeth together. He'd only made a difficult situation worse. And Libby was positive *that* fact didn't bother him in the least.

"Go on, *git!*"

Libby jumped back at the nearby shout. A heartbeat later a drunken cowhand came flying through the saloon doors. On wobbly legs he staggered across the boardwalk, stumbled off the edge, and fell into the street.

From inside, Libby heard a chorus of male laughter with just a sprinkling of female voices chiming in. She stared down at the hapless man lying in the dirt and, despite herself, felt a stirring of sympathy. Spreadeagled, he lay faceup, staring at the night sky through wide, vacant eyes. As she watched, he smacked his lips together noisily, mumbled incoherently, and slowly braced his hands on either side of his body to roll over onto his stomach.

A horse tied to the nearby hitching rail skittered sideways, but the man didn't even seem to notice the animal.

His battered brown hat lay only a foot or two from him, but when he tried to crawl toward it, he lost his balance and sprawled face first into the dust. Libby took a half step closer, thinking to help him up, when she heard his muffled laughter and stopped dead.

Mouth against the dirt road, arms and legs spread wide, the young cowhand's dirt-encrusted shoulders shook as his chuckles grew louder and louder.

Her lips twisted, Libby stared down at him, and memories of Robert filled her. Instead of the cowhand, she saw her late husband as she had too many nights in the past.

Drunk. She remembered his staggering loss of balance as she tried to guide him to his room. She remembered listening to his unending stream of complaints about her, Bobby, the ranch, and life in general.

All too well she remembered lying in her own bed, watching the doorknob, hoping it wouldn't turn under his efforts to get in. She recalled vividly propping a ladder-backed chair under the brass knob and hoping it would be enough to dissuade him long enough for the drink to rob him of any desire for her.

And clearly, she remembered the "morning

after." She knew that come tomorrow at dawn, the giddy cowhand lying in the street would be groaning with the agony of a head that threatened to split wide open. She knew he would be sullen, regretful, and still certain that the night before had been worth the pain of waking up.

Certainly, Robert always had. Her lips quirked suddenly as she also remembered how often she'd found it necessary to clang her iron skillet against the stove on those mornings her husband sat slumped over the kitchen table. A small thing perhaps, but at the time she'd felt it was a simple way of making her feelings clear.

Although on that score, Libby was positive that Robert had never had any doubts about what she was feeling at any particular time. It had taken her more than a year to realize that he just didn't care.

Her resolve suddenly strengthened, Libby turned her back on the fallen man and her memories. She'd stood up to her husband. She'd managed to maintain an illusion of contentment for her family's sake. She'd given birth to a child and nurtured him alone. And upon her husband's death she'd found a buyer for their ranch and made her escape.

After all that, certainly Cord Spencer and his cohorts weren't enough to send her packing!

She was home again now. She would raise her son in Harmony. And she didn't want to spend the rest of her life explaining to Bobby just why the men he admired spent so much time in a barroom.

Facing the saloon, she told herself that if men didn't have sense enough to protect themselves and their families, then by God, it was up to *her* to do it for them!

She shoved at the doors and stepped inside.

Once again the noise died away with her entrance and she felt the stares of everyone in the place. At least tonight she was ready for it.

"Good evening, Mrs. Wilder," Cord called out from near the bar. "We've been expecting you! Please, come in!"

Libby looked around suspiciously. But the men surrounding her looked . . . harmless.

"Are you alone tonight?" Cord asked, a grin creasing his handsome face as he pretended to look behind her. "Ah, I see you are. What a shame. No drums? No horns? No parade of women coming to close down my den of sin?"

"No," she said, then swallowed and added more loudly, "I'm alone."

"And no less welcome for that fact," he offered, extending his hand graciously and waving her forward.

She stayed put and watched him curiously from a distance of not more than twenty feet. Why was he being so . . . *nice*? Her eyes narrowed just a bit. Something was going on. Something she was unaware of.

"You know why I'm here?" she asked.

"Yes, indeed."

"Will you close your saloon?"

"No, indeed."

The men seated at the tables around the bar burst into wild laughter at the exchange, and Libby shot the closest man a look that silenced him immediately. The florid-faced farmer ducked his head and stared determinedly into his beer.

"Mrs. Wilder," Cord coaxed from his position at the front of the room, "why don't you step right up here where everyone can see you?"

"No, thank you," she replied quickly. "It's apparent that most of these men have been here *quite* awhile." She let her eyes sweep the room, pausing occasionally on a particularly blurry-eyed man. "They'll probably be able to see me better from right here."

An appreciative chuckle sounded from the back of the room, and Libby noticed one of the bar girls wink at her.

Cord grinned and nodded. "All right, fellas!" he shouted, holding both hands out toward the crowd. "What d'ya say we all keep quiet for a bit and let the lady have her say?"

"You *want* me to talk to your customers?" Libby asked.

"That *is* why you're here, isn't it? To tell us all about the evil of sin?"

"Sin!" another voice called out. "A gift from Above!"

"Amen, brother," someone else answered.

"Well, Mrs. Wilder?"

It was a challenge. Pure and simple. Libby watched the saloonkeeper and saw what Samantha must see. Good humor shining in his eyes and a decidedly wicked grin. But should she take him up on his offer? Or was it some trick to make her appear a fool?

Slowly, one more time, Libby looked around the crowded, smoke-filled room. A sea of faces, turned toward her, waiting expectantly for whatever was to come. She recognized most of them. Several farmers who usually came into town on the first of the month, young ranch hands, a gambler or two. In the far corner she spied Zeke, the barber, a pleasant smile on his face as he waited for the "show" to start. At the same table was Kincaid Hutton and another, older man Libby thought just might be the new doctor she'd heard Minnie was so enamored of.

Charlie Thompson stood behind the bar, his hands braced on the shining wood surface, a sympathetic look on his face.

From the corner of her eye she saw someone stand up and walk toward the center of the bar.

Travis.

He moved slowly, lazily, until finally he stopped, turned his back to the bar, hooked one bootheel on the brass railing, and leaned his elbows on the bar top. His head cocked, he watched her through cautious brown eyes, waiting.

She hadn't expected her heart to give such a leap of welcome simply at the *sight* of him. But there was something in his too-casual stance. Some tightly leashed *readiness* that made her mouth dry and her palms damp.

With a wrench Libby tore her gaze from him. It was impossible to think clearly while looking directly into his eyes.

And above all, she *had* to think clearly.

"Well, Mrs. Wilder?" Cord asked again. "Would you care to speak to the men? Or will you be leaving us already?"

Chapter Seven

TRAVIS TOLD HIMSELF THAT HE OUGHT TO stop the whole thing. But in the next instant he realized that Libby would have his hide if he tried to butt in now.

He watched her carefully. In the hazy light of the saloon she looked completely out of place. Like a diamond in a pile of stones. Or a flower in a patch of weeds. From her tidy, upswept hair to the high-necked, long-sleeved blue dress she wore, everything about Libby Wilder screamed out—*Lady*.

He flicked a quick glance at his surroundings and wasn't surprised to see signs of impatience lining the faces of the men nearest him. Libby was a distraction.

A pretty one, sure. But a distraction nonetheless. Men who came to Cord's place didn't want a lecture. And they didn't want their drinking interrupted. The novelty of her visit was beginning to wear off, and Travis wished she'd get the hell out of the bar before there was real trouble.

But until she did something illegal or Cord asked her to leave . . . there was nothing Travis could do. Except wait.

He saw the indecision on Libby's features slowly become determination, and he knew that she'd made up her mind. She was going to take Cord up on his offer. Of course, he'd never doubted that she would. He only hoped she wouldn't start a riot once she started talking.

"Most of you know me," she started, and a few of the men grumbled acknowledgment.

"For those who don't, my name is Liberty Taylor Wilder."

"And I'm Buck, honey! How do?"

Travis's gaze narrowed, and he stared toward the far corner, trying to figure out who'd spoken.

Libby paid no attention, though.

"I'm here tonight because I want to ask you all to go home. To your families."

A snort of laughter interrupted her. "Hell, lady. Why d'ya think we're here in the first place?"

"Whiskey is only trouble," she tried again, louder this time.

"Amen, sister!"

"Damn right!"

Her cheeks flushed, Libby's temper was slowly rising to the boiling point. Not that Travis blamed her any. But on the other hand, what more did she expect? Did she really think to convince these men to set their drinks down and run home? Just because *she* said to?

"No woman wants a drunkard for a husband!"

"Hey, Mike," someone called out, "reckon if that's true, mine'll leave?"

Travis winced. Things weren't going well at all. Libby looked fit to be tied. Her patience was fast disappearing. But to give her her due, she wasn't a quitter!

"Do you really want to spend *all* of your hard-earned money on liquor?"

"Shit! The little lady's right!" a booming voice from near the door shouted out. "Hey, Cord, how 'bout you buy a round for a change?"

"Sorry, boys," Spencer answered with a grin.

Her hands were clenched at her sides, and her back was ramrod straight. Travis shook his head in admiration. No one but him would probably notice those small signs of Libby's anger. To everyone else, she looked perfectly composed.

He watched her sharp eyes move over the ever noisier crowd before she spoke again.

"Think what you could do with the money you saved!" she went on, struggling to be heard over the low-pitched grumbling in the room.

"True, true, darlin'. I could spend more time at Lottie's, that's for damn sure!"

Someone slapped the speaker on the back, and a few more voices were added to the growing laughter.

Then one voice carried over the rest. A deep, gravelly voice without a trace of humor in it. "C'mon, Cord! I didn't come in here for no preachin'! And if I was to listen to a damned sermon, it wouldn't be from no woman! Now, you shut the lady up or I will."

"Who said that?" Libby shouted back, turning first one way, then the other, trying to identify the speaker.

A burly man with a full beard lying across a dirty, red flannel shirt pushed himself to his feet. "*I* said it."

Travis straightened up from the bar.

Libby faced the man standing only a few feet from her and lifted her chin defiantly. "How *dare* you tell me to shut up?"

The man's small eyes narrowed even further, and he ran one thumb under a suspender strap. "Lady, you got a mouth on you that fair splits a man's head. Why don't you run along home and leave men's business alone?"

"Business?" she challenged and took two steps forward. Chairs scraped against wood as men in the way scuttled out of her path. "Drinking yourself into a stupor is *business*?"

"Darlin'—" her adversary said.

"Don't call me darlin'!" Libby shot back and stepped closer still.

Travis moved away from the bar and started inching his way toward Libby. He had a terrible feeling that everything was about to go wrong.

He recognized the big man antagonizing Libby. A sometime shotgun rider for the stage-line and all-around no-account, he'd drifted into town a few days before and had already been in three fights.

And, though Travis told himself that surely the man wouldn't hit a *woman*, there was simply no way to be sure about that.

As Libby stopped only inches from the big man's chest, Travis heard Zeke call out from behind him, "Now, now! I think this has gone far enough. . . ."

The crowd drowned the older man out. Every man in the place had an opinion, and it seemed they'd all decided to shout it out at once. But Travis didn't pay attention to any of the others. His gaze was locked on Libby and the man who towered over her with the height and breadth of a mountain.

"You know, darlin'," the bearded gent said,

"up close you're kinda pretty. I reckon a man could make allowances for that harpy's tongue of yours!" His thick hands shot out and snatched hold of Libby's waist. Easily lifting her off the floor, he chuckled at her puny efforts to get free.

"Here now, pretty lady . . . why don't I show you what a little whiskey can do for ya?"

A red haze of anger blurred Travis's vision. All he could see . . . all he could think about . . . was that fella's hands on Libby! His ears filled with the roaring thunder of his own blood racing through his veins, Travis pushed his way through the crowd. His only thought was to reach Libby. But it was as if he was in a dream. He couldn't seem to get any closer, no matter how quickly he moved.

He no sooner pushed one man out of his way than another sprung up in front of him. He'd never reach her in time, he knew it. Trouble was about to explode in Cord's saloon.

And the big man still holding Libby was only a small part of it.

From several feet away, as he determinedly shoved people out of his way, Travis saw Libby reach down to the table behind her. When she raised her arm, a whiskey bottle clenched in her hand, he wasn't even surprised.

And when Libby bounced that bottle off the big man's skull, Travis was close enough to hear the loud smack and see the burly drifter's eyes roll back. Travis also saw her satisfied grin as the man started sliding down to the floor. Then her smile faded to a look of panicked dismay as she was carried down along with her victim.

At once bedlam broke out in the crowded

saloon. Chairs sailed through the air, crashing through the windows facing Main Street. Tables were tossed aside as if they were nothing more than kindling. Beer mugs and whiskey bottles arched high and slammed back to earth, taking a few of the battle's participants with them.

And still, Travis couldn't reach her. As he ducked a punch aimed at him, he thought he caught a glimpse of blue, but it was gone so quickly, he couldn't be sure. It seemed as though the crowd had swelled to hundreds of men, even though he knew it wasn't so. Every man in the place suddenly turned on the man beside him, friend or foe, eager to get into the brawl.

Someone loomed up in front of him, fist drawn back, and Travis hit him. The man dropped like a stone. Shaking his aching hand, Travis took another step and fell across a wounded warrior stretched out on the floor. On his hands and knees he heard Cord shouting from somewhere in the back of the room for the men to stop, but Travis knew a shout wouldn't do it.

If it wasn't for Libby, he'd fire a few rounds into the air until the damned fools paid attention. If, he told himself as someone fell over him, he could get up off the floor. But as it was, the only thing on his mind was finding her and getting her out of harm's way before she got hurt.

His palms flat on the plank floor, a bootheel ground into the fingers of his left hand. Travis yelped, grabbed the booted ankle, yanked on it, and listened with a pleased smile to the heavy *thump* of the man hitting the floor.

Finally he managed to push himself to his feet and immediately headed for the last place he'd seen Libby. A few steps into the fray, he spotted her. Travis stopped dead at the sight.

Brown hair tumbling down over her shoulders, her dress torn at the collar, one sleeve hanging loose around her left wrist, and already the beginnings of a beautiful shiner on her right eye, Libby had thrown herself into the fight. She stood in a circle of battling men like an avenging angel, her head turning this way and that, looking for her next target.

Even as he watched, Travis saw her kick one man in the shins. Then, as another man foolishly made a grab for her, Libby picked up a glass and tossed raw whiskey into his eyes.

A creaking groan screamed out overhead, and Travis looked up. One man, hanging from the wagon-wheel chandelier, swung across the room, the soles of his booted feet only inches from the heads of those below. And as Travis watched, the fixture pulled free of the ceiling and fell in a splintering crash onto the crowd.

Only a few of the oil lamps were still lit when it landed, but as the kerosene spilled across the floor, tiny blossoms of flames skittered along the edges of the oil, quickly spreading and growing.

Immediately shouts of alarm went up, and men forgot about their fight in the effort to stamp out the fire before it had a chance to catch and build.

In the momentary confusion Travis saw that Cord and the others had the situation in hand enough that his help wasn't needed. Instead, he raced across the last few feet separating him from Libby.

Her dirt-streaked, triumphant grin greeted him, but he ignored it.

Without a word he bent low, grabbed her legs in an iron grip, and let the upper half of her body flop down against his back as he stood. Even as she shouted angrily and pounded on his back with her fists, Travis pushed his way through the surrounding men. Not until they were outside did he slow his steps, and even then he made no move to let her go.

On Main Street a small group of people, mostly curious customers from Lottie's, stood huddled together, trying to see into the saloon. Apparently, they had the sense to stay clear of the fight itself. No one seemed to notice them as Travis cautiously crossed the street. Circling around the edge of the First Resort, he hurried his steps again and kept walking along behind the row of clustered buildings that formed the heart of Harmony.

Past the mill, the livery stable, and Jane Carson Evans's dress shop. Libby squirmed in his arms, and he tightened his grip, determined to hold on to her until he could talk to her somewhere quiet. Her furious voice ringing in his ears, Travis continued past the depot, the mercantile, and the entrance to the hotel.

When he finally stopped just outside of town, near the foot of the bridge spanning the Smoky Hill River, Travis dropped Libby to her feet in front of him.

Before she was even sure of her balance, she swung one fist at him, and he ducked as it came in, then grabbed both her hands in his.

"Let me go, Travis!"

"Not until you tell me you're through fightin' for the night!"

She sucked in a gulp of air and seemed to steady herself in the same motion. Travis tried to keep his mind clear enough to think, but standing that close to her, in the dark, *alone* . . . well, it wasn't easy.

"All right." She sighed. "You're completely safe, Travis. Now let me go."

He released her immediately.

Pulling her sleeve uselessly up to her shoulder only to watch it slide back down the length of her arm, Libby stared at it ruefully before turning back to look at the man in front of her.

"Just what was that all about?" she asked. "How do you think it looked to everyone in town to see you carrying me around like a sack of flour?"

"It probably looked a damn sight better than you would have looked bein' tarred and feathered by that crowd in the saloon!"

Hmmph!" She pushed her hair out of her eyes with the back of her hand. But the heavy mass fell forward again and lay across her cheek. "Tarred and feathered indeed. I was doing just fine by myself, y'know."

"Yeah," he said grimly. "I saw." Deliberately he reached out and gently touched her bruised eye. When she flinched, he lowered his hand again. "Sorry."

She waved his apology away. Her own fingertips gingerly explored her aching cheekbone. "Does it look awful?"

"Not yet, but I expect by tomorrow it ought to be a real beauty."

"Oh, Lord," she said on a groan. "A black eye. At *my* age." Libby sank to the ground, and her wide blue skirt pooled out around her. Crossing her legs Indian style, she braced her elbows on her knees and propped her chin in her hands. "How will I explain this to Bobby?"

How could she explain it to herself? she added silently. For heaven's sake! She'd been in a barroom brawl! And, she acknowledged silently, she'd enjoyed every minute of it! Splintered images of the fight rose up in her mind. Once again she saw the surprised expression on that big man's face when she hit him with the whiskey bottle.

She glanced again at her torn sleeve and couldn't remember exactly when that had happened. Of course, she thought wryly, she couldn't remember being punched in the eye, either.

But she *did* remember all too clearly the excitement of being in the middle of such a scuffle and holding her own.

Guiltily a tiny smile curved her lips and Libby found herself biting the inside of her cheek to keep from laughing out loud. Visions of the saloon girls running for cover and the nameless man swinging across the room on the chandelier flashed across her brain. She could almost hear Cord shouting for quiet only to be drowned out by the sound of breaking glass.

And Travis. Libby sneaked a quick glance up at him. Pushing through that crush of men to reach her with the single-minded determination of a mother bear desperately trying to save her cub. Then the memory of him falling to the floor and being stepped on rushed into her mind, and she had to look away again before he saw her smile.

She pulled in a deep breath of the cool night air and let her head hang back on her neck. Staring up at the blanket of stars, she realized that for the first time in too many years, she felt . . . *good.*

"What are you thinking?" Travis whispered and squatted down beside her.

"Oh . . ." She didn't look at him. Instead, she kept her eyes locked on the North Star, almost directly overhead. Lying down on the soft green grass, Libby let the cool dampness soak into her and finished evasively, "Just that my 'speech' didn't go exactly as planned."

"I'm glad to hear that."

"What?"

"I said," Travis went on and sat down on the grass beside her, "I'm glad you didn't *plan* that brawl."

"It wasn't *my* fault, Travis." She looked over at him, but didn't move.

"Sure it was, Lib. You were the first to raise a hand. Or, in your case . . . a whiskey bottle."

"But—"

"Oh, I'm not sayin' he didn't deserve it, mind you." He looked down at her, and Libby told herself that she didn't remember his eyes being such a *deep* brown. "But hittin' a man over the head with a bottle ain't the way to make him see your side of a thing."

Her lips quirked and she fought down the threatening smile only to lose her composure entirely when a fit of giggles seized her. She couldn't help it. The look of surprise on the big man's face rose up in front of her again, and this time she didn't fight the compulsion to laugh.

Libby's shoulders shook and her chuckles spilled out into the otherwise quiet night. After only a moment or two Travis's deep voice joined hers, and for several minutes the only sound was their mingled laughter.

When he finally drew in a deep breath and calmed himself again, he said, "Jesus, Libby! When that fracas started, I thought sure you'd be trampled in the dirt."

"But I wasn't," she reminded him.

"No"—he snorted a half laugh—"and you damn sure surprised a few of those ol' boys."

"But not you?" she asked, still struggling to compose herself.

He leaned down on one elbow and looked into her face. The moon's indistinct light threw shadows across his features that made his expression hard to read. But Libby couldn't seem to tear her gaze away.

"Nope," he finally said with a grin. "Not me. Y'see, I *remembered* that girl in the saloon. *That's* the Libby I used to know."

"A barroom brawler?"

"A woman who dives right in to whatever she thinks is her business. No matter what anybody thinks or says."

Her breath stopped at the base of her throat. She could feel her heart pounding in her chest. There was—*pride* in his voice when he said that. Libby could hardly believe it. But, looking up into his eyes now, she saw that he meant it.

"It almost sounds as if you *liked* that Libby."

She wanted to call the words back as soon as she'd uttered them. But it was too late.

"Oh," Travis answered gently, "I liked her a lot. Admired her, too."

"*Admired?*"

"Sure. No matter what, *that* Libby always stood up for what she believed."

"Hmmph!" Libby shook her head slightly and let her gaze slip away to the night sky again. In all the lectures she'd been forced to listen to in her youth about her "wild" ways and unladylike behavior . . . never once had anyone said they *admired* her actions.

And now, well. No doubt the entire town would be talking about this night for years to come. She sighed heavily. Libby could just imagine what her *mother's* reaction would be to her *latest* escapade. Thoughtfully she touched her bruised eye again. How on earth would she ever explain a black eye to *Lillie?*

Then a voice in the back of her mind asked, Why should you explain it at all? Aren't you an adult? Yes, she shot back silently, but even an adult is accountable to others.

"Back to worryin' over what'll happen tomorrow?"

"Yes," she admitted and turned to look up at him. It didn't even surprise her anymore that he seemed to know what she was thinking.

"I'll tell ya somethin', Libby," he whispered and leaned down closer to her. "Maybe you *should* be worried. Back in the saloon, when you started that fracas, I was torn between stranglin' you myself and kissin' you so hard you couldn't see straight."

Chapter Eight

LIBBY BLINKED. HIS FACE WAS SO CLOSE TO hers, she felt his warm breath on her cheek. The familiar scent of peppermint swirled around her on the slight breeze from the nearby river. From somewhere out on the prairie, a wolf howled, and in the distance Libby could still hear the sounds of people at the Last Resort.

But in the space of a moment everything except Travis faded away. She knew she should leave. Go back to the hotel. To safety. Then a soft smile curved his lips, and Libby admitted that she didn't *want* to leave. Not yet. Not without feeling again that indescribable lurch of emotion that swelled in her whenever his lips touched hers.

She wanted to know again, however briefly, the tingling sensation that felt as though her blood was on fire. She wanted to feel his arms enclose her again and listen to the thundering of her own heart in her ears.

For a just a moment she wanted to feel *alive* again.

"Libby . . ." he whispered just before his mouth claimed hers.

His arms closed around her, and she arched into them as her hands slipped up to encircle his neck. Her fingers snaked through his too-long hair, and Libby sighed when he stretched out on the grass beside her, pulling her close.

Just as before, her body flickered into life, and when his tongue traced her lips, Libby opened for him in silent welcome. With his first damp, warm caress, she groaned in the back of her throat before returning his kiss with unpracticed eagerness.

Travis levered himself up on one elbow and loomed over her, never pulling his mouth from hers. His left hand slid over her waist and up her rib cage to cup her breast. When his thumb and forefinger stroked deliberately at her nipple, Libby gasped and broke the kiss. Even through the fabric of her gown, his touch inflamed her until she thought she might die if she didn't feel his flesh against hers.

Then he dipped his head and kissed the hardened bud. Her fingers wove through his hair and held his head to her breast. With every stroke of his tongue, the damp fabric rubbed against her tender flesh, sending ribbons of desire snaking through her body with all the intensity of a summer storm.

She never wanted him to stop. She wanted . . . Libby arched her head back and opened her eyes wide. Staring blankly at the sky overhead, she admitted that she didn't know what she wanted. Not really. How could she?

She'd never known these feelings before. This . . . *urgency*. This need.

Somewhere in the back of her mind, Libby realized that Travis's hand had moved to the tiny buttons at her throat. As she felt them freed, one by one, she told herself that she should stop him. That it was up to her to call a halt to what was happening before it was too late.

But she couldn't. Not if it meant her life.

The night air brushed against her skin, and she inhaled deeply, breathing in the heavy scent of the river. Her heart pounded with the strength of a blacksmith's hammer. Then Travis's teeth nipped at her nipple, still buried beneath folds of material, and she banished all thoughts from her mind.

She didn't want to think. She wanted to feel. Giving herself over to his touch, Libby bit at her bottom lip and struggled to breathe.

As his teeth raked over her sensitive flesh again, she twisted her body slightly, moving with the aching warmth that flooded the center of her. Eyes still locked on the star-studded sky, Libby's fingers moved through Travis's hair, silently urging him on, hoping against hope that he wouldn't stop before she could experience more of what he offered.

When her dress lay open, unbuttoned to the waist, Libby pulled in a shaky breath and risked one glance at Travis. Slowly he tugged the fine fabric of her ivory chemise down until her breast was bared to him. She swallowed heavily and squeezed her thighs together in response to an overwhelming curl of pleasure winding through her.

As she watched, Travis lowered his head to her breast and took her erect nipple into his mouth. Libby groaned and closed her eyes tightly, giving herself up to the incredible feel of his mouth on her breast. His tongue flicked against her tender flesh while at the same time he began to suckle her.

Streaks of fire coursed through her body. Libby felt the flames licking at her soul and welcomed them even as her brain screamed at her to stop him. The delicious damp warmth of him invaded her, claiming her as nothing else ever had.

No man had ever touched her as Travis did now.

She'd never known that such feelings existed, and if she had, she knew she could not have lived without them.

Travis's left hand moved over her stomach, across her abdomen, and slowly dipped to the hollow between her thighs. He determinedly separated her clenched legs and cupped the aching core of her body with gentle fingers.

She twisted and moved her hips in unspoken need. Her tongue darted out to smooth across suddenly dry lips as Libby struggled to draw air into her straining lungs. When Travis lifted his head from her breast, she almost cried out at the separation.

Instead, she forced herself to meet his hooded gaze.

Lost in the depth of his eyes, Libby raised up slightly to plant a tiny kiss at the corner of his mouth. When she laid back down, he followed her and whispered against her lips, "I love you, Libby. Marry me."

As if she'd been tossed into the cold river water, Libby stiffened. What was happening? What was she doing? What had she been thinking?

And then reality dropped over her. She hadn't

been thinking at all. That was where she'd made her mistake.

While she still had the strength, she rolled away from him and came to her knees.

Travis lay on the grass only a foot or so from her, but he might as well have been miles away. His whispered words had put a distance between them greater than anything on a map.

Love?

Marry?

Good God.

With fumbling fingers, Libby drew the edge of her chemise up to cover her breast, still damp from his attentions. Frantically she worked at the buttons on her dress, all the while screaming silently at herself for her stupidity.

How could she have let this happen? Hadn't she promised herself at Robert's death *never* to allow a man too close again? Hadn't she made a solemn *vow* never to marry again?

Huh! That traitorous voice at the back of her mind laughed at her. What she'd been feeling had nothing to do with the sanctity of marriage! She'd *been* married, for heaven's sake! She wasn't an innocent anymore. She knew that the marriage bed didn't contain any pleasure for the woman beyond the relief felt when a husband completed his "duties" quickly.

Travis inched toward her, and Libby scooted back, still avoiding his eyes.

No. What she'd been feeling in his arms was more akin to what Lottie's girls must experience. It shamed her now just *remembering* her groaning and writhing under Travis's touch.

"What's wrong, Lib?"

"Nothing," she lied and pushed herself to her feet. She ignored the unfamiliar aching in her body and told herself it was the price she'd have to pay for her wanton lack of self control.

"Dammit, Libby," Travis countered as he stood to face her, *"something's* wrong." He shrugged and took a half step toward her but stopped as she almost leaped away. "All right, maybe I shouldn't have . . ." Travis inhaled sharply and blew the air out in a rush. "But, Libby, I *love* you. I want you to marry me."

A harsh laugh escaped from her throat before she could call it back.

"Libby—talk to me."

"There's nothing to say, Travis." She couldn't look at him. She'd probably never be able to face him again. Every time she saw him, she would see his mouth at her breast, feel his hands on her body, hear her own sighs of pleasure . . . Oh, God. "I, uh . . . have to go back to the hotel now. Bobby will—"

". . . be asleep by now, probably."

"Yes, but . . ."

Travis stepped close and grabbed her upper arms before she could scoot away again. Deliberately Libby kept her gaze locked on his sheriff's badge. As always, the star was pinned a little crookedly to his shirt pocket. She noticed a tiny tear in the material and a small dent on one of the star's points.

She *couldn't* look at him.

"Libby, tell me what's goin' on in that fast-movin' mind of yours."

She shook her head.

He tilted her chin with his fingertips, forcing her head back and her gaze to meet his.

His so familiar features swam before her. Libby blinked furiously, trying to clear her vision, but he remained blurred by the unshed tears filling her eyes.

For one heart-stopping moment she allowed herself to think on what might have been. If only Travis had noticed her years ago. Before Robert. Before she married.

But such thinking was useless, she knew. She couldn't wish away the last four years. And wouldn't even if she could. To do that, she would also wish away Bobby . . . and Libby couldn't imagine life without her son. Bobby was the *one* thing Robert Wilder had done well.

"Please, Travis," she whispered finally, "just leave me alone."

"What?"

"I won't marry you, Travis. Not ever."

He pulled her to him roughly, his fingers curling into the flesh of her arms. "Why the hell not?"

Libby studied his face and saw the utter confusion on his features. She could hardly blame him. After all, she'd just acted the whore in his arms. Why wouldn't he be surprised?

"Because I will never marry *anyone*. Not again."

"Do you still love him *that* much?"

A short bark of laughter that sounded harsh even to her own ears escaped her. Love? Robert?

"Libby . . ."

"No," she said quickly, "I don't still love

Robert." Then more quietly she added, "Sometimes I wonder if I ever did."

"What?"

Travis's hand tightened again on her arms, and Libby tried to ignore the warmth of him. A small part of her wanted desperately to lean into his strength. To feel his arms close around her and know that it would always be so for them.

But another wiser, wearier part of her knew that such a gamble was not worth the price she would have to pay if she was wrong.

"Libby . . ." Travis whispered urgently, "you're makin' me crazy! If it ain't your dead husband . . . then what is it? *Marry* me!"

"No, Travis." She shook her head and forced herself not to look away from him. She owed him at least *this* much, Libby knew. "I already have one child. I don't need another."

"What in the devil are you talkin' about?"

"Husbands."

"Yeah. I want to be your *husband*. Not your child."

"Robert said that to me once, you know. He told me how much he loved me. How he wanted to marry me." Briefly she raised one hand and stroked his jaw. Her fingertips slid over the dark stubble on his cheeks, and she bit her lip hard before letting her hand drop to her side again reluctantly. "But he didn't want a wife, Travis. Oh, maybe he thought he did. But what he really wanted was a mother."

She pulled away from him and took a couple of paces back. Straightening her shoulders and lifting her chin slightly, she continued. "He wanted someone to carry him up the stairs when he'd had too much to drink—which was almost every night."

"Libby . . ."

"Don't stop me, Travis." Libby lifted one hand to silence him. "You might as well know this from me—even though no one else does. You already know that Robert was a drunk. What you don't know is that he wasn't a much better husband when he was sober.

"*I* took care of the ranch. *I* paid the bills and saw to it that the stock was cared for." Her breath caught and she felt the first of her unwanted tears slide down her cheek. "After Bobby was born, *I* raised him and prayed every night that Robert would be too drunk to come to my room because I knew I couldn't bear to raise another child around him."

Travis's features were carefully blank, and Libby rushed on, wanting to finish talking and find a hole to hide in for a while.

"Thankfully," she said with another snort of laughter, "my 'charms' didn't seem to hold much appeal for Robert." Libby shook her head, lost in the memories. "Do you know how Robert died?" she asked suddenly.

"Yeah . . ." he said slowly. "Your folks said he died in a fall from his horse. Broke his neck."

"That's only partially true. He fell, all right," she said and sucked in a gulp of air to continue. "He was drunk. Coming home from the saloon. He fell from his horse as he was crossing a small creek. Robert fell facedown and was too drunk to move. He *drowned* in a creek that a child could walk across in three steps."

"Jesus, Libby. I'm—"

"Don't be sorry. I've already told you I don't want your pity."

"I'm not offering pity!" His shout seemed to hang in the silent air between them.

"I'm sorry your husband was such a damned fool. But I'm not sorry he's gone." He pushed one hand through his hair viciously, as if looking for something to hit. "If that makes me some kind of bastard, then I'll just have to live with it. And I'm not sorry you're home. In Harmony. Where you belong."

Libby shifted from foot to foot nervously as he took a step closer.

"I *am* sorry it's gonna take me awhile to convince you that not every man in the damn world is lookin' for a woman to take care of him. I *am* sorry that whatever that bastard husband of yours did to you, it made you afraid of your own body!"

"What?" she gasped.

"I saw you, Libby. I held you and felt you tremble."

"Stop it!"

"No. By God, you may be tryin' to pretend that nothin' happened between us, Lib. But don't expect me to help you any." He reached out for her, but when she stepped away, he let his hand drop. "When I touch you, everything inside me lights up. And I know it was the same for you."

"No." She shook her head firmly, determined to set him straight on *this* at least. She would deny what she'd felt with her last breath. No "lady" would respond to a man like that, and she knew it. "That's not true. I am not one of Lottie's girls, Travis. I am a widow. A mother."

"You're also a woman, Libby. And if I have to remind you of that every time I see you, then so be it." He reached for her and pulled her into his arms before she could break away.

One more time he bent his head to hers, and Libby's pulse pounded and her blood raced in response. Despite her every effort her entire body throbbed at his nearness. And then the kiss ended and he stepped back. She swayed unsteadily for a moment, before regaining her balance.

"Well, Libby?" he asked. "Can you tell me you didn't feel anything?"

"Nothing, Travis," she answered quietly, almost choking on the lie. "I felt nothing."

He shook his head, a soft smile curving his lips. "Your heart's poundin', Libby. Your mouth is dry and there's a hunger deep inside. You may be afraid of it now, Lib . . . but it's there. And it ain't about to go away. I won't let it."

The strength of his gaze demanded that she not look away.

"And I'm gonna stoke that fire of yours, Libby. I'm gonna pile so much kindling on that little flame that we'll both be swallowed up in the blaze."

"No," she whispered, even though her body leaped to life at his promise.

"Oh, yes," he assured her, then added unnecessarily, "and I build a *helluva* fire, Lib."

Libby choked down the knot in her throat, then turned away and blindly hurried toward the hotel. As she broke into a stumbling run, she sent up a silent prayer that he wouldn't follow her.

Libby wasn't sure she had the strength to withstand him again. Not now.

"Where the hell did she go?" someone demanded.

"Shit," a thin man holding a wadded-up bandana to a bleeding cut on his forehead answered, "I didn't see her at all after the fight started."

"Ain't that just like a woman?" Another voice hooted in the darkness. "Start a fight, then run off?"

The voices carried easily down the length of Main Street, and Travis sighed softly in response. There was no avoiding it, he knew. Even though all he wanted to do was go back to the hotel, crash through Libby's closed door, and *demand* that she acknowledge what lay between them . . . he couldn't. At least not yet.

Besides, he was fairly certain that Cord Spencer had plenty he wanted to say to the town sheriff.

As he neared the crowd, Travis pushed thoughts of Libby to the back of his mind. In the faint glow of lamplight spilling from the open saloon doors, Dr. Jacob Tanner was moving among the injured.

The older man's shock of gray hair stood practically on end and even at a distance of some twenty feet, Travis saw that the man's shirt was torn.

Cord looked up as he neared the small group. "I was wondering what happened to you," he called.

"Everybody all right?" Travis asked, ignoring Cord's implied question.

The other man's eyebrows lifted momentarily. "Yeah. Nothing serious, anyway."

"What about the fire?"

"No damage to speak of," Cord assured him. "Except, of course, the chandelier lying flat on the floor."

Travis nodded and came to a stop beside his friend.

"Libby all right?"

"Yeah. Yeah," Travis said, "she's fine."

"She might not be by tomorrow."

"What d'ya mean?"

"Only that some of the men are pretty het up right now." Cord shrugged and nodded at a few of his still-grumbling customers.

"What about you?" Travis asked, studying his friend's features. "You gonna want to press charges?"

Cord snorted. "This isn't the *first* time I've had my place roughed up in a fight, Travis. And it won't be the last. You got to figure on trouble sometime, if you run a saloon."

"Thanks."

"Don't mention it." The saloonkeeper tugged at his collar, then glanced at the other man again. "You know, I *was* going to ask you if you thought she was really worth all this trouble . . ."

Travis ignored the other men only a few feet away and stared at the man beside him. He didn't even bother to wonder *how* Cord had guessed about his feelings for Libby. "What changed your mind?" he asked instead.

His eyebrows wiggled and Cord grinned. "If you remember, friend . . . Samantha was more than her share of trouble."

Travis nodded, recalling his friend's recent, rocky courtship.

"Well," Spencer concluded finally, "she was *more* than worth it."

Smiling to himself, Travis stood still and watched the other man as he walked away.

Chapter Nine

SHE HID FOR THREE DAYS.

For three solid days Libby didn't stick her head outside her hotel room. She saw no one except Faith, who dutifully brought her friend's meals upstairs on a tray.

And Libby was eternally grateful to Faith, not only for keeping Lillie Taylor from charging into her daughter's room demanding explanations for her "heathenish" behavior . . . but for not asking questions herself.

Libby lifted the brass-backed hand mirror and studied her reflection objectively. Her "black" eye had now faded into a deep purple-and-yellow stain on her flesh. Gently probing the bruise with her fingertips, Libby winced and told herself she was lucky that Bobby was staying with his grandmother. A four-year-old would *definitely* ask questions and demand answers!

"Answers," she muttered, then stuck her tongue out at the mirrored Libby staring back at her. Dropping the glass to her lap, she let her head fall back against the white iron bedstead.

The cool, twisted metal felt good against her neck. For a moment she tried to empty her mind of all the whirling thoughts that had plagued her for the last three days. But it was no use.

Travis's image popped into her brain with the resilience of a cork bobber on a fishing line. And with it came the searing memories of his touch, his kiss, his whispered promises.

Libby's fingers curled into the ivory lace bed coverlet, and she gripped the fine material tightly. She didn't want to remember. She didn't want to think about any of it. And she surely couldn't risk *believing* him.

Somewhere downstairs a door slammed, and Libby sat straight up, listening.

A voice. Shouting. A *female* voice shouting.

Libby cocked one ear toward her closed door and strained to hear. The voice was becoming clearer. *Closer.* Then another woman's voice rang out. Arguing. And footsteps. Hurried footsteps, charging up the stairs.

Swinging her feet to the floor, Libby stood up and faced the still empty doorway. Waiting.

The strident tones were clear as a bell now. Only the words were muffled. And knowing the owner of that voice as well as she did, Libby could guess what was being said.

When the door to her room flew open and Lillie Taylor careened into the room waving a copy of the Harmony *Sentinel* in one hand, Libby braced herself.

"Have you utterly *lost* your mind?" the older woman shouted, shaking the paper as a puppy would a bone. "What could you have been *thinking!*"

Two steps behind her, Faith staggered into the room, saying between gasps for air, "Sorry, Libby. But I couldn't stop her."

"It's all right, Faith." She sighed and silently

admitted that *nothing* would have stopped her mother this time.

"Stop me?" Lillian shouted. "Stop *me*?" She turned on Faith like a snake. "Why didn't you try to stop *her*?"

"Mother . . ."

"Don't use that tone with *me*, young woman!" The older woman was trembling, she was so furious. "That my *own* daughter would subject her family to such . . . such . . . ridicule!"

Libby sucked in a gulp of air and prayed for patience. After all, she'd known quite well what would happen when the edition of the *Sentinel* carrying her announcement came out.

However, she thought, with a wary glance at her mother, she hadn't thought Lillie would take it *this* badly.

Her mother was usually immaculately turned out, but today she looked as though she'd gotten dressed in a dark closet. The buttons on her green shirtwaist were done up crookedly, leaving huge gaps of material that displayed a half-tied corset. Lillie's skirt, a deep red-and-navy-blue striped silk, had been made to accommodate a bustle—which was missing—causing the skirt to hang in a puddle of fabric behind her.

And, Libby noted distractedly, her mother was even wearing mismatched shoes, one of which had a higher heel than the other, giving Lillie a slightly tilted appearance. The older woman's gray-streaked hair had begun to tumble from a too hasty knot at the top of her head, and her cheeks were positively *flaming* their legendary apple red.

"Well!" Lillie demanded. "Have you *nothing* to

say for yourself? Hmmph! I should think not! Why . . . what on earth *could* you say, for heaven's sake!"

"Mother, if you'll—"

"Oh no, you don't. I haven't finished yet, by heaven!"

Libby exchanged a quick look with Faith, who finally seemed to be getting her breath back from the hurried rush up the stairs.

"Look at me when I speak to you, Missy!"

"Mother, there's no reason—"

"There certainly *is* no reason for you to have humiliated your own family in such a fashion!" Lillie began fanning herself with the crumpled pages of the *Sentinel*. Then her eyes caught the banner of black ink again and she said stiffly, "*Temperance League! Good Lord!*"

"Where is she?" A faraway shout cut into her mother's tirade.

Good heavens, Libby sighed inwardly. *Now* what? Her gaze flicked to the wide open door, and she listened to Maisie's still distant voice with a growing sense of dread.

"Speak up, Kincaid! Where is Libby?"

"Who is that?" Lillie whispered frantically, with a wild-eyed look about the room. "Maisie? Oh, Good God! The fat's in the fire now. . . ." She turned a malevolent eye on her oldest child. "See what you've done?"

"Mother, if you would just let me . . ." Libby tried to speak again, even knowing that it would be useless.

She was right.

"I believe you've done quite enough already, thank you very much!" Lillie turned then and glared at Faith. "Don't just sit there, Faith Lind! Get up and bar that door!"

Reacting as much from instinct as anything else, Faith leaped up as commanded and slammed Libby's door shut.

"It's *Hutton*, Mother."

"What?" Lillie shot a distracted glance at her daughter.

"I *said*," Libby repeated, "Faith's name is *Hutton* now, not Lind."

"Oh." Waving her hand as if she were swatting flies, Lillie mumbled, "Lind . . . Hutton . . . she's still Faith, for heaven's sake. Now hush!"

In seconds heavy footsteps sounded in the hall, then came to a stop directly outside Libby's room.

Lillie held both hands up for silence, glaring at the two younger women opposite her as if daring them to speak.

"Libby!" Maisie's voice carried easily through the heavy oak door. "We know you're in there. Open this door *this* minute."

"Don't you dare," Lillie whispered when her daughter took a half step forward. Then more to herself than to the two young women with her, she mumbled distractedly, "*We*. She said *we*. Who's with her? I wonder. Minnie, no doubt. Hmmph! *She* never misses much!"

"Mother . . ." Didn't the woman see that it was pointless to hide from Maisie?

"Hush!" Lillie said a little too loudly and winced at her own tone.

"I heard that, Lillie Taylor!" Maisie crowed.

"Buckets, nails, and the Devil's tail!" Lillie

muttered viciously, and Libby fought down a smile at her mother's creative way of cursing.

"You might's well open this door, 'cause we ain't about to go anywhere till we talk to Libby!"

Lillie crushed the newspaper in her hand and shook her other, empty fist in frustration.

"C'mon, Lil! We saw you hotfootin' it over here just a breath or two ahead of us! Now, open up!"

"Mrs. Taylor," Faith finally said, "we really should open the door. I have other guests in the hotel, and Maisie is disturbing them."

"Then have your *husband* throw her out!" Lillie snapped.

"Maisie is his *aunt*!"

"Only by marriage."

"Mother!"

Gritting her teeth, Lillie glared at her daughter one last time, then snarled, "Who's with you, Maisie?"

"It's just Minnie and me, Lil. Who'd ya think? I ain't had time to go roundin' up a crowd . . ."

"Yet," Lillie muttered.

"You gonna open up, or am I gonna have to yell for Kincaid to bring me and Min a couple of chairs?"

"This is all your fault, Missy!" Lillie spat at Libby, then straightened up and squared her shoulders. Narrowing her eyes at her daughter, she shook the paper at her. "And I'm not finished with you by a long shot!"

Libby rolled her eyes and managed to stifle a laugh as her mother clomped unevenly toward the door and reluctantly turned the brass key in the lock.

Maisie and Minnie practically fell into the room. Minnie smiled at the others, and Maisie squinted at Lillie. "Lord have mercy, woman! You get caught in a tornado on the way over here?"

Faith coughed delicately to hide her chuckle, then sobered instantly when Lillie's steely gaze settled on her.

"All right, Maisie, you're in. What do you want?"

"Take it easy, Lillie." The tall, thin, gray-haired woman stepped jauntily into the room with a lightness that belied her age. "We just want to find out a little more about this here *Temperance League* of Libby's!"

"Oh, Lord!"

"Now, Lillie dear," Minnie crooned soothingly. "This might be a very good idea, y'know."

Lillie snorted at her.

"Did ya even *listen* to her yet, Lil?" Maisie tossed in.

"I don't see that that's any of your business, Maisie Hastings!"

"Don't climb up on that high horse of yours now, Lil." Maisie's squinted gaze swept over her old friend. "You ain't dressed for it by half!"

Lillie glanced down at herself and for the first time, noticed what she was wearing. A horrified gasp left her throat just before the red in her cheeks fanned out to encompass her entire face. She took several quick, deep breaths before moaning softly and falling into a graceful heap on the floor.

"Mother!" Libby shouted, dropping to her knees beside the fallen woman.

"Mrs. Taylor!" Faith covered her open mouth with her fingertips.

Maisie plopped down on the edge of the bed and patted the mattress beside her as a signal to Minnie to join her. When she was seated, Maisie looked away from Lillie's prostrate form and cocked her head at her twin.

"Well, Min?" she asked saucily. "What do you think? I'd say that one was one of her best."

"Oh, yes, Sister. Much more elegant than the last one."

"What?" Libby turned on her mother's friends. She couldn't believe the two of them were happily chatting while her mother might be in mortal danger! "More elegant than her last *what*?"

"Why her last 'swoon,' of course, dear," Minnie chimed in.

Travis leaned back in his chair and tried desperately to quiet the pounding in his head. Slanting a glance at the three angry men standing around his desk shouting at him and each other, he told himself that it was going to be a *long* day.

Idly his fingertips smoothed over the hand-delivered edition of the *Sentinel*. He didn't have to read Libby's announcement again. He already knew it by heart.

And even if he hadn't read it himself . . . so many others had read it *to* him that morning, usually at the top of their lungs, he *still* would have memorized it.

Sighing inwardly, Travis told himself that he should have known Libby wouldn't stop. He should have guessed that the brawl in the saloon wouldn't be enough to deter her.

Unconsciously, at the memory of the fight, he moved his jaw and winced slightly at the still-present ache. Whoever'd hit him that night had carried quite a punch. Of course, he hadn't really noticed the pain until the following morning.

During the time he'd spent with Libby under the stars, he wouldn't have noticed if his boots had been on fire! It was small wonder then that a few aches and pains had gone undetected. Just remembering that night with her, though, brought an all too familiar ache to another part of his body that wasn't so easily ignored.

He shifted uncomfortably in his chair and told himself that it was a good sign that she'd been hiding from him. And he was convinced that's exactly what she'd been doing. At first, when he'd seen her announcement in the paper, he'd thought that she'd been staying out of sight until after everyone had seen it.

But then he'd realized that that wasn't the reason. Any woman who could stand toe to toe with a room full of brawling men wouldn't concern herself with a few lines in a newspaper.

No, he smiled to himself. She was hiding from him. From what she'd felt with him. What they'd felt together.

"I don't see what's so damn funny, Travis!" an angry voice shouted, shattering his thoughts.

"Yeah!" another man tossed in. "What's this gonna do to the other females in this town?"

"It ain't a good thing, Travis." This last voice spoke calmly, solemnly.

Travis looked up at the last speaker. His long,

thin face was haloed by wispy strands of gray hair standing on edge along his scalp. Norton "Hangdog" Harper was the gloomiest man for miles in any direction.

The scrawny farmer saw black clouds everywhere. He was the only man Travis had ever known who could look up at a bright summer sky and predict a twister. No matter how well things were going for him, Hangdog always expected an ax to fall.

"Hangdog" — Travis sighed and lowered his booted feet from his desk to the floor in one easy move — "folks have got the right to put whatever they want to in the paper. There's nothin' wrong with Libby's announcement."

"Nothin' wrong!" shouted the first man, a fat farmer dressed in tattered, stained overalls.

Travis looked askance at him. He knew the man only slightly. His name was . . . Frank something. He had the overbearing manner of a bully, and Travis took an immediate dislike to him as the big man continued.

"What's wrong is, this female is gonna stir up the others. And we all know what happens when a *female* tries to think!"

"That's right, Sheriff," the fat man's admiring, shorter friend echoed.

"Yeah?" Travis set his elbows on the desktop and propped his chin in his hands. Silently he counted the women he'd known in his life — beginning with his late mother — who could think circles around the puffed-up farmer. When he reached thirty, though, Travis stopped. He could have gone on forever, no doubt, but it wouldn't get the annoying man and his bootlicking pal out of the office. "Why don't you tell me what happens, Frank?"

"Well . . ." Frank stammered, crushing his sweat-stained hat in one hand and his copy of the *Sentinel* in the other, "they get 'notional.' Start complainin'. Tellin' a man what he should be doin'. Some *could* start gettin' uppity."

"Uppity?"

"Yeah, Sheriff. Uppity." The man drew a deep breath, and Travis watched his body swell to an enormous size. "You ain't got you a woman so you don't hafta worry none about this female stirrin' things up. But the rest of us has got to keep our females in line."

His lips thinning, Travis told himself that arguing with a halfwit was a useless undertaking. And yet, he couldn't stop himself from asking, "And you keep your wife 'in line,' do you, Frank?"

"You're durn tootin', I do." He jerked his head and ripples of fat moved and shuddered.

"Well, then," Travis said through clenched teeth, "you have nothing to worry about, do ya?" Silently he sent his best wishes to the unfortunate woman who'd actually *married* the poor excuse for a man!

"Course not! But *I* think—"

"Thanks for stoppin' by," Travis interrupted, barely managing to hide his disgust. "I'll be handling the situation as I see fit."

"Well, sure ya will, Sheriff," Frank whined at the commanding tone of the younger man opposite him. "We"—he jerked his head again at his smaller friend, and Travis turned away from the resulting ripples of flesh—"we only wanted to

let ya know how we stand on this here . . .
sit-you-ashun."

"'Preciate it, fellas." Travis nodded distractedly and looked down at his desktop. The best
way to handle that kind of man, he knew, was to
ignore him. Blankly staring at the newspaper, he
didn't look up until he'd heard the jailhouse
door open and close again.

Startled, he jumped slightly to find Hangdog
still standing in front of his desk.

"Did you want something else, Hangdog?"

"Nah, Sheriff." The gloomy man sighed. "Just
wanted to tell ya, I got me a bad feelin' about all
this here."

A reluctant half smile curved Travis's lips.
Absently he wondered if Hangdog had ever had
a *good* feeling about anything.

"Yessir," Hangdog went on. "Bad times is
comin' for Harmony. I feel it in my bones." He
bobbed his head solemnly. The thin wisps of hair
waved and danced with his movement. "Just
thought you ought to know that, Sheriff."

"Well, thanks, Hangdog. I'll keep it in mind."

"Fine, fine." His narrow shoulders slumped
dejectedly, he settled his dust-brown hat, in
surprisingly good condition, on his head. Then,
with a weary sigh, Hangdog Harper turned
slowly for the door. His steps heavy, he crossed
the room as if marching to the gallows.

It made Travis tired just to watch. He held his
breath until the older man opened the door and
stepped onto the boardwalk.

At last, he told himself. Peace.

He could sit quietly, get his thoughts together,
figure out what to do . . . then go to see Libby.

The jailhouse door suddenly flew open and slammed into the wall. Travis looked up, then let his head drop back onto his chest.

"Did you *see* this?" his latest visitor yelled.

"C'mon in, Cord. I've been expectin' you."

Chapter Ten

"HER *LAST* SWOON?" LIBBY CRIED, FRAN-
tically slapping her mother's wrist. "What are
you talking about?"

Faith had opened the windows and a hot,
dusty breeze swirled through the room, lifting
Lillie's loose hair from her forehead teasingly
before dropping it again.

"Just what I said," Maisie snapped. "And you
can stop pattin' her hand, too, Liberty. Lil ain't
gonna wake up till she's damn good and ready."

Despite the other woman's tart words, Libby
kept right on slapping gently at her mother's
flesh, hoping for some sign of life. But there was
nothing. Since Lillie had dropped to the floor,
there hadn't been so much as a flicker of an
eyelash.

Libby ground her teeth together in frustration.
She would never forgive herself if anything were
to happen to her mother!

And she was having a hard time holding on to
her temper. She could hardly believe that two of
her mother's oldest friends didn't seem the least
bit upset by what had happened to Lillie!

"Libby, dear," Minnie soothed encouragingly,
"she really is all right, you know."

"Hell, yes, she's all right." Maisie snorted a

laugh and patted her sister's black-clad knee. "Sister, I do believe Lillie's gettin' better at this all the time."

"I believe you're right, Sister."

Libby glanced at Faith, but her friend simply shrugged helplessly. There was no help for it. If she wanted any information, she'd have to ask the two sisters chortling over her mother's predicament.

"Very well," she said finally. "Will *one* of you tell me what's going on?"

"Sure, sure, we will, hon. Now get up off your knees and set down proper," Maisie urged, waving her hand at a nearby chair. Turning to her sister, she said, "What do you think, Sister? I believe that Lillie's best effort yet was over to the store . . . ?"

After a thoughtful moment Minnie's face cleared, and a smile creased her weathered features. "Oh, of course. The Sissy episode. Yes, yes, Sister. That one would get my vote, certainly."

"Vote?" Libby asked as she settled down into the overstuffed, floral fabric-covered chair. She shook her head slightly and mumbled, "The 'Sissy' episode?"

What on earth, she asked herself, could her sixteen-year-old sister have to do with their mother dropping into a dead faint?

Ever since she could remember, Lillie Taylor had been completely in control of herself. Oh, she'd lost her temper occasionally, naturally. But as far as Libby knew, the woman had *never* fainted. In fact, Libby didn't have a single memory of her mother's being sick a day in her life.

Sick. Oh, Lord, she thought, suddenly frightened. What if Lillie was really ill? But if that was true, would two of her oldest friends be so unconcerned?

"What is happening?" she asked. "And what does Sissy have to do with any of this?"

"Now, now . . . it's easily enough explained," Maisie said quickly. She looked at her sister as if asking permission to be the one to tell the tale. Minnie gave her a slight nod, and Maisie launched into the story.

"First off, don't worry about this faintin' business."

Libby glanced worriedly at her mother. She hadn't moved.

"This here's been goin' on for a few months now."

"*What* has been going on?" If they didn't say it quickly, Libby was going to start screaming.

"The faintin', of course." Maisie nodded her head jerkily, knocking loose a few tendrils of curly gray hair. "But Lillie calls it 'swoonin'.'" She snorted indelicately and pointed at the fallen woman. "Few months back Lil read one of them *Ro*-mance books?" At Libby's nod, she went on. "Well, it seems that the girl in the book was all the time keelin' over, real dainty like? And the hero was forever totin' her around the countryside."

Maisie straightened and tugged unnecessarily at the fit of her gown. "Sounded real foolish to us," she said, indicating her sister, "but Lil there said it was romantic."

"Romantic?" Libby's eyes widened. "My *mother*?"

"Sure seems to work on James right enough," Maisie acknowledged. "Lil drops like a rock and James trots to her side. Course, he can't hardly *carry* her. Lillie ain't exactly a *small* woman . . . but she manages to lean against him real pretty." She sighed and added, "Then he helps her off to bed and well . . . *You* know."

Stunned, Libby looked from the woman on the floor to the women opposite her and back again. "My *mother*?"

Minnie leaned toward her just a bit and said softly, "Just because a woman is um . . . gettin' on in years don't mean she ain't interested in . . . well!" She sniffed and sat back.

"*Anyway*," Maisie said pointedly, "Lil commenced this 'swoonin'' after she read that durned book."

"But what were you saying about Sissy?" Libby asked with a quick glance at her mother's prone form.

For some reason, she still had quite a hard time imagining her parents behaving . . . "romantically." Concentrating, she stared at Lillie's unconscious body. Had she moved just a bit? Libby didn't remember that slight frown on her mother's lips. After a moment she told herself that she simply must have missed it before.

"Oh, my!" Maisie clapped her gnarled, work-worn hands together delightedly. "That was her best effort yet!"

"Oh, heavens, yes!" Minnie agreed.

Faith shrugged at Libby's questioning look.

"Faith, you missed that one. You, Kincaid, and Amanda was off to Ellsworth that week."

Faith nodded and Maisie went on.

"Well, it happened like this." She took a deep breath. "When Lil found out about His Worship and Faith's sister, Zan?"

His Worship? Libby wondered silently. Then in a flash of memory, she recalled her mother writing to her about the two Englishmen who'd taken a ranch nearby. As she recalled, the younger of the two had some sort of fancy title or other.

"I mean, o' course, that Edward Winchester?"

"Yes," Libby broke in. "I know who you mean. Mother wrote me about them."

"I don't wonder!" Maisie snorted, then chuckled lightly. "Lil had her sights set on His Highness. She figured to snare him for either Mary or Sissy . . . then Zan Lind up and lands the big fish without hardly tryin'!" The older woman hooted with laughter.

"Maisie!" Faith gasped.

"Lillie was fit to be tied." Minnie piped up.

Maisie shot her twin a warning look. "Who's tellin' this story, Sister? You or me?"

"Oh, you, Sister. Of course. Go right ahead on."

With a wary last look at the woman beside her, Maisie turned back to Libby. "Anyhow, when Lil found out that His Mightiness was off the marriage market, she fell into a swoon that folks talked about for three days!"

"What?"

"That's so, dear," Minnie's voice chimed in.

"She went into this real elegant turn and kinda spun around till her skirts was flyin', then she just dropped like a stone." Maisie shook her head admiringly. "I swear, she looked pretty as a picture a-lyin' there in the dirt."

"I was *not* in the dirt, Maisie Hastings!" Lillie sat straight up and shook her index finger at the woman opposite her. "You know very well indeed that I was 'overcome' while inside my own store!"

"Mother!"

Maisie's brow wrinkled. "You sure about that, Lillie?"

Libby stared openmouthed as her mother shot to her feet and towered over the two sisters, still sitting on the edge of the bed. She wasn't sure whether to be relieved that her mother was obviously in fine health . . . or *furious* that she would worry her so needlessly.

"I believe *I* ought to know *where* I swoon!" Lillie pushed her hair out of her eyes. "And I would *never* swoon in the dirt! It's most unbecoming. All that dust, you know."

"If you say so, dear . . ."

While the three women argued amongst themselves, Libby turned to Faith. Somewhat relieved to find her own confusion etched onto her friend's features as well, Libby leaned back in her chair and waited for her mother's temper to turn back on her.

"What d'ya say, Jacob?" Zeke asked the doctor as he trimmed the man's hair.

"What? About the Temperance League, you mean?"

"Sure. Isn't that what everybody in town is talkin' about?"

"Well, I believe I'll keep my opinion to myself on this one, if you don't mind, Zeke."

The barber chuckled to himself. "Not the bravest way to go, Doc. But surely the safest!" He spun his customer around to face the mirror and smiled at the man's reflection. "Looks like there's gonna be some interestin' times headed Harmony's way, real soon."

"True, my friend. All too true."

"Did ya see it, Lottie?" Cilla ran into the Madam's bedroom, paper in hand.

"Of course I saw it, girl. I'm not blind, y'know."

The younger woman plopped down on her stomach across Lottie's mattress. "I talked to her the other day. Libby Wilder, I mean."

"Yes?"

"She says she ain't interested in comin' after us next."

"Well," Lottie replied as she smoothed rose-scented cream on her well-cared-for hands. "I certainly hope she meant it, dear. I've come to care for Harmony quite a bit. I'd hate to have to move at this late date."

"Move?"

"You never know, dear." Lottie turned to face the younger girl and suppressed the rush of memories of herself at that tender age. "There's no telling *what* might happen when a 'good' woman goes on a rampage."

"Ride 'em, cowboy!" A voice from the corner shrieked. "Take your boots off! Have a drink!"

Lottie stood up and moved toward the decanter of brandy on a small table in the corner.

Nodding briefly to her parrot, she answered, "Thanks, friend. I believe I will."

"I don't see why you're so upset, Alex," Jane Carson Evans said to her husband. "After all, it was only good business for Samantha to accept Liberty's *paid* announcement."

Alex ran one hand through his thick hair and looked at his pretty wife, still slightly befuddled by his good fortune in finding her.

"Alex?"

"Hmmm? Oh!" He smiled to himself. It was hard to keep his mind on anything besides her. "I know you're right, Jane. But I can't help wishing Sam had used a bit more common sense. She must have known what such an announcement would do to this town." He looked down at the paper in his hands for the umpteenth time. "A Temperance League! It's like waving a red flag in front of a bull! The men in town won't stand for this!"

"It appears that they'll have to," Jane commented dryly and checked her stitches on the dress she was altering for Mary Taylor.

"And Sam's own husband the owner of the saloon!"

"Yes, dear."

"I tell you, Jane. The men will never allow their wives to join this Temperance League! This will only mean trouble!"

Her hands suddenly stilled in her lap. Jane looked up at her husband. "Did you say *allow*?"

Abby Sutherland bounced her daughter Dinah on her hip and absentmindedly listened to the baby's delighted laughter. Not even the ringing of the blacksmith's hammer disturbed little Dinah. She'd become accustomed to her "adoptive" father's business quickly.

Her eyes raking the black-bordered announcement in the paper, Abby stepped into the unbearably hot smithy.

At first sight of her, Jake laid his hammer and tongs aside and grinned in welcome. Being a husband and father was fresh enough that just the thought of his new family brought a smile to his once shy, closed features.

"Jake, did you see this?" Abby held out the paper.

His gaze flicked over the bold-faced announcement quickly, then up to Abby's concerned features. "What's wrong, darlin'? It's just a meeting."

She chewed at her lip thoughtfully. "Yes, but don't you see? What if the next thing to come is someone trying to chase off Cousin Lottie?"

Jake gave her a wide smile. How like his wife to be so worried for someone else. But he'd seen this kind of thing before. He knew that for most women, these kinds of "leagues" never lasted longer than the momentary fascination with something new . . . different.

Chances were, the meeting wouldn't even be held! It wasn't likely that Liberty Taylor Wilder would find more than a couple of women to join her in a town the size of Harmony.

And what harm could a few women do?

"Don't you worry, Abby. Lottie'll be just fine. You'll see." Hell, he told himself silently. The men in town would never stand for Lottie to be chased off anyway. "Now, why don't you and Dinah let me get cleaned up, and then we'll all go over to the hotel for some coffee?" He leaned toward the baby that so delighted him and chucked her chin with one thick finger. "And some milk for you, button!"

Dinah rewarded her father with a drooling, toothless grin.

"Well, James, you can't say you weren't expecting *something* of this sort."

James Taylor packed tobacco into the bowl of his pipe and looked up at Charlie Thompson's smiling face. You would think, he told himself, that a *bartender* would be just a bit concerned at the mention of a Temperance League!

But instead, Charlie seemed to be enjoying James's discomfort far too much to be worried.

He finally sighed. "I suppose not, though I *had* hoped that Libby would settle down a bit as she got older."

"Apparently," Charlie countered on a laugh, "that's not the case."

"Apparently." James's gaze flicked up to meet the other man's sharp black eyes. "What did Cord have to say about it?"

Shaking his head, Charlie ran one long-fingered hand over his curly, closely cropped hair. "Plenty, I'm afraid. He wasn't pleased at all. But as far as I could tell, he was more upset with his wife than with your daughter!"

"Hmm. Makes sense, I suppose. After all, Samantha didn't *have* to run the durn thing."

"Ah, but you know Samantha. There's nothing she likes better than a bit of excitement."

"Excitement?" a man called out as the bell over the mercantile's opening front door rang out. "What excitement?" Frederick Winchester stepped up to the counter, nodded to Charlie, and looked quizzically at James. "Did I miss something?"

"In *Harmony*?" a younger version of the clipped British voice asked. "Excitement?"

"Hello, Ed," James said to the young man just closing the door. He paid no attention to the slight wince on Edward Winchester's face at the familiarity of the greeting. "Fred" —James turned to Ed's uncle— "it's my daughter."

"Which one, dear man? Which one?"

"The oldest. Liberty. Don't believe you've met her yet."

"Liberty?" Ed mumbled.

Charlie scooped the newspaper off the counter and handed it to Ed with a smile. While the young man read the notice, James explained the situation to Fred.

"But that's marvelous!" Ed chortled as he folded the newspaper neatly.

"Marvelous?"

"Yes, Mr. Taylor. Don't you see? If your daughter and her female gladiators are successful, we may finally rid ourselves of that hateful brew you people insist on referring to as 'whiskey.'" He grinned and reread the notice. "It's past time that we imported some fine liquors. Wines, brandies, and the like. The type of thing a *gentleman* can relish on occasion."

"You don't seem to understand, Ed."

The younger man looked up at Charlie.

"If the ladies win this little 'war' . . . we won't have *any* liquor."

"None?"

"None."

"But," he babbled, "surely they can't mean to do away with *brandy*!"

"Yes."

"Champagne?"

"Yes."

"Certainly not . . ." Ed asked, clearly appalled, "*cognac?*"

Charlie nodded. "Afraid so."

"Great heavens!" Ed looked at the other men. "Whatever will be next in this benighted country?"

"Travis . . ." Cord pulled in a deep breath and looked down at his friend. "You have got to do *something* about Libby."

"Yeah, I know."

"I was willing to go along with all of this. I figured she'd cool down, forget the whole thing after a while." He threw his hands high. "Hell! I didn't even press charges when she all but wrecked my saloon! But now *this*!" He shook the paper again.

"Calm down, Cord."

"Calm down, y'say?" The tall man walked to the window, stared out blankly for a moment, then turned and walked back to Travis's desk. "I'm under *attack* here, Travis! My livelihood. My business. My *life*!"

"Yeah." Travis hid his grin. He'd never seen Cord so upset. But he knew the man well enough to know that in an hour or so, cold logic would replace the anger he was feeling now. "And by your own wife, too!"

"I know!" Cord nodded frantically. "I couldn't believe it myself! Stabbed in the back by those I hold most dear!"

"You'll survive, I think," Travis observed.

The other man laid both palms down on the cluttered desk and leaned toward the apparently unconcerned sheriff. "Yes, I will, Travis. The question is, will those two women?"

"Women always survive, Cord. You should know that."

A long, tension-filled moment passed as the two men stared at each other. Then slowly, like steam falling away from an unfired kettle, Travis watched the anger slip from Cord's body.

The other man gave a half laugh and pushed himself away from the desk. "You're right, Travis. Women *do* survive. Most times, better than we."

"Don't worry about this, Cord. I'll speak to Libby."

Cord nodded, folded the paper, and slipped it under one arm. "You do that, Travis. I wish you luck." He turned for the door and stopped for a moment to look back. "You might do the same for me. . . ."

"Huh?"

"Wish me luck?" Cord grinned and shrugged. "I'm about to go have a 'talk' with my loving wife."

As Spencer left the jailhouse, Travis told himself that they would both need all the luck they could get.

He stood up suddenly, walked around the

edge of his desk, and snatched his hat from the peg on the wall. And he would need his share of that luck now.

It was time to face Libby.

Chapter Eleven

He heard them from the street.

With the windows open their voices carried easily on the still, almost expectant air of Harmony. Travis wasn't sure exactly what he'd been anticipating. But a *party* was not it.

As he entered the hotel and quietly closed the door behind him, he paused in the entryway, trying to identify the different female voices floating down the stairs.

Libby's, he had no trouble at all recognizing. Even muffled as it was by distance, her voice stirred something deep inside him.

It had been too long since he'd heard it, too. Three long, endless days and even longer nights. As much as he'd wanted to, Travis had decided not to track her down and demand that she speak to him. When she'd gone into hiding, he'd simply told himself that maybe she needed the time to think.

And, he was willing to admit, if only to himself, that he was hoping a few days apart might convince her that she wanted him as much as he wanted her. If she wasn't ready to hear him say that he loved her, at least she should be willing to admit that there was *something* between them.

He wasn't a kid to be fooled by a woman's response. He knew damn good and well when a woman was interested—aroused. And by thunder, Libby'd felt the passion at their first touch burst into life as surely as he had. And where there was *that* kind of fire, there had to be *feeling* as well.

Maybe she was afraid of the word *love*—and from what little she'd said about that husband of hers, he could hardly blame her. But Travis wasn't about to let her turn her back on him *or* love just because she'd made one mistake in the past.

He'd convince her. Somehow. Maybe she needed courting. But *courting* was for getting to know someone. She already *knew* the kind of man he was. Hell. He'd known her most of her life! And if anything should have proved that they belonged together, those few minutes alone in the night should have done it!

Lord knew, they'd convinced *him*! That short time with her had proved everything he'd ever imagined about her to be true. And the reality of touching her was better than any of the countless dreams he'd had of her over the years.

Shit! He'd hardly gotten any sleep at all since that night. Just the memory of her touch, the feel of her flesh under his hands . . . groaning softly, he swallowed, pushed those thoughts aside, and told himself to remember the rest of it as well. The hurt, angry words she'd thrown at him. The unshed tears in her eyes when she'd described her "marriage."

Travis sighed and realized that it was going to take much more than a few heat-filled kisses and breathy promises to wipe away her distrust of the very word *husband*. But somehow, he had to do it. Because, dammit, he wasn't about to be satisfied with crumbs.

He didn't want to spend the rest of his life sneaking down to her house in the dark for a few brief hours of passion. He wanted everything. Marriage. Kids. Fights. Making up.

Everything. And this time he was going to get it. He wasn't about to let Robert Wilder ruin his plans again! This time from the grave!

But for now, he told himself with a shake of his head, he'd do better to keep his mind on what was happening.

Listening carefully, he separated the other voices quickly. Maisie, Minnie, Faith, and, of course, Lillie. He should have known that Lillie would be the first to storm her daughter's walls, with Maisie and Minnie not far behind. Faith, he assumed, had simply gotten caught in the middle.

"Terrifying, isn't it?"

Travis turned and watched Kincaid Hutton toss a wary glance at the staircase. He hadn't even heard the man walk up.

"Huh? Terrifying?"

"Yeah." Kincaid swiveled his head to meet the sheriff's gaze. "Anytime you hear a bunch of women laughing like that—it means trouble for a man."

"Kincaid!" Travis grinned and slapped the man on the back. "I do believe you're gun-shy! And with a wife like Faith, too."

"So would you be, if you had any sense." Kincaid shuddered slightly when Maisie's howl of laughter shot down the stairs. "And it has nothing to do with Faith. Believe me, no one knows better than *I* do what a wonderful woman she is."

"Then what the hell are you talkin' about, man?"

"Simple." Kincaid leaned his forearms on the polished oak newelpost. "Man and woman. Meant to be together—but mortal enemies!"

Travis exploded into laughter. "Enemies?"

"Close enough." He pointed his index finger at the man opposite him. "You ever try listening to a bunch of women when they're together like that?" He jerked his head at the top of the stairs.

"Not really, I suppose." He hadn't had much opportunity for that, Travis told himself. After all, except for Maisie and Minnie, he was never around enough women at one time that they would qualify as "a bunch."

"You ought to try it sometimes." Kincaid nodded grimly. "I have . . . and believe me, it's not for the weak-hearted."

"How do ya mean?" Intrigued in spite of himself, Travis listened to Kincaid even as he acknowledged that the feminine laughter floating downstairs had taken on a whole different sound.

"I mean," the man said softly, "they talk about things together that men *never* mention."

"You mean like—"

"I mean *everything*." Kincaid nodded again solemnly. "No subject is safe. No *man* is safe. Every woman in this town knows exactly what every *man* in this town does in his own home."

Travis whistled.

"Exactly. They share secrets and swap advice like horse traders at an auction." He breathed deeply and went on in a more hushed tone. "If Charlie Thompson's snoring is keeping Cora up nights . . . one of the women will have a cure. If some poor fool thinks to slip an evening with a floozy past his wife—Lord help him. That . . . *sisterhood* will know about it, and before he gets home, his wife will be ready and waiting."

Travis nodded and licked his suddenly dry lips. "And you say you've *heard* them talkin' about—"

"Yeah." Kincaid shuddered again and straightened up. "But I didn't listen long. I didn't want to hear what Faith might say about me!"

Travis understood that reaction completely. The thought of being the center of talk at a quilting bee was enough to turn a man's hair white.

He looked worriedly at the staircase. "How long has that been goin' on?"

"Today, y'mean? The laughing?" Kincaid shook his head. "Only a few minutes. The shouting?" He rolled his eyes. "Quite a while. And I *prefer* the shouting."

"Hmmm." Maybe it would be better if he came back later, Travis told himself. After all, he didn't want to talk to Libby in front of an audience, anyway.

"Papa?"

Both men jumped and Travis turned just as Kincaid said on a relieved sigh, "What is it, honey?"

Amanda Hutton, eight years old and full of

beans, stood in the parlor doorway. Her puppy was right behind her, balanced on his hind legs, his needlelike teeth buried in the hem of her short green skirt.

The girl swiped at her dog and missed. She grinned when Boom tried to bark with his jaws clamped shut.

"Me and Boom're hungry, Papa."

"'Boom and I,'" Kincaid corrected.

"We figured you might be, too," she agreed.

Travis hid a smile as the puppy lifted his back paws off the ground and swung lazily, hanging from his mistress's skirt by the strength of his teeth.

"See?" Kincaid muttered from the corner of his mouth as he looked down into his little girl's angelic expression. "They learn early just which smile goes the farthest with poor old papa."

"Yeah. And you look real upset by the whole thing, Kincaid."

"Oh, I am." He shot the sheriff a quick grin, then bent down, loosened the puppy's grip and lifted his daughter into his arms. With Boom leaping at his knees, Kincaid smiled at Amanda and received a loud, wet kiss for his trouble.

Looking past her at Travis, he said, "As you can see, it's much too late for me, my friend. But take my advice—"

"What's that?"

"Have sons."

"Papa!"

"I only meant Travis, honey." Kincaid smiled and winked at the child he held so carefully. "Me . . . I prefer beautiful daughters and scruffy puppies!"

"Boom's not scruffy!" she argued as her father carried her toward the kitchen.

Travis watched them go with more than a touch of envy. Sons, huh? Well, if he could get Libby to agree—he could have a son in the next couple of weeks. *Sooner* if it was up to him! Bobby was a fine boy, and he'd like nothing better than a chance to be his pa.

Then an image of Libby's belly, rounded with *his* child, rushed into his mind, and it was all he could do to breathe.

They could be so good together. She and Bobby and him and any others the Lord might think fit to send them.

Travis gritted his teeth as a sharp burst of laughter floated down the stairs to him. If he could just make her *see.* Resolution swelling in his chest, Travis began climbing the stairs. Come hell or high water, he was going to convince her that he was nothing like Robert Wilder . . . or *die* trying!

He only hoped those females would stop laughing before he got there.

"Oh, Lordy!" Maisie chuckled, wiping her eyes with the back of her hand. "I'd have give money to see that fight!"

Libby looked at the women in astonishment. It wasn't until after Lillie had quite recovered from her "faint" that she'd noticed her daughter's black eye for the first time. But as soon as she had, she'd demanded to know the entire story of the brawl.

Never, Libby told herself, would she be able to figure out her mother! Just when she thought she'd done it, Lillie surprised her. Why, she'd spent three days in her hotel room to avoid the lecture she'd expected her mother to deliver at first sight of the shiner. Instead, Lillie'd calmly asked how she'd gotten it, then demanded details.

This was *not* the mother she remembered. The always prim, proper Lillie Taylor should *never* have so thoroughly enjoyed the story of her daughter's fight in a saloon!

And Maisie, Minnie, and Faith were no better, she concluded silently. They'd had her repeat her story so often she could say it in her sleep and still they weren't satisfied. There was a lesson somewhere at the bottom of all this, Libby told herself.

If only she knew what it was.

"Oh, Zeke had a knot the size of a hen's egg on his forehead for two days. . . ." Minnie laughed delightedly. "And he *insisted* that he'd walked into a door!"

"As if we'd believe that!" Maisie added.

"Good heavens," Lillie said, "did those men actually think we *missed* seeing the destruction at Cord Spencer's place?"

"Well," Faith threw in, "I still don't understand how that cowboy reached the chandelier in the first place . . . let alone pulled it right out of the ceiling!"

"I don't know, either," Libby confessed. "I just looked up and there he was—and then he fell and the little fires started up and everyone started shouting . . ." She shook her head.

"And who was it you bonked on the head, dear?" Lillie asked for the fifth time.

"I'm not sure, Mother. I don't think I've seen him before."

"Don't imagine you'll see him *again*, either!" Lillie smothered a laugh behind her hand. "At least not if he sees you first!"

Maisie gave the other woman a friendly shove, and they leaned together, laughing.

"Travis!" Minnie shouted to be heard.

"What?" Libby asked.

"You said Travis picked you up and carried you to safety?"

"Uh . . ." Well, she thought. He *did* carry her. She hadn't been sure at the time if it was safety on his mind—or murder. And as it turned out, she reminded herself, it was neither. "Yes, that's right, Min."

"Oh, my." Lillie leaned her head back against the iron footrail of the bed. "Isn't that romantic?"

"Here we go!" Maisie shouted. "Back to that durned book again!"

"Mother, it wasn't *romantic* at all," Libby said hurriedly. Thunderation! If there was *one* thing she didn't want her mother focusing on, it was a "romance" between her and Travis!

Heaven knew *he* was doing plenty of that for himself!

Besides, how romantic could it be to be tossed over someone's shoulder like a side of venison?

"It sounds very romantic, dear." Sobering suddenly, Lillie seemed to remember whom she was talking to. "Of course, it wasn't seemly at *all* to allow a man such liberties as cradling you close to his heaving bosom—"

"Heaving *what*?" Maisie gaped at her.

"Bosom, Maisie," Lillie snarled. "Bosom. Don't

you ever read anything besides knitting patterns?"

"I sure as hell don't need to read a book to know that men don't have bosoms, Lil. They have—"

"*Travis!*"

Every eye in the room turned at Faith's shouted greeting.

Libby felt the flush sweep over her and knew there wasn't a damn thing she could do about it. The open doorway seemed almost crowded by his broad shoulders. He stood leaning against the doorjamb, his booted feet crossed negligently at the ankles, a half smile on his face.

Frantically Libby thought about the last few minutes of conversation and wondered just as frantically how long he'd been standing there listening.

"Ladies . . ." he finally said, and his deep voice sliced through the few feet of space separating them and cut deep into Libby's soul.

"Didn't you ever hear of knockin', Travis Miller?" Maisie pushed herself to her feet and squinted at the interloper.

"Yes, ma'am. But the door was open." He grinned and shrugged. "I said hello, but you ladies didn't hear me. You were too busy"—he looked at Libby—"talkin'."

Libby's eyes widened. He'd apparently heard too much!

"Well." Lillie Taylor stood up, smoothed her mismatched outfit, and tilted her head to look up at the tall man. "Is there something you wanted, Sheriff?"

He flicked a glance at the woman he hoped to

make his mother-in-law and, to his credit, didn't even blink at her outrageous attire. "Yes, ma'am. I have to speak to Libby. Official business."

"Official, is it?" Lillie narrowed her gaze slightly and pursed her lips. "Is this about the saloon? Or about the newspaper announcement?"

"I'd rather talk about that with Libby, Mrs. Taylor."

"I'm sure you would, young man," Lillie countered.

From behind her, Libby watched open-mouthed as her mother defended the actions she'd been furious about only an hour before.

"However," Lillie continued quickly, "I don't know how you can describe anything my daughter's done as illegal, Sheriff. Furthermore . . . I don't think it wise to leave an unchaperoned woman alone with a man in a hotel room."

"Lillie . . ." Minnie put in.

"Mother, it's all right." Libby wasn't sure if it would be or not . . . but she *was* sure she didn't want her mother or the others listening to what Travis might have to say.

"Now, dear," her mother said pointedly, "I think it best if we all stay here and see what the *sheriff*"—her nose wrinkled slightly—"has to say."

Libby groaned quietly and glanced at Travis. There was a telltale smirk hovering around the edges of his mouth. He was *enjoying* this!

"I'm afraid I insist on privacy, Mrs. Taylor," he said softly.

"Is my daughter under arrest, young man?"

"No, ma'am."

"Then, for heaven's sake why should I—"

"Lil—" Maisie grabbed her friend's arm and whispered something in her ear.

Libby watched her mother's expression carefully and had no trouble at all guessing what Maisie was suggesting. Lillie Taylor's eyes narrowed, widened, then softened speculatively.

She glanced from her daughter to Travis and back again. The beginning of a smile curved her lips as she finally pulled away from Maisie and announced, "Very well, Sheriff. If you insist."

"Thank you, ma'am," he muttered, not bothering to hide his smile.

"Libby, dear . . ."

Libby tore her gaze from the tempting man in the doorway and looked at her mother.

"We'll be going now." Lillie pushed her hair off her forehead, leaned forward, and planted a quick peck on her daughter's cheek. Then she turned away, saying, "All right, then. Maisie. Minnie, Faith, girl. Come along. Official business, you know." She ushered the others out the door ahead of her like a mother hen herding chicks. Then she walked unevenly to the door with as much grace as she could manage in the situation. Before she left the room, though, she stopped beside Travis for an instant.

"Yes, ma'am?" he said, and Libby watched her mother's eyes widen slightly when the power of his dark gaze fell on her.

Lillie cleared her throat and said, "The door will remain *open*."

"*Mother!*" A hotter, deeper flush stained Libby's skin as she sank down onto the nearest chair, her face buried in her hands.

What else, she asked herself miserably, could *possibly* happen today?

"Lillie," Maisie commanded from the hall, "come on outa there!"

As the voices faded away, Libby heard Maisie add, "So help me, Lil, if you swoon again, I'll leave ya right there on the steps!"

A deep, throaty chuckle that sent ripples of sensation through her body echoed in the room just before Travis closed the door.

Chapter Twelve

THE ROOM SEEMED SUDDENLY SMALLER than it had five minutes earlier.

Libby looked around her hotel room, letting her gaze move over the huge oak wardrobe, a small corner table holding a pink-and-cream pitcher and bowl, and the dressing table with its matching etched-glass mirror. Reflected in the shining glass was the white iron bed and Travis, watching her from his post near the door.

Quickly her gaze slid away until she was staring helplessly at her clasped hands in her lap.

"Libby?"

How could *anyone's* voice be that deep? she wondered agitatedly.

"Libby, I ain't goin' anywhere till you work up the nerve to look at me. Even if it takes all day!"

Reacting to the challenge immediately, Libby looked up at him. "I'm not afraid to look at you, Travis." I'm afraid, she added silently, of what looking at you *does* to me.

It had been three days since she'd seen him, and unwillingly, her eyes moved over his features hungrily. Where had this *longing* sprung from? she asked herself. When exactly had her body started reacting to his presence with such a start?

And why did his eyes have to be such a deep, liquid brown?

"Eye hurt?" he asked, leaning negligently against the closed door.

"No," she answered too quickly, her right hand reaching up to touch the bruised flesh. "Not much, anyway."

A long, disturbing silence stretched out between them, and Libby felt as though every inch of her body was coiled to snap. Why didn't he say what he had to say and leave? Why did he keep looking at her? And why did he close that door?

It was so hot in the tiny room, Libby felt as though she couldn't get enough air. She ran one finger under the tight, high collar of her soft yellow day gown and wished mightily that she could undo the buttons at her throat before she strangled.

A drop of perspiration rolled down her back beneath her dress, and she shifted uneasily with the soft, teasing sensation. His steady gaze was still on her. She felt it. And the strength of his stare brought the same gentle, tingling sensation to a completely different part of her body.

"You ready to talk to me now?" he finally said, and Libby went limp with relief when the silence was broken. Surely *anything* would be better than that tension-filled hush.

"About what, Travis?"

"Take your pick, Lib." He pushed away from the door and took two steps closer.

Immediately she leaped up from the chair, walked around behind it, and raised the window another few inches. The white lace curtains didn't move. Not a breath of a breeze stirred the steamy air. She felt as though she was trying to breathe through a blanket. And Travis's presence wasn't helping any.

Please, she whispered silently and stared up at the steely blue Kansas sky, please make him keep his distance.

She spun back around to face him and saw that he had indeed stopped. Right next to the foot of the bed. She gulped past the knot in her throat.

"Well?" Travis asked, the timbre of his voice rumbling along her spine. "What'll it be?"

He yanked off his hat, tossed it to the table behind him, and ran a hand through his sweat-dampened hair.

"Hmmm?" She tried desperately to pull her gaze away from the lock of hair that curled and fell onto his forehead.

"I asked you what you wanted to talk about first, Lib. The saloon? The newspaper?" He paused briefly before adding softly, "Or us?"

Her concentration snapped, and she found herself looking directly into his eyes. She could almost *see* the flames of desire dancing there. The incredible heat reached across the room for her.

What was happening?

"Us?"

"Excellent choice." Travis moved around the edge of the bedframe and plopped down onto the mattress. The bedsprings screeched in protest, and Libby's gaze flew to the closed door.

Were her mother and the rest of them standing out on the landing, listening?

"Get up, Travis," she ordered swiftly. "If someone should hear that sound, they might think . . ."

"What, Lib? What might they think?" His full lips tilted at one corner, he watched her.

"That we . . ." She waved one hand frantically at the bed. A flush swept over her. He knew precisely what she meant. The sparkle in his eyes was proof of that.

He bounced.

"Travis!"

"Good, Libby." He grinned and winked. "Call my name again. Louder this time!"

Lord! The bed screeched and groaned with his every movement, and when it didn't make enough noise for him, he bounced harder.

"Libby!" he shouted, still with that grin in place.

She cast one quick glance at the door before turning back to him. "Travis!" she yelled at him. "Don't! Stop!"

He grinned even wider, held on to the iron rail at the foot of the bed, and jumped up and down on the mattress until the rails at the head of the bed pounded against the wall.

"Don't worry, darlin'," Travis called out, "I won't stop!"

"That's not what I meant!" But she couldn't even be heard anymore over the screams of the bedsprings and the heavy thumping of metal against the wall.

Then just as she began to moan his name in exasperation, he stopped bouncing on the bed and the shrieks died away, leaving her "Oh, Travis" hanging much too loudly in the air.

"Ah, Libby!" Travis echoed and flopped back

onto the mattress with a lusty groan. "Honey, I have to rest a bit. I'm just too wore out to do that anymore right now."

She stared at him and felt her jaw drop. What had he done? Her hand at her throat, Libby couldn't seem to tear her eyes away from the bed and his prostrate form. Even from where she stood, she could see that his self-satisfied smile was still in place.

As she watched him, Travis crossed his arms behind his head and crossed his feet at the ankles. He looked as though he had no intention of leaving anytime soon.

A soft noise from the hall outside her room brought Libby spinning around to face the door. She closed her eyes and listened for the slightest sound.

There! Her eyes flew open again. A tiny creak of the floorboards on the landing. Someone *was* there. Someone who'd heard every creak of the bed and everything they'd said to each other. Then she heard the unmistakable sounds of quick, hurried footfalls, running down the stairs.

Her hands curled into helpless fists at her sides as Libby stared at the plain white surface of the painted door. Whoever it was . . . and she didn't think she wanted to know for sure *exactly* who . . . had certainly gotten an earful.

A tiny voice in the back of her mind laughed at her. With the ruckus Travis kicked up, everyone in the *building* had heard him. She'd be lucky if folks weren't standing around in the street, waiting for round two!

And now what? she asked herself. Step out that door and pretend nothing happened? Face down the curious looks and say nothing? *What?*

Her glance flew back to Travis, and the wink he shot her did nothing to calm her temper. "How could you do that?"

"Do what, Lib?" His grin faded into a soft smile. "Bounce on a bed? Hell, every kid alive's done that at least a time or two."

"But you're no kid and that's *not* your bed!"

"It could be. . . ."

She stiffened. Just the thought of *that* sent runners of chilled flesh all over her body. In a blinding flash Libby saw the two of them, in bed, arms wrapped around each other. A warm curl of excitement, centered down low in her belly, spread to her thighs until she was sure they were too weak to support her.

It was wrong. She knew it. No woman with any morals at all should feel those damp, hungry yearnings. Deliberately she locked her knees and lifted her chin. Sucking in a great gulp of air, she said calmly, "No, Travis, it couldn't."

He turned onto his side, leaned up on one elbow, and looked hard at her. "Why not? There's gonna be quite a few in this town now who'll think it *is* already."

"I can't help what they think."

"So you'll just let 'em talk."

"That's right," she decided suddenly. After all, she didn't have much choice in the matter, did she?

"And you won't tell 'em yea or nay, is that right?"

"Yes." Though after the performance *he'd* put on, she seriously doubted that anyone would believe her even if she tried.

"Uh-huh." He sat up and swung his long legs off the side of the bed. His hands curled over the edge of the mattress, he said softly, "If they're gonna hang you anyway, ya might as well be hanged for a lion as a sheep."

"What's that supposed to mean?"

"I think you know."

She did know. All too well. The memories of his touch, his kiss were still so fresh in her mind, she could almost taste him. But if she became as he put it, a lion, would she ever again be able to be the sheep?

Once in his arms, would she ever be able to walk away from the feelings he kindled in her? And could she risk finding out?

No.

He must have read her answer on her features, she thought, because he pushed himself off the bed and faced her without the slightest hint of a smile.

"All right, Libby," he said softly, "I'll let it rest for now."

Thank heaven!

"But I won't quit, Lib." He gestured at the bed behind him. "This here, folks *will* talk. And I want 'em to."

"Why?"

He took three quick steps that brought him to her side. Reaching for her hands, he uncurled her fingers, and his thumbs moved over her palms delicately. His gaze bored into hers, and Libby's breath caught at the tenderness shining down on her.

"Because I believe I'm gonna need all the help I can get to talk you into marryin' me."

That word again. She tried to pull her hands free, but his grip tightened just enough to prevent her escape.

"I know, Lib. You've *been* married."

She bit the inside of her cheek and forced herself to breathe slowly, evenly.

"But can you really judge all men by the no-account your husband was?"

"He's all I have to judge *by*."

"Nah." Travis smiled again, that crooked tilt of a smile that touched her like nothing else ever had. "What about your pa? What about Faith's pa? And Samantha's?"

"It's not the same thing at all, Travis."

"Why not? For God's sake, Lib! You've known lots of men in your life. Why shortchange all of us because of the rotten apple you married?"

"The men I've known," she said firmly, "I've known as fathers—friends. The only *husband* I've had was Robert." Libby yanked her hands free and crossed her arms in front of her chest. "And a *husband* is something very different from a *father*."

"True." His hands fell on her shoulders now and pulled her close. "But a good man is good in most things he does, Lib. And a rotten apple is rotten with everything and everyone."

Maybe, she thought, maybe he had a point. But she couldn't risk it. Hadn't Robert seemed a perfectly nice, charming man before she married him? Hadn't he said and done all the right things? Courted her? Flattered her?

But, her mind taunted, weren't there a few doubts even then? What about the times Lillie had tried to tell her daughter that Robert wasn't the man for her? What about the unfriendly silences between her father and the man she married?

A small trickle of confusion wormed its way through her thoughts. Was it possible, she wondered, that all the signs of Robert's weaknesses were there—in the open—*before* the marriage, and she was simply blind to them? Could she really have been that duped by an illusion of sophistication?

Libby tried to think clearly, logically, but the warmth of Travis's hands on her shoulders was making it difficult. And suddenly there was so much more to think *about*.

Had she really, because of her own stubbornness, walked into a marriage that should never have happened in the first place?

Was Travis *right*?

His eyes seemed to be looking through her, into her mind, her heart. He watched her with a tender hunger that threatened to swamp her entirely.

As he bent his head slowly closer, even her anger over what he'd done, the position he'd placed her in, faded. Suddenly all she cared about was the touch of his lips on hers. Libby wanted to feel that quick flash of fire racing through her veins. She wanted to feel her heart pounding as though it would fly out of her chest.

Even if she never allowed herself that luxury again, just this once, she told herself.

And then his mouth claimed hers, and all thought vanished.

His arms enfolded her, drawing her tightly against his chest. The warm strength of him surrounded her, and that fire she remembered so clearly danced to life in every nerve of her body. He parted her lips skillfully and slipped his tongue inside her mouth to caress her with gentle strokes.

And when the gentleness had fanned the flames of her desire, Travis held her tighter and pulled away from her mouth to follow the line of her throat with his lips. Libby shuddered slightly and tipped her head to one side, welcoming the feel of his breath on her neck, his mouth on her flesh.

The strange blossom of warmth she'd experienced before was born again under his touch. This time, though, the feeling was stronger, more urgent. This time she felt the strength of her own need for this man right down to her toes.

Her eyes flew open, and she stared blankly at the ceiling, caught in the wonder of her body burning from the inside out. Hands clenched tight against his back, Libby pulled him closer, luxuriating in the notion that his heart beat frantically in tandem with hers.

He took a half step and then another. Libby followed, suddenly willing to go wherever he took her. Her eyes squeezed shut again, and she determined to shut everything but Travis—and that moment—from her mind. She wanted to find out what more there was. She wanted to know if this burning in her veins had an end.

Another step and he leaned back, drawing her with him. He was slowly lying down on the bed. She knew it. She felt the soft mattress beneath her knees as he laid her down gently beside him.

Libby moved her hands to the back of his head, raking her fingers through his thick hair.

She felt the top button on her gown as he slipped it free. Then another and another and Libby knew she should stop him. The tiny voice in the back of her mind screamed at her to think! To stop!

Libby pulled in a deep breath of the warm summer air and silenced the voice of reason with a sigh.

Travis's hand cupped her breast, and he shifted position, leaning over her. The bed shrieked in protest when his lips first touched the hollow at the base of her throat. His thumb and forefinger teased her hardened nipple as his mouth moved over the pale flesh of her chest.

Libby stiffened slightly, arching toward him almost unconsciously, offering her breast to him, silently pleading for his touch. Then he moved again, dipping his head lower. His fingers tugged at the fine material of her chemise until she felt the sultry air on her exposed breast.

She opened her eyes and looked at him as he slowly took her nipple into his mouth. Libby groaned softly as his tongue moved over the sensitive bud. Her fingers threaded in his hair, she held him to her and welcomed the familiar curl of desire that shot through her belly and thighs.

With his mouth at her breast, he lifted her slightly and inched them both back farther onto the mattress. This time the bedsprings screeched so noisily, the sound seemed to echo in the tiny room long after they were still again.

And in the momentary hush when the springs were silenced, Libby heard it.

A voice.

In the hall.

On the landing.

"Good God, they're at it again!"

Then another voice, quickly urging, "Hush! They'll hear you!"

Chapter Thirteen

"WHY IS EVERYBODY SO MAD AT MAMA?"

James Taylor looked down into his grandson's eyes. How to explain to an almost four-year-old boy that most adults didn't make much sense? Even *he* didn't understand the things so-called "grown-ups" were capable of sometimes.

In the two hours since the *Sentinel* came out, more people had poured through the doors of the mercantile than he usually saw in a week. And every last one of them had had plenty to say about Libby.

Shaking his head, James sucked in a gulp of air and told himself that this would all blow over. Harmony was a small town. Everything that happened, no matter how unimportant, created some kind of stir.

At the same time he had to admit that the newspaper announcement was hardly unimportant. At least not to his customers.

Irate fathers, husbands, and young men of courting age had come together for a common cause. To silence Liberty Taylor Wilder.

In turn, they'd demanded that James *order* his daughter to stop her "rabble-rousing," cancel the temperance meeting, and stop making a spectacle of herself at the saloon!

James sighed heavily. As if he could do any of those things! He'd learned long ago what it seemed his customers had not. It was impossible to stop a woman from doing whatever she darn well pleased. At least, he told himself—the women in *his* family.

Even his youngest daughter, Sissy, treated him as if he was a slightly dim-witted, though well-meaning, child. Nope. If the men from Harmony thought he had the tiniest bit of say-so over the women in his family—they were greatly mistaken.

And Bobby had seen and *heard* them all. Just like his mother, the child had a talent for being exactly where he shouldn't be. And no matter how James had tried to keep the boy out of the store, he always found a way to come back.

"Grampa?"

Bobby tugged at the worn, but spotlessly clean white apron James wore when working at the store.

Forcing a smile, James ruffled the boy's soft blond hair. "I don't know, Bobby," he lied. "But don't you worry, all right? Not *everybody* is mad."

"Gramma is," the child pointed out.

"Hmmm . . ." There was no denying that! Lillie had flown out of the store like her skirts were on fire. James looked away from his grandson and turned to stare out the shining windows facing Main Street. What could he say to the boy about his grandmother?

One corner of his mouth lifted in a wry grin, and James told himself that as much as he loved Lillie—she was one of the adults he had the most trouble understanding.

It had been hard enough holding her down after that saloon fight! Once she'd heard that Libby had been in the thick of things, she'd lain in wait for her daughter at the store. And when she hadn't shown up, James had accepted that little gift gracefully from whatever gods protected husbands and fathers from their families.

Even Lillie had seemed almost pleased. Almost as though she figured Libby was ashamed of herself and hiding out until the initial reaction to the fight blew over. But with the announcement in the paper, Lillie tossed caution to the wind and took out after her daughter.

Now all he had to do was try to make Bobby see that no matter how mad Gramma got . . . her upsets were usually short-lived. One thing you could say for Lillie. If you survived the first explosion of temper . . . in five minutes she'd be fine again.

"Yes, Gramma *is* mad, boy." He paused and smiled at the little face so like his own children's. "But, well—sometimes your ma gets mad at you, doesn't she?"

"Uh-huh. *Lots.*" Bobby pushed Travis's dirty, beat-up hat to the back of his head. "Like when I mess up my new clothes before church or when I eat candy before supper or when I—"

"Yes," James interrupted, knowing full well that Bobby's list could go on for hours, "I know. But she never *stays* mad for long, does she?"

"Nah." Bobby shook his head violently, and the hat tilted and rocked. "She always smiles and gives me kisses."

"That's right. Well, you got to remember that your Gramma is your mama's mama." He wrinkled his brow. That sounded confusing even to him. "Anyhow . . . Gramma won't be mad for too long."

"You sure?"

"Yeah, I'm sure." To take the boy's mind off things, James stuck his hand into a nearby jar, pulled out a long black licorice whip, and handed it to him. "Why don't you go on out and find your uncle Harry?" With any luck, he added silently, by the time the boy got back, maybe most folks would be through with their complainin'.

Bobby stuck one end of the thick black rope into his mouth immediately. Grinning, he nodded and raced for the door.

It never ceased to amaze James just how quickly children were able to put their problems behind them. With a chuckle he sucked in a gulp of air and looked around the empty mercantile with a pleased smile on his face. At last. A few minutes to himself. Quiet. Peace.

The bell over the door had hardly stopped ringing after Bobby's exit when two farmers marched inside, one of them shaking a copy of the *Sentinel*.

"Taylor!" the man shouted. "Where's that daughter of yours?"

James sighed, reached into the licorice jar, and pulled out a whip. He leaned his forearms on the counter, stuck one end of the candy in the corner of his mouth, and waited.

Travis groaned and pushed himself into a sitting position. Behind him, he heard the telltale rustle of fabric as Libby pulled herself together again.

"Who was it?" she whispered. "Could you tell?"

"No." He fixed a glare on the door and was glad he couldn't see through it. It would be much better for the snoopers if he didn't know *exactly* who it was.

"My mother, probably," Libby muttered, more to herself than to him.

Travis snorted. "I doubt it. If that was Lillie, I figure she'd have come right through that door."

It was his own fault. He knew it. And dammit, he hadn't *planned* on seducing her. At least not now. Of course, if he hadn't made such a big damn joke over bouncin' up and down on the bed, *no one* would've been listening at the door! And he wouldn't be in such a painful condition now.

Finally he stood up and carefully walked to a few feet away from her. If he ever expected to walk comfortably again, he needed some space between them.

While Libby rearranged her clothing, Travis let his mind wander to the rooms downstairs. To the snoopers and the rest of the people who'd no doubt heard his performance earlier. He could well imagine what *they* were thinking right about now. In fact, he could almost *see* the looks he and Libby were going to be getting as soon as they left the safety of her room.

And maybe that was a good thing, he told himself thoughtfully. Maybe . . . that was *just* what Libby needed to push her toward him. He rubbed his jaw distractedly and tried to envision

Lillie Taylor and how she would be reacting to what had supposedly happened between him and Libby.

A half smile crossed his face, but he wiped it away immediately. It wouldn't do to let Libby see how pleased he was with the way things were working out.

After all, what kind of man did it make him to ruin a woman's reputation in order to convince her to marry him?

A *desperate* one, he silently acknowledged.

"Travis," Libby's voice came from right behind him. Without even turning, he knew from her tone that the passion would be gone from her features.

"Travis," she said again. "I think you should go now."

Slowly he looked over his shoulder at her. As he'd known, her face was pale, stiff. Her eyes no longer looked warm and welcoming, and even her mouth had tightened into a rigid line. In spite of his best efforts, Travis felt a small spurt of anger well up inside him.

Here he stood, nearly torn in two with the strength of his need for her, and all she could do was tell him to leave? Did she really think it was that easy? That nothing she did had the slightest effect on him? That he could kiss her and hold her and much too briefly know what it was to run his hands over her body and then just . . . *stop*?

He never would have thought that Libby could run so hot and cold. But looking at her now—from her pale face to her "buttoned up to her ears" dress—no one would ever guess that five minutes ago she'd been everything he'd ever dreamed she would be.

Well, dammit, Travis told himself angrily. He wouldn't be brushed aside—and he damn sure wasn't gonna pay retribution for Robert Wilder's sins! And it was high time she found that out, right now!

Turning quickly, he clutched her to him before she had a chance to slip from his grasp.

"Travis, don't." She pushed ineffectually at his chest. "Just go away. Please."

"Not yet, Libby. See, whether you want to know it or not, I'm a man."

"Don't be ridiculous! Of course you're a man."

She twisted a bit in his arms, but it was futile. He wasn't ready to let her go. Not yet.

Instead, he pulled her tight against him. One hand slipped to the small of her back, and deliberately he pulled her hips close. Close enough that she could feel what she did to him. Close enough that there could be no doubt left in her mind about whether he really wanted her or not.

Libby went completely still in his arms. After a moment, his grip loosened, but she didn't move away. He felt her tremble. "This stoppin' and startin' business is beginnin' to wear a little thin, Libby."

"I never once asked you to do anything, Travis. This was *your* idea." Her voice shook and he smiled.

"Oh, I'm willin' to admit to that."

Her gaze snapped up to his and he nodded.

"Hell, I'll be proud to tell ya, I've wanted you since you were sixteen years old."

Her eyes widened and she shook her head, denying his words.

"Yes, Libby. It's true. And I waited. And waited." His anger drained away as if it had never been. Looking into the face he'd loved for so long made it impossible to stay mad at her.

She looked so . . . confused. Bewildered. Travis stifled a sigh. How could he make her understand? How could he make her see that taking a chance on him was worth the risk? Somehow, he had to show her that not all men should be judged against Robert Wilder.

Slowly he lifted one hand to cup her cheek gently. "By the time I figured you were old enough, Wilder arrived, and before I knew what was happening, he'd sneaked you right out of town."

"He didn't *sneak*."

"Might as well have." Her green eyes were locked on his, and Travis felt the old, familiar pull of them. He'd waited so long to hold her. To feel her pressed against the length of him. To see himself reflected in her eyes and know that he was the only man in her heart, as well. He sighed and added, "As soon as he hit Harmony, you couldn't see anybody else for dust."

She bit her lip, and all he could think about was touching those lips with his tongue.

"Before I knew it, it was too late. You were gone."

Libby dropped her gaze as if unwilling to discuss the past, her husband, anything. He lifted her chin with the tips of his fingers until their eyes met again.

"But like I told you before, Lib. You're back

now. And I ain't about to set around and wait again."

"Travis, I—"

"I know. You *told* me. You don't ever want to get married again 'cause Robert made such a miserable mess outa things."

"That's right." Under his watchful gaze, she took a deep breath as if steeling herself for an unpleasant task and added, "But it wasn't just his fault. It was mine, too."

"How?" he whispered. He wanted to keep her talking. He wanted to know everything.

"Right from the beginning, I think I knew that marrying Robert was a mistake." Surprise lit her eyes for a moment, then a wry smile curved her full lips. Her fingertips brushed lightly across his chest, and he had to grit his teeth to keep from groaning. "Strange," she continued. "That's the first time I've ever admitted that out loud."

"Good."

"Good?"

He nodded. "I'm glad *I* was the one you said it to."

"You're hopeless, Travis." A wary smile touched her features.

"Ain't I just?" He winked at her before asking softly "If you knew it wasn't right . . . why the hell'd you do it?"

Libby sighed, and as he held his breath, she slowly laid her head on his chest. "Stubbornness, I guess. Pride. I just couldn't bring myself to admit to my mother that she was right about him." She straightened again. "But he *seemed* a good man—steady . . . successful . . ."

Travis winced. One thing you could give to

Wilder, anyway. The man had had more to offer her than a small-town sheriff.

Hardly daring to speak, afraid he might break the spell that held them together, Travis nonetheless asked, "What happened, Libby? What went wrong?"

Her spine went rigid. He felt the tension as it crept over her and wanted to bite out his own tongue for ruining their brief moment.

In a chill, distant voice she answered, "I discovered shortly after our marriage that Robert much preferred a whiskey bottle to me."

"Well, then," he tried, "that should have nothin' at all to do with you and *me*. I ain't a drinker, Lib."

She glanced up at him. "I didn't think Robert was, either."

"But you *know* me!"

"I've seen you in the saloon, Travis."

"I didn't say I was a *saint*." It felt as though he was cradling a piece of wood in his arms. All her softness, all the remaining shreds of passion had fled. "I have an occasional drink. Like most men."

She snorted.

"There's nothin' wrong with that, Libby." He heard the desperation in his voice. How was a man expected to argue with a woman whose head was solid rock?

"The *saloon* is wrong," she shot back.

"Then you won't quit what you're doin'?"

"No."

"Dammit, Libby . . ."

She pulled herself free of his grip and took a

halting step back. Jaws locked, she said stiffly, "We simply can't agree on this, Travis."

"We could if you'd listen to reason."

"Reason?" A short bark of laughter escaped her, but it did nothing to remove the hurt wariness shining in her eyes. "The only *reason* you're interested in, is back on that bed!"

"Not the *only* one." Travis wanted to go to her, hold her, demand she listen to him. *Hear* him. Instead, he held his ground and added, "Besides, you can't deny you enjoyed our 'time' together as much as me." There. He'd caught her on that. He knew damn well she couldn't deny the fire between them.

"Yes, I do deny it."

"*What?*"

"A *lady* doesn't enjoy such . . . 'duties.'" She sniffed, lifted her chin, and glared at him. "And a gentleman surely wouldn't take an opportunity to embarrass a woman he cared for."

He allowed himself one step closer and didn't take it back even when she stepped farther away from him. For God's sake, where in the hell did she get such wild-hair ideas?

"First off," he ground out, "I don't know if I'm a gentleman or not . . . but I *do* know that I ain't a bit embarrassed by what we were doin'. Why should I expect *you* to be?"

"Because—"

"My turn," he snapped and held one hand up for silence. "And as for the other . . . what d'ya mean 'duties'?"

She crossed her arms protectively over her chest. He watched her fingers bite into her upper arms until the flesh turned white. "The, uh . . . 'marriage' duty, of course."

"Uh-huh," he mumbled through clenched teeth. "And just who was it told you about your 'duty'?" he asked, although Travis was pretty sure he knew what her answer would be.

"Robert."

Yep, he told himself. He should've bet money on that one. "And what about these 'rules' for ladies? He tell ya that, too?"

"Of course." Her lips thinned into a straight line. "Who else but my husband would teach me those things?"

Travis laughed. "And you *believed* him?"

"Certainly."

As his chuckles grew into a deep-throated laugh that filled the tiny room, he saw Libby's hackles rise. He blinked back the water in his eyes and told himself that when she put her mind to it, she could make herself look as stiff and starchy as any razor-lipped old maid.

"What is so funny?" Her foot tapped against the shining wood floor.

He held one hand up and struggled to calm himself. After drawing several deep breaths, he finally managed to ask, "Why?"

"Why what?"

"Why'd you believe him?"

"Because—"

"You didn't trust him on anything else!" Travis interrupted. "From what you've said about the damn fool, you wouldn't've believed him if he told you grass was green!"

"But—"

"No *buts*, Libby."

"No!" she insisted, her features a mask of confusion. Her arms fell to her sides, and she shook her head slowly. More to herself than to him, she said, "It *must* be true. With Robert I never felt anything like . . ." She stopped and let her voice fade away. After a moment she glanced at him from the corner of her eye.

Travis grinned. It pleased him more than anything else had in his life to know that it was *he* who'd shown her pleasure. That it was only *he* who'd made her tremble.

Crossing quickly to her side, he laid one hand on her shoulder until she looked at him fully. The smile fell from his face as he said, "If that's true, Libby, then your husband was a bigger damn fool than I thought. He didn't care enough or *know* enough to bring you pleasure."

"No," she whispered, her eyes sliding from his.

"Yes, Libby," he countered and lifted her chin before placing a brief, gentle kiss on her upturned lips. "Between us, Libby . . . between us, it would all be so different. So good. So . . . right."

Chapter Fourteen

THREE DAYS LATER SHE WAS JUST AS CON-fused as she had been when Travis left her hotel room. Libby closed her eyes briefly and let herself remember that last, gentle kiss. The firm warmth of his mouth on hers. The steady beat of his heart beneath her hands.

Given free rein, her treacherous mind also reminded her of the hard length of him pressed against her. She recalled every tremor of her own body and the hours it had taken for the fire in her blood to fade. And even then it hadn't gone completely. Only changed into a bone-deep, smoldering need that gave birth to an ache she'd never experienced before.

Libby's eyes flew open again at the shout of laughter. Shaking herself, she mentally tamped down the flickers of warmth that had flooded back into her blood at the mere thought of Travis. She had to stop this, she knew. But somehow, that was much easier *said* than *done*.

Libby sat at Faith's desk, pulled in a deep, calming breath, and looked at the handful of women who'd come to her temperance meeting. A poor turnout, she told herself, then silently placed the blame for *that* as well as her own personal torture, on Travis.

As the women talked amongst themselves, Libby busied herself with a pencil and paper. She'd wait a few more minutes before beginning, even though she suspected no one else was coming. Glancing at the idle sketch she'd drawn, she wasn't surprised to see a dagger, complete with drops of blood.

Her brows lifted. Obviously one part of her mind wanted to kill Travis. He'd made her life hell! From the moment they'd finally left her hotel room, Libby'd felt the curious, sometimes appalled stares of the citizens of Harmony.

It shouldn't have surprised her in the least to find out that it was Maisie and Minnie who'd taken up the listening post outside her room. Or that the two women had nearly killed each other on the stairs in their eagerness to report what they'd heard.

Libby sighed then and remembered her conversation with Faith. Her friend had grinned and assured her that even if the twins *hadn't* done their share of talking—*everyone* downstairs had heard Libby's bed pounding against the wall.

No one had needed to be told anything after that. They'd all drawn their own conclusions.

And though the bed bouncing incident had happened three days ago, people were *still* talking. Every time she entered a room, whispered conversations came to an abrupt halt. Children giggled when she walked past. Her own sister Sissy looked at her with a wide, moonstruck gaze. Curious, *interested* eyes followed her at every turn.

Her own father had hardly been able to look her in the face without blushing! And her *moth-*

er's reaction had gone beyond anything Libby'd expected. After "swooning" at Maisie's report that "Libby and Travis was makin' that bed scream with pleasure again," she'd taken to wearing black.

She'd even gone so far as to wear a heavily veiled hat on the day following Libby's "disgrace." Of course, she thought with a reluctant smile, after her mother'd walked smack into the same hitching post twice in one hour, she'd abandoned the thick, black veil.

No one believed her that nothing had happened. Of course, Travis wasn't helping there, either.

He refused to say *anything*. He just grinned a lot.

In fact, he wasn't even talking to *her*. She watched as her pencil drew a stick figure complete with badge and brand-new hat directly beneath the tip of the dagger. During the last three days, every time she turned around, Travis was there. Smiling. He didn't speak. He didn't try to touch her. He kept a respectable distance at all times. But he watched her.

The pencil in her hand made the tip of the dagger longer, sharper.

She felt his eyes on her all the time. And the self-satisfied smile on his face had become a part of him. Even *Bobby*—her own *son*—had fallen under Travis's spell. He mimicked his hero's walk, talk . . . *everything*. Not for the first time, she told herself that it was a good thing Bobby was living with her parents right now. Not only was there more room for a young boy to play . . . but if she had to live with a miniature version of Travis day in and day out, there was no telling *what* might happen!

Libby felt as though her nerves were stretched as tight as piano wire. One wrong move and she would snap.

She drew little Xs over the stick figure's eyes.

"Libby!"

She looked up, startled, and shuffled the drawing to the bottom of the stack of paper.

"When're you gonna start this meeting, girl?"

Maisie. Naturally. She shifted uncomfortably under the older woman's sharp eyes. "I thought I'd wait a few more minutes, Maisie," Libby said with a shrug. "There may be others coming."

"Nope. We're it."

Libby's gaze shifted to Minnie. "How do you know?"

"Folks've been talkin' about this meetin' for days, Lib." She paused and winked. "Along with . . . *other* things." A muffled titter shot from Maisie's throat, but Minnie ignored it and finished. "We ought to know who's comin' and who ain't."

Libby sighed heavily. If Minnie was right, this was a poor start indeed. She let her gaze move over the other women seated around the schoolroom.

Faith, Maisie, Minnie, Jane, and Lillie, still dressed in black. Libby sighed and after a moment glanced at her younger sisters, Mary and Sissy. Out of seven women, *three* were her own family members!

The schoolroom doors opened briefly, allowing a shaft of afternoon light to slice down the middle of the building. Samantha Spencer stepped inside and smiled. She held up a pad of paper, and Libby reminded herself that Samantha was there only as a reporter.

Well, just because they were starting small didn't mean they'd *stay* small. From tiny nuts grew mighty oaks!

"All right then, ladies," Faith said, "why don't we begin?"

"What do we do?" Jane asked.

"Begin what?" Maisie threw in.

"Well," Libby interrupted, "perhaps we should simply talk about *why* we're here, first. And then we could move on to what we'd like to accomplish."

Her sharp eyes moved over the woman, looking for a spark of interest. Nothing. Then her sister Sissy's hand shot up.

Thank heaven. "Yes, Sissy?" she asked. "What would you like to say?"

Sissy pushed herself off the bench seat and stood up as if she were reciting in school. "I think it would be a good idea to have some of those cookies and punch. Maybe it would make everybody feel better."

Libby sighed.

"Sit down, young lady!" Lillie fixed a stern eye on her youngest daughter. "There'll be no cookies for you, today."

"Ma . . ."

"Maybe we should talk about why we believe in temperance," Libby almost shouted to be heard over her sister's whine. "Faith? Why don't you go first?"

The woman glanced from side to side furtively, then finally looked up at Libby helplessly. "Well, I . . ."

"It's all right, Faith, just say what you think. Tell us why you're here."

"But, Libby . . . uh . . ." Faith smiled and shrugged her shoulders. "I really came today out of friendship. I just didn't want you to be here alone, is all."

A sinking feeling started in the pit of her stomach. Libby looked from one face to the next and read almost the same expression every time.

They were all here for that reason! It should have pleased her, she knew. They were her friends. They cared about her. But she'd hoped for so much more. Didn't they understand that she was doing this for them as much as for herself?

"Now, Libby," Maisie said firmly, "don't take on. I'm sure there's folks around here who feel like you do. They just . . ."

"Just what?"

"Well, dear," Minnie cut in, "some of them were a little put off by what, uh . . . *happened* at the hotel the other day?"

"*Nothing* happened."

"Uh-huh." Maisie's lips twitched.

"Maisie," Libby tried again for what seemed the hundredth time, "there is an explanation for everything you heard."

"Uh-huh," she said again, "and I know what it is."

Libby groaned.

"I may be old, honey. But I ain't *that* old." Maisie snorted, tugging at her shirtwaist, and added, "Just 'cause I don't hear the tune much anymore, don't mean I don't remember the dance!"

"Don't hear it *much*?" Minnie snorted. "Sister, your band's been dead for years."

"That's all *you* know, Sister."

"Poo!"

"Poo?" Maisie stood up and glowered at her sister. "I'll have you know, Minnie Parker . . . I still get around a mattress every now and then."

"Changing the sheets don't count!"

"Why, you old . . ." Minnie inhaled sharply.

"You're as old as me, remember!"

"Old is as old does!"

"You made that up."

"All old sayin's got made up at one time or another!"

"Not by you!"

"*Ladies!*"

Libby shook her head and stared at her mother. She'd been so caught up in the twins' fight, she hadn't even seen Lillie stand up.

"I *hardly* think this topic of conversation is 'suitable' for ladies to be having. Especially" — she jerked her head at her two unmarried daughters— "'Little pitchers have big ears,' you know."

"Mama!" Mary's insulted tone let them know exactly how she felt at being excluded from their conversation.

"Hush!" Lillie turned, then flicked a glance at her other daughter, hovering near the cookie tray. "Sissy!"

Sissy's outstretched hand dropped like a stone. This was *not* going well. Libby looked to the rear of the room and saw Samantha busily scribbling at her pad, a smile on her face. Oh, dear.

"Why don't we get back to the subject at hand?" Jane suggested, and Libby could have kissed her.

"Which is?" Maisie asked.

"Temperance," Libby stated flatly. "And how to get more women to these meetings."

"These?" Sissy complained. "There's gonna be more than one?"

"Of course. We'll meet until we've succeeded in closing down the saloon."

"Now, Libby, there's a place for everything in this world, dear," Minnie spoke again. "Most of the women around here look forward to their husbands going to Cord's place for a while. Gets them out from underfoot, you understand."

"Besides," Maisie added, "a beer or two never did any harm when it come to a quick romp!"

"Maisie!" Lillie frowned.

"Ah, Lillie," the older woman countered quickly, "they got to learn sometime. 'Sides, you sayin' you don't appreciate a little trot around the mattress time to time?"

Libby watched her mother, fascinated. Somehow, she was still having trouble imagining her parents doing anything the slightest bit "romantic." Still, with as many kids as they'd had . . . Libby shook her head.

Lillie took one quick step toward Sissy, slapped her hands over the girl's ears, and whispered, "I like to dance every bit as much as you do, Maisie Hastings! And I daresay my band plays a good deal more often than yours!"

"Her band's dead." Minnie's lips twitched.

"My band's just tunin' up, Sister!"

"Poo."

"Oh, for heaven's sake!" Samantha interrupted sharply. "We all like to 'dance.' But we didn't come to talk about our 'bands,' did we?"

Libby shot her a grateful smile.

"All right, fine, Miss Newspaperwoman," Maisie said. "Then how about you tell us how to get more women to Libby's meetings?"

"Well . . ." Samantha's pencil tapped against her front teeth.

"We could have cake," Sissy suggested, stepping away from her mother's hands.

Lillie rolled her eyes.

"Nope. Ain't enough," Maisie said flatly. "The menfolk around here are almighty mad at you, girl." She shook one finger at Libby. "They don't take kindly to bein' told what to do anymore than you ever did. Just about every one of 'em's told their women that they can't come to your meetin's."

"Oh."

"That's right, 'oh.'" Maisie jerked a nod. "Now, the women of Harmony don't take orders any better than their men do, so I'm thinkin' there're a few who want to come to your meetin'. Even if it's just to show their men that they won't be dictated to."

Not exactly what she'd had in mind, Libby thought tiredly.

"But," Maisie went on, warming to her theme, "we need something to make the women feel sorry for ya."

"*Sorry* for me?" That went against the grain. If

there was *one* thing she didn't want, it was people feeling sorry for her.

"That's a good plan, Sister."

Maisie grinned at Minnie and said, "And I think I know just the thing to do it, too!"

"What?" In spite of her reluctance Libby had to ask. It was the old fascination of the rabbit for the snake about to eat it.

"Get yourself arrested."

"What!" Libby hadn't thought it possible for Maisie to surprise her any further. But somehow, the woman had managed it. Get arrested? By Travis? Be locked up in a cell with him only a few feet away?

And what about her son? What would Bobby think if his new hero locked up his mother?

An instant later she found herself thinking that Maisie might have stumbled onto just the thing that would sway Bobby away from whatever plans he might have for making Travis his new father.

"Sure. You get arrested, and every woman in these parts will come runnin'."

"Maisie Hastings, you have taken leave of your senses!" Lillie shouted at her old friend. "Suggesting that *my* daughter . . . a respectable widow with a small son . . . allow herself to be thrown in jail like a common—"

"I'm not talkin' about prison here, Lil." Maisie frowned. "I'm talkin' about the Harmony jailhouse. She'd be right down the street. We could visit her. Bring her supper and such. . . ."

"And what about Bobby?" Lillie asked, her foot tapping against the floorboards.

"Hell, Lil. You're his granny! You mean to say

you couldn't keep watch on the child for a few days?"

"Of course not, but what would the boy *think*? Seeing his mother locked away like a common—"

"I could bring her cookies," Sissy offered, but no one paid any attention.

"It might work," Minnie conceded. "Might give the women just the push they need."

"And if it doesn't?" Lillie demanded.

"Well, no harm done."

"No harm?" Lillie waved one hand at her daughter. "What about Libby's reputation? She could hardly spend the night in that jailhouse with Travis!"

Maisie's eyebrows wiggled. "If you'll recall, Lil . . ."

"Oh, Lord," Lillie mumbled as the bed-bouncing incident came rushing back into her mind.

"Well, Libby?" Maisie turned on her suddenly and asked. "What do you think about it?"

Libby's gaze moved over the women in the room. She'd known most of them her whole life, and yet, in the last few conversations with them, she'd learned so much about them.

Strange, she told herself. Until a girl was grown and married, she never really knew the other women around her. It was almost as if there were a secret club. A club where your membership dues had to be paid with experience. She glanced at her mother.

Since she'd come home, despite the occasional lapses of advice and controlling attempts, Lillie'd treated her like an equal. It was as if, now that Libby'd been married, had a child, she was finally welcome into the circle of women. The laughter, the talk about things Libby'd never imagined her mother'd ever *thought* of, the trust.

It was all there for her now. She'd finally grown up. And with being an adult came the responsibility of making your own decisions.

If being arrested would rally more women to her side, then that's just what Libby would do. And she had a sneaking suspicion that her mother would be proud of her for doing it.

Sucking in a great gulp of air, Libby stood up and faced her friends and family. "It's a perfect idea, Maisie. I'll do it."

"But how?" Jane asked quietly.

"I'm not sure yet," Libby admitted. "But I'll think of something." She glanced at her mother again. Behind the sheen of concern in her eyes, Libby was positive that she read *pride* shining in Lillie Taylor's eyes.

Libby's house lay in cartons, crates, and piles, scattered over the ground just at the edge of town. Travis stared at the spot where the building would soon stand and imagined it as it would look, with the shade of the cottonwoods surrounding it. With surprisingly little effort, his mind created the image of he and Libby, sitting on a front porch swing at the end of a long day.

The shadows lengthened, stars peeked out of the night sky, and she cuddled closer to him for warmth. Soft lamplight spilled out the shining windows, creating a pale yellow path through the darkness that Bobby, after a day at play, would follow home.

A dreamy smile touched his lips, and he

pulled his still uncomfortably new hat off to wipe the sweat from his forehead.

Glancing down, he noted that Bobby had done the same thing. Smothering a grin, he watched the boy drop his hat back on his head, then spread his short, chubby legs wide and plant his hands on his hips.

It was almost eerie, watching your own mannerisms on someone else. But at the same time Travis felt a swell of pleasure blossom in his chest and grow. He'd grown so accustomed to Bobby's company, he hardly remembered what it was like to make his rounds about the town alone.

And he didn't care to, either.

Hell, he couldn't even wish away the last four years anymore. If he did that, if he wished that Libby had never left Harmony . . . then Bobby wouldn't exist. He smiled down at the child. Travis couldn't imagine his world without the boy.

"It's gonna be a big house, Travis."

"Hmmm?" he said, distracted by his imaginings.

"Too big for just me and Mama," Bobby pointed out with a quick glance up at the tall man beside him.

"You think so?"

"Uh-huh." The boy rubbed his shirtsleeve over the "deputy" badge Travis had given him only the day before. "I was thinkin'."

"What?"

"Maybe you could live with us, Travis?"

He didn't say a word. He couldn't. The knot in his throat was much too big for that.

"I mean," the boy went on, a little more haltingly, "you like me, don'cha?"

"Sure I do, Bobby." Travis's voice sounded strangled.

"And you like Mama . . . and we like you, too. So maybe you could stay with us and pretend to be my papa? Just a little bit?"

"A little bit?"

"I promise to be good, Travis." The boy turned his wide green eyes on him, and Travis flinched under the direct stare softened by a sheen of wistfulness. "Honest I do."

Immediately he squatted down beside the child. Forcing a smile, he said, "I'd like that a lot, Bobby. But your mama and me got to talk about it first, all right?"

"But you want to? You want to be my pa?"

"I sure do, Bobby. I'd like that fine."

The boy chewed at his bottom lip, rubbed one eye, and hesitated only a moment before throwing his arms around Travis's neck. As the sheriff held him, Bobby whispered, "Can you and Mama talk real soon, Travis?"

Travis's heart staggered a bit, but his arms only tightened around the small, sturdy body. "Soon, Bobby. I promise. Real soon."

The boy was right. It was time. He'd waited and watched long enough. He hadn't said anything about that afternoon at the hotel. Instead, he'd let the town gossips take care of that.

Travis had wanted Libby to come to him. But maybe, he told himself, he'd waited more than long enough. Lord knew, he and Libby were past due for the "talk" he had in mind.

About four years past due.

Chapter Fifteen

At an emergency meeting of the Temperance League, two days after their first one, Libby told the women her latest plan. It had come to her only the night before. It was better than getting herself arrested. And it was so simple. So easy. It *had* to work.

At the very least, it should serve notice to the men in town that their women would not be ordered about. And, she thought, the women wouldn't have to sacrifice a thing!

Libby smiled at the slightly larger crowd filling the schoolhouse. Abby Newsome had joined the group along with Faith's mother and sister Zan and several wives from the outlying farms.

Oh, she knew quite well that most of these women had rallied to her banner only because they didn't like their husbands ordering them not to speak to her. But with her new plan, all that would change. The women would come together, and the men would have no choice but to agree.

Eventually.

Soon Harmony would be back to normal. And the saloon would be closed. After all, a business couldn't stay open if it didn't have any customers, could it?

"Ladies," she said firmly and waited for the chattering voices to fade away. "I think I've found a way to force the men of Harmony to agree to closing the saloon."

"I'll believe *that* when I see it," Maisie snorted.

Libby frowned. "Last night I was remembering a story I'd read once and—"

"Fairy stories!" Someone laughed. "Now she's gonna tell us fairy stories!"

"It was called *Lysistrata*," Libby went right on.

"Lisis-what?"

"*Lysistrata*," she said with a smile at Abby. Letting her gaze slide around the room, Libby caught the knowing gleam in Samantha's and Faith's eyes. Those two at least knew where she was headed with this. "It's about . . . well, it doesn't really matter what it's about. But in the story, the men and women of this town couldn't agree on something. And the women found a way to win."

"Shotguns or rifles?" someone in the back of the room asked, and the other chuckled nervously.

"Neither." She paused until she was sure she had everyone's attention, then said, "They simply refused to allow their husbands any 'liberties.'"

"Liberties?"

"Sex, Faith," Maisie shot back. "Sex."

"For heaven's sake!" Lillie reached across Sissy, grabbed a cookie, and shoved it into the girl's mouth. "Chew," she ordered. "Loudly."

"You mean you want us to cut our men off?"

Libby smiled at the thin farm wife in the back. "Exactly. If we band together in this . . . refusing the men—well, in a few days, they'll be so anxious to call a halt, they'll agree to closing down the saloon."

"Libby," Samantha called from her post by the door.

"Yes?"

"Even if your idea works, what makes you think that Cord would be willing to close down?"

"Well, Samantha," Libby said softly, her fingers twirling a pencil, "I was hoping that you, too, would join us."

"Me?"

"Sure. If we're not all in this together, it won't work."

"But I'm not a member of your league . . . remember?"

"I know, Sam," Libby conceded. "But you *are* a woman."

Lips quirked, Samantha nodded and leaned back against the closed door.

"Does this mean no kissing, too?" Abby Newsome chewed at her full bottom lip.

For just a moment Libby let herself remember Travis's kiss. The touch of his mouth against hers. The incredible heat of his tongue invading her. Deliberately she shoved the traitorous thoughts aside and forced a smile. "Yes. It means no *anything*."

"There's still Lottie and her girls to think about. . . ."

Turning to Maisie, Libby said quickly, "All right, there isn't much we can do about Lottie's place. But am I right in guessing that most of the husbands don't go there anyway?" She let her gaze slide slowly over the small group of women. "Aren't her customers mainly the ranch hands or drifting cowboys?"

Some of the women nodded.

Henrietta Norton, Hangdog's wife, finally answered, "I don't know about the rest of you, but my man's been told time and again . . . go to Lottie's, don't come home."

"True, true," someone chanted.

"And what about you?"

"Pardon?" Libby asked, looking around the room for the speaker.

A tall, heavy-set woman in a faded gray dress stood up. "I said, what about you? As far as I can see . . . you got nothin' to lose at all in this. You ain't even got a man."

"That's not what *I* heard . . ." another voice whispered.

Lillie shot to her feet, glaring at the woman. "Who said that?"

"It's all right, Mother," Libby inhaled sharply and said, "You're right. I don't have my own man now. But I was married. I know what I'm asking you to do. And frankly, I can't understand why it bothers any of you." She shrugged. Memories of Robert's rough fumbling in the dark rose up, and she quashed them down. "It's more like I'm offering you a vacation."

"*Vacation?*" Maisie muttered, narrowing her eyes at Libby. With a shake of her head, she added, "It's plain to see I thought more highly of *Travis* than I should have."

"Sister!"

Libby ignored them. She wouldn't think about Travis. She'd been avoiding him very nicely the last couple of days, and she wasn't about to let him invade her thoughts now. Besides, what she'd felt in his arms was better not even considered. A ribbon of gooseflesh crept up her spine, but she pushed it aside. Those . . . *feelings* had nothing to do with what was happening now.

And if the women went along with this idea of hers, it would give her an *extra* reason to stay away from the handsome sheriff. As if she needed another reason, she laughed silently. Quickly she crossed her fingers and said loudly, "Well? Are we agreed? Shall we try this? For a few days, anyway?"

A few reluctant heads nodded, and Libby waited breathlessly until the small cluster of women finally agreed to give her plan a try.

As the women left the schoolhouse, though, Libby couldn't help wondering why so many of them had looked at her so piteously.

That afternoon Travis stood outside the mercantile. She'd managed to avoid him for two days. She wouldn't even open her hotel room door. And when he stood on the landing shouting, Faith had insisted he leave because he was disturbing the other guests.

Travis frowned slightly as he recalled Kincaid's helpless shrug, but he couldn't hardly blame the man for avoiding a fight with his own wife over something that wasn't his concern in the first place.

He glanced over his shoulder at the nearly empty Main Street. It seemed everyone in town had an opinion they were too eager to share with him.

The women all made clucking noises with their tongues, shaking their heads at him as if he were a boy caught stealing apples. Life at the boardinghouse hadn't been any too pleasant lately, either. Maisie and Minnie were women with strong opinions and had not the slightest hesitation in sharing them.

Then, when he'd seen them not fifteen minutes ago, leaving yet another of Libby's "meetings," he would have sworn there was a disappointed look in Maisie's eyes.

Travis sighed heavily. He'd also heard more about the "goings-on" at the hotel than he'd ever thought to. And he found himself almost wishing he'd never pulled that stunt of bouncing and jumping on Libby's bed.

Besides, he heard that the men in town weren't treating her too well because of that incident. Of course, they were all careful to watch their mouths around *him*. But Zeke had told him that one or two of the men from the outlying farms had fairly *ordered* her off their property when she'd tried to speak to their wives.

Apparently, Travis told himself, he'd thoroughly *ruined* her reputation with that scene at the hotel. This whole thing had gotten way out of hand. All he'd wanted to do was try to convince her to marry him . . . and now he'd made her out to be some kind of fallen woman!

And she wouldn't even *talk* to him!

Well, he thought grimly, he was about to change all that. He'd finally decided that the thing to do was simply camp out at the mercantile. Sooner or later she'd show up at her parents'

store. And when she did, she'd find him waiting.
If Lillie Taylor didn't shoot him first.

Still smiling over how well her meeting went,
Libby crossed the boardwalk in front of her
parents' store. She pushed the mercantile door
open and heard her mother shouting, "You have
quite a nerve, Travis Miller, showing your face in
here! After what you did!"

"Now, Lillie," James soothed.

"Don't 'now Lillie' me, James! You didn't hear
that thumping and banging! And the groaning!"
Lillie waved one hand at her face. She looked up
at Libby. "*You* groaning."

"Mrs. Taylor," Travis said, with a quick glance
over his shoulder at Libby. "*Lillie*, it's not what
you think. . . ."

"Oh, really, young man!" Lillie straightened
up, lifted her chin, and glared at the sheriff. "I
suppose you want me to believe that you were
jumping up and down on the bed like
children . . . just to make noise?"

"As a matter of fact—"

"Don't insult me!" Lilly sniffed.

Libby stared at Travis. It was the first time he'd
even mentioned that day at the hotel. And even
though she was pleased to hear him admit that
nothing had happened between them, she also
knew that it wasn't any use.

"Mother," she said quietly, "could we please
stop discussing that afternoon?"

"I only wish it were possible," Lillie moaned
and sagged against her husband. James staggered.

"Unfortunately, no one in town seems the least

bit inclined to forgive and forget." Lillie shot a nasty glance at Travis. "You could at least have asked her to marry you. Done the decent thing."

"MOTHER!"

"I did."

"That's what I thought," Lillie went on, racing right past Travis's quiet statement. "You have no more respect for her than she had for herself when you—"

"Lillie," James interrupted, watching Travis with a quiet intensity. "Lillie! Hush a minute here."

"Hush up?"

"Travis," James asked. "What did you say a minute ago?"

"I said"—Travis pushed his hat to the back of his head, glanced first at Libby, then turned back to her parents—"I *did* ask her to marry me."

"What?" Lillie's jaw dropped.

Libby's throat closed. It was difficult to breathe.

"When?" James asked.

"Right after she came home," Travis said, then turned to grin at Libby.

"Well, for heaven's sake!" Lillie pushed away from her husband's side, raced around the edge of the counter, and went to Travis. Pulling him down to her, she planted a kiss on his cheek, then shook her head at her daughter. "If you two aren't the silliest things! Why didn't you *say* you were betrothed? Why, *no one* would hold a little, shall we say . . . 'eagerness' against a properly fianced couple. All this time wasted." She clucked her tongue, then clapped her hands together and rubbed the palms briskly. "James!

Get your order pad. There's so much to be done! Oh, my! A wedding!" Her eyes narrowed slightly. "This will teach the busybodies in town! Have you decided on a date? Oh, never mind. I'll take care of that for you. James!" She turned on her heel and strode back to the counter. "Hand me that calendar!"

A cupboard slammed upstairs, and Lillie looked up. "Sissy! Get out of that cabinet!" Glancing back at her husband, she said, "You should hire some of the extra farm hands to help put the new house up quicker, dear."

"Good idea, Lil," James agreed.

"Lillie," Travis said.

"Mother," Libby echoed.

"Hmmm?" Her index finger ran along the calendar until she stopped with a grin. "Three weeks! That should be plenty of time to get the champagne in from Salina."

"Three weeks?" James said with a worried frown.

"Champagne?" Libby said. "*Mother*, I'm the head of the Temperance League!"

"Champagne doesn't count, dear. Everyone knows that!" Lillie flashed her a smile. "Besides, what's a wedding without a little champagne?"

"There is no wedding."

Silence dropped like a heavy curtain over a badly acted stage play. Three pairs of eyes turned to Travis. He shifted uncomfortably, but held his ground. Until Lillie spoke, in a voice so laced with venom, it was a wonder he didn't drop dead on the spot. Instinctively Travis took a step back.

"What do you mean, there is no wedding?"

"Just what I said."

"But you *said*," Lillie snarled, "that you proposed."

"I did."

The older woman inhaled slowly, as if gathering her strength. "Then what seems to be the problem?"

"Your daughter."

"Libby?"

"She said no."

Libby watched her mother's head swing slowly in her direction. She winced at the power of that stony glare and thought briefly about hiking her skirts and sprinting through the door behind her. But that wouldn't solve anything. It would only serve to drag this whole unpleasant situation out longer.

Unpleasant. She risked one glance at Travis and told herself that he didn't look in the least bit discomfited. Quite the contrary, in fact. He looked almost pleased. And, she thought wryly, why shouldn't he? He'd turned her family against her and gained himself some allies.

Then she caught the dark, hungry look in his eyes and barely managed to suppress a shiver. In an instant, fires swept through her, boiling her blood and choking off her breath. He ran his tongue across his lips, and Libby's mouth parted slightly as if ready to welcome him.

A damp warmth centered down low in her belly, spreading fingers of desire down her thighs until she thought she might fall over. Her breasts felt heavy, and her nipples, she knew, were hard and straining against the bodice of her dress.

All this from a single look.

She pulled in a deep, shuddering breath and deliberately shook her head, trying desperately to dislodge the memories. The need.

But deep inside herself, Libby knew that if they hadn't been interrupted by Maisie's shocked whispers . . . she and Travis would have done exactly what the entire town was convinced they'd done already.

"What is all this nonsense about you saying no?" her mother demanded.

Her gaze snapped to Lillie's outraged features. "It's not nonsense, Mother."

"But you had no trouble saying yes to a *dance*," her mother said meaningfully, closing the distance between them with a few quick steps.

Behind her mother Travis and James looked at each other in confusion. But Libby knew exactly what Lillie was talking about. She remembered all too clearly Maisie's memories of bands and tunes and "dances." A telltale flush spread over her cheeks, but she straightened her shoulders and faced her mother down.

"I've told you—"

"Yes," Lillie snapped, "nothing happened. Well, let me tell you something, missy! Something did indeed happen! Half the town heard you and Travis doing your best to knock down the hotel!"

"Mother!" Good God. Would people be talking about that day for the rest of her life?

Yes, she answered herself silently. They would. Just as *she* would remember it for the rest of her life. Whether she wanted to or not.

"Lillie," James crooned, "calm down now, dear . . . you don't want to have an attack. . . ."

She waved a hand at her husband to show him she'd heard, but she didn't take her eyes off her daughter. "Now, missy, you didn't listen to me four years ago . . ."

Libby blanched. Her mother had never once referred to the last-minute talk they'd had. But Libby remembered it as if it were yesterday.

With only fifteen minutes until the wedding, Lillie Taylor had urged her oldest child to call the whole thing off.

"Don't worry about a thing, dear," she had said. "Your father will explain to everyone. You don't *have* to go through with this, Libby."

But she couldn't back out. She couldn't bring herself to admit that she wasn't ready. That she'd made a mistake. She couldn't face the humiliation.

Libby almost laughed. *Humiliation?* Since returning to Harmony, she'd become adept at handling humiliation. But now she was faced with almost the same situation as the one she'd been in four years ago. Only *this* time her mother was on the would-be groom's side.

"But you're damn well going to listen to me now," Lillie continued. "You *will* be getting married. Just as soon as the new house is finished."

"No, I won't." She wouldn't be bullied into making another bad decision. Not by Travis. And certainly not by her mother.

She'd learned her lesson the first time. Unless she was absolutely sure . . . unless she had no doubts at all . . . she would *never* get married again.

And Libby couldn't imagine being without her doubts.

"Travis!" Lillie's gaze locked with her daughter's, but she snapped out an order to the man behind her.

"Yes, ma'am?"

"Buy a ring."

Chapter Sixteen

Before she could open her mouth again and dig an even deeper hole for the both of them, Travis grabbed Libby's elbow and spun her about.

"Where are you going?" Lillie demanded.

"For a walk," Travis ground out and dragged Libby toward the door. She pulled against him, but he kept on, his strength overpowering her heel-dragging.

Out the door, off the edge of the boardwalk, and around the corner of the mercantile, Libby still fought him. Tugging and yanking, she kept trying to free herself from his iron grip. But nothing worked. He kept going, past the hotel, down to the river's edge, under the shade of the cottonwoods.

When he finally stopped, he dropped her arm, and she immediately turned to leave.

He reached out and grabbed her again. "Dammit, Libby, don't you think it's time you and me talked?"

"I have nothing to say to you, Travis. Nothing."

"Fine," he snapped. "Then *I'll* talk. You listen."

The mutinous expression on her features told him she would bolt at her first chance. Since he wasn't about to let her leave until he'd had his say, Travis held her shoulders tightly, his fingers digging into her flesh.

"You're hurting me," she finally said.

"Sorry," and his grip loosened just a fraction, "but, Libby, you're about to drive me out of my mind."

She stood stiffly, staring past his shoulder, refusing to meet his gaze.

"Look, Libby," he said, "I ain't gonna apologize for tellin' your parents that I asked you to marry me."

"No need."

"Yeah, I can see that. But," he added, pulling her a hair closer, "I also don't want you to marry me just 'cause your ma says so."

"You needn't worry, then, Travis." Her gaze flicked to him, then snapped quickly away again. "I have no intention of marrying you."

"No, you don't understand, Libby. I want you to marry me 'cause *you* want to."

She snorted.

"There's something between us, Lib. Something so big it almost scares me sometimes." Her rigid stance dissolved just a bit. "Whenever I'm near you, I can *feel* it. And so can you."

"No."

"Denyin' it don't make it so, Lib." He lifted her chin, holding it firmly with his fingertips, and forced her to look at him. "I love you, Liberty. And I think you love me, too."

"You're wrong," she said, but her voice trembled slightly.

"Am I?" He lowered his head and brushed his lips across hers, gently. Reverently. When he pulled back again, a tender smile curved his lips. He stared down into her shining green eyes and had to force himself not to crush her against him.

Her feelings for him were written plainly in her eyes. He couldn't be wrong. But she was so damned stubborn, he hadn't a clue as to how to make her admit it.

Reluctantly he was compelled to use his only argument. Her reputation.

"This is a small town, Libby." His voice whispered against her face, and he inhaled the soft, flowery fragrance of her. "Folks talk."

He didn't have to feel the tension return to her body to know it was there. Her eyes gave away her slightest feeling. And right now they shimmered with a slow-building anger.

"I don't care," she said.

"Sure you do. If not for you, then what about Bobby?" It was a low blow and he knew it. But he was getting desperate.

"Bobby's fine."

"Now. But what about later? What about when he starts hearing all the comments folks're makin'? What about if he asks you what happened at the hotel? What will you tell him?"

"The truth."

"We've already tried that with everybody else," he countered quickly, pressing his advantage. "Did they believe?"

Her lips pressed together grimly.

"Did they?" Travis pulled her closer and let one hand slide down her rib cage and over her hip. She shifted away, but he followed her movement. "Or did they think what they wanted to?"

"Bobby would be different. He'd believe me."

"Even if he did . . . would it make a difference? Wouldn't he still hear the whispers?
Wouldn't it still hurt him to hear folks talking
about his mother?"

Tears welled up in her eyes, and Travis called
himself every kind of a bastard. He hadn't
wanted it this way. He'd wanted to win her over.
To woo her.

But she wouldn't let him. And by God, he
wasn't going to lose her. Not again.

"We could leave Harmony. . . ."

Her voice was soft, so . . . *lost*-sounding, he
almost missed it. But when he realized that she
just might be serious, something cold wrapped
around his heart and lungs, making it almost
impossible to breathe.

Leave Harmony?

"This is your home, Libby. Bobby's home now,
too. He loves it here. He *belongs*." Travis knew his
desperation was evident in his voice, but he was
helpless to hide it. Just the thought of her leaving
again was enough to send daggers of pain slicing
through him.

Because if she left *this* time, he knew she'd
never come back.

"Bobby *belongs* with me," she said flatly.

"And you *belong* with me."

The time for talking was past. Travis pulled
her close, wrapped his arms around her, and
slanted his mouth over hers. He felt her breath
escape her in a rush and as her lips parted for air,
his tongue swept inside her mouth. Caressing,
teasing, he poured all the longing that had been
a part of him for too many years into his kiss.

His hands moved over her body with the

eager need of someone too-long denied. Her breasts, her back, her softly curved behind. And every touch only fed the desire for more.

He felt her hands curl around his neck, felt her press her hardened nipples into his chest. Her tongue matched his stroke for stroke, and Travis knew that even if her mind couldn't accept that they belonged together . . . her body *knew* it. Her heart *accepted* it.

And when he thought he would never be able to draw another breath, she pulled away. As she struggled to draw air into her heaving lungs, he watched her with a hunger that had only been stoked by the taste of her.

Her eyes shone glassily, her lips were puffy and red from his kiss, and her glorious deep brown hair had begun to straggle down from its topknot. He reached for her, but she shook her head and took a step back.

"I . . . can't do this, Travis. Now, more than ever."

"*Now?*" he asked, his own breath labored. He watched the play of shadows drifting over her face with each movement of the tree branches overhead. A puff of wind lifted a tendril of her hair and laid it teasingly across her cheek. "What do you mean," he ground out, "*now* more than ever?"

She inhaled deeply, and he fought to keep his eyes from her breasts.

"We," she said and swallowed heavily, "we women have called a sex strike."

"*What?*" She couldn't be serious!

"That's right. A strike." She lifted her chin and stared at him through still hazy eyes. "Until the men agree to stay away from the saloon . . . there won't be any . . ."

"Any what?"

"Any of"—she waved her hand at him—"*this.*"

"You're joking!"

"I've never been more serious."

"It won't work."

"Of course it will work."

Travis tore his hat off and threw it to the ground. Staring at the dirt and the strands of grass that had managed to grow despite the covering shade of the trees, he challenged, "And what makes you think so, Libby?"

"The men will never be able to stand it. They'll miss their . . ."

"*Duties?*" he snapped.

She blanched a bit at his sarcastic tone, but Travis ignored it and continued.

"And what about the women? Don't you think *they'll* miss it?"

"No. Why should they?" Libby's eyes screwed up, and she cocked her head at him questioningly.

"Why?" He snorted a laugh that had not a trace of amusement in it. "Jesus, Libby! You don't even *know* what it is you've given up. Or what you've asked the others to do without."

"Of course I do. I'm a widow, not some simpering virgin!"

"You might as well be a virgin for all you know about making love!"

Defiance suddenly sparkled in her eyes. "I know enough to know that I'm not interested in finding out more!"

"Is that right?" His voice was low, dangerous. He took a step toward her, and he could see that she desperately wanted to move back. But she held her ground. Stubborn, he told himself. Hardheaded, stone cold, stubborn. "Then maybe you'll tell me who it was I was just kissing?"

She swallowed nervously, and he continued his attack.

"Who was it pressed her breasts against me, breathed into my mouth, and near stole away my own breath?"

"Travis . . ." Libby's tongue snaked out and licked her lips.

"That's right, Libby," he whispered throatily, "it was *you*. Hot, hungry, and eager to touch and be touched."

"No."

"You can say whatever you like, Libby. You can pretend that you felt nothing. You might even be able to convince yourself. But not me." He shook his head and let his gaze move over her slowly, lovingly. "I held you. I heard your sighs, felt your trembles. Whatever you want to think, Libby, you enjoyed it. And you wanted more."

Seconds slid by into minutes, and still the silence between them hovered like a living, breathing creature. Travis watched the play of emotions on her face and prayed that she would finally admit what each of them knew to be true.

But when a grim resolve settled on her features, he knew she wouldn't. Not yet.

"Whatever you or I may think, Travis . . ." she said finally, "the point is, we called a strike and we're going to stick with it. Until the saloon is closed."

"All of this, just to close Cord down?"

She nodded jerkily.

"You're gonna tear this town apart, Lib," he warned. "You're gonna pit the women against their men all for no reason."

"There *is* a reason!" she countered hotly.

"Accordin' to *you*," he said. "You're doin' this for *you*."

"Not just for me. The whole town will be better off. It will be safe." She spoke quickly, hurriedly, as if trying to convince herself, not him, that she was right. "No one else will have to die because of whiskey."

"No. Liquor was no more responsible for your husband's death than a match is responsible for a house fire."

She didn't say anything, and he went on.

"Just like you can't blame a gun for killing somebody any more than you can hold a knife accountable for slicing your finger." He took two steps closer and laid his hands on her shoulders. She didn't move away, but she didn't come to him, either. "Sooner or later, Libby," he said quietly, "we *all* make choices. And we have to take the responsibility for those choices. Robert *chose* to drink himself stupid. A man who kills with a gun *chooses* to be a killer. It's not the whiskey or the pistol to blame."

She shook her head. "But if the liquor or the gun wasn't there . . . it wouldn't happen."

Travis smiled grimly. "People find ways, Libby. Folks who can't buy their liquor brew their own. *Moonshine?* And you think nobody was ever killed before somebody made the first gun? Hell, no. Before guns, they used rocks, or clubs." He tilted his head to look into her wary eyes. "You gonna chop down every tree so nobody can swing a tree branch at somebody else?"

"But—"

"No *buts*, Libby. Every man and woman has to live with their own mistakes. Their own choices." He inhaled deeply, then blew it out again in a rush. "If there hadn't been whiskey around and available . . . what would Robert have been like?"

"He'd have—" she started quickly.

"No, take your time, Lib. *Think* about it." Travis cupped her cheek gently. "Remember him as he really was, Libby. And this time, don't hold a whiskey bottle accountable."

She shook her head and stepped back. He could see her mind working on everything he'd said. He watched her eyes cloud over as she pulled deep within herself, examining her past. And Robert.

After a long moment, when she stepped away from him and turned back toward town, he let her go. She had a lot to think about, he knew. And she'd have to do it alone. He only hoped that when she was finished working things out, she'd come to him.

Standing in the shadows of the huge trees, Travis kept his gaze locked on her until she disappeared around the edge of the hotel. Only then did he release the pent-up breath imprisoned in his chest.

*   *   *

By the third day of the strike, there wasn't a smile to be found in Harmony.

Even Minnie's perpetually tilted lips were pulled into a thin, straight line. Tempers flared, fights broke out over the slightest of reasons, and both the men and the women were glaring at Liberty Taylor Wilder.

"Sissy!" James ordered sharply. "Get your hand out of that licorice jar this minute!"

Libby watched her sister's surprised expression and felt a stab of sympathy. As far as she knew, that was the first time their father had ever snapped at Sissy about her snacking. When tears welled up in Sissy's eyes, James, too, must have realized how harsh he'd sounded.

"Go ahead, hon"—he tried to smile—"you have as much as you want."

"I'm not hungry," Sissy sniffed. Then she lifted the hem of her dress and marched past her father with her nose in the air.

James's shoulders slumped for a moment, then he straightened deliberately and stared hard at his oldest child.

Though he didn't say a word, Libby knew full well what he was thinking. This was all *her* fault. Well, good heavens, she hadn't expected the men to become so . . . *cranky!*

"James!" Lillie's voice screeched from upstairs.

"Don't shout!" he hollered right back.

"I'll shout if I've a mind to," came the reply, and Libby winced at the sharp tone. Silently she admitted that it wasn't only the *men* who were out of sorts! "Now, you get up here this minute," Lillie continued, "and help me with the material for Libby's curtains!"

"Of all the . . ." James slammed his pencil down on the countertop and moved toward the stairs muttering viciously under his breath.

Quietly, carefully, Libby backed toward the door. And even as she stepped out onto the boardwalk and squinted into the morning sun, she asked herself where she could go.

At the hotel Faith and Kincaid were at each other's throats . . . Maisie and Minnie hadn't seemed the least bit pleased to see her the day before . . . and even Samantha had brushed past her only a half hour ago without a word.

She walked to the edge of the boardwalk and leaned against the porch post. Letting her gaze drift out over the small, dusty street, Libby told herself that nothing was working as she'd planned.

The men were supposed to be upset, of course. Though she hadn't expected the *women* to be complaining. But it was obvious that neither side was going to be able to hold out much longer. And if she were completely honest with herself, she would have to admit that even *she* missed seeing Travis.

He'd been playing turnabout since their last talk at the river. Instead of waiting for her to avoid him, Travis had managed to stay away from her, this time. And if he was doing all this to give her time to think . . . it was working.

She'd had a lot to think about, not least of which was the kiss they'd shared at their last meeting. All too clearly she recalled his touch, his scent . . . the *feel* of him pressed tightly against her.

But more than that, she remembered his

words. And as much as it pained her to admit it, he'd given her plenty to think about. Though it had been painful, she'd forced herself to examine her recollections of Robert.

But even reliving ugly memories wasn't enough to convince her that Travis was right. Oh, she thought grudgingly, even *sober*, Robert hadn't been much good. But if there'd been no saloon handy . . . perhaps everything would've been different. Better.

Now, though, she would never know for sure. And even if Travis *was* right . . . could she back down now? Could she go to the women in town and say "I was wrong? Saloons aren't bad places after all?" No. How could she? After everything she'd said and done since returning to Harmony, she would look a perfect fool.

There had to be another way, she told herself grimly. There had to be a way to rally the women to her. Strengthen their resolve to win this battle with their men. If they backed down now, the men would never let them forget it.

Her fingers idly plucking at the splintered wood of the post behind her, Libby's gaze moved along the row of buildings until she'd settled on the Last Resort.

In the background she heard the telltale pounding of hammers and the harsh rasp of saws as the men her father'd hired built her house. She inhaled sharply and remembered her mother's words about a wedding when the house was finished.

Well, Lillie would be disappointed. Although she was willing enough to admit that her marriage was hardly a common example to judge by . . . Libby was still not interested in marrying anyone.

Especially Travis. The things he did to her, the way he could make her feel . . . no. It *couldn't* be right. It just *couldn't*.

She blinked away thoughts of Travis and concentrated instead on the saloon, halfway down the street.

As she watched, a cowboy flew through the batwing doors and sprawled in the street. From somewhere nearby came the heated sounds of an argument, followed by a slamming door.

Travis was right. Harmony was coming apart. She had to do something that would bring this strike to an end quickly—and still allow the women to win.

Slowly she smiled.

Of course.

How could she *possibly* have forgotten?

Something to bring the women together again. Make them strong in their stand against the men.

She would get arrested.

Tonight.

Chapter Seventeen

GETTING ARRESTED WAS NOT AS EASY AS one might think.

She'd thought about it all day and hadn't come up with a proper "crime" to commit until that evening.

After all, it wasn't as if she actually wanted to do anyone real *harm*. And she certainly didn't want to have to stay in jail for any length of time! All she wanted to do was garner enough sympathy from the townswomen that they would be strengthened in their battle against the men.

Her stomach churned with swarms of butterflies dipping and swaying with each new burst of nerves that shot through her. If only there were some other way, she thought, staring at the Last Resort, just across the street. But there wasn't. She knew that only too well.

And something *had* to be done. Quickly. Only an hour ago she'd seen a definite softening in Faith's eyes when her husband reached for her hand after supper. If something didn't happen soon to firm up the women's resolve . . . well, Libby thought that Faith wouldn't be the *only* woman in town to surrender to her husband's demands. She'd seen enough in the last few days to know that the "sex strike" was taking its toll on quite a few people.

Her own parents were hardly speaking. Sissy had lost her appetite, and Mary refused to talk to Libby. The younger woman blamed her sister for Danny Vega not coming to call the last time the stage rolled through town.

Libby sighed. And *she* wasn't much better than any of the others. Her own temper was frayed, and most of the time she felt as though her insides were tied up in knots. The worst part was, she didn't understand why. After all, she didn't even *have* a man to miss! Except Travis, a voice in the back of her mind whispered.

Travis. Just the thought of him was enough to start her heart racing and her blood boiling. The knot in the pit of her stomach tightened, and she ground her teeth together. This wasn't going at all how she'd planned. Even her own body was working against her.

A warm evening breeze swept in off the prairie and Libby lifted her face to meet it. For a moment she let the familiar scents of a summer wind fill her, reminding her of happier times. Times when her only concern was which dress to wear to an upcoming barn dance.

Was it only four years ago? Had she really changed *so* much? She'd thought coming home to the warmth and safety of Harmony would help her become the person she used to be. But recently she'd realized that that was not the answer. She wasn't that young girl anymore. She was a woman. A widow. A mother.

And her life waited for her in the future . . . not the past.

She sighed again, straightened up, and turned her gaze on the vast, star-sprinkled sky overhead. As she had all too often in the past few days, she found herself thinking of Travis.

Libby'd tried to push the memory of their last moments together out of her head. Over and over, she'd heard his words echoing in her head and heart. And when the sound of his voice died away, other memories rushed in. She'd tried to forget the feel of his mouth on hers. The warmth of his hands encircling her. The steady beat of his heart.

But it was impossible.

Even when her brain wasn't conjuring up his image, her body would suddenly stir to life as if responding to a phantom touch. No matter where she went or what she was doing, an uncanny *sense* of him was with her.

And that frightened her even more than the thought of arrest.

Libby sucked in a great gulp of air, squared her shoulders and gripped the river rock in her hand tightly. Grimly, she pushed the aggravating thoughts aside and told herself to get on with it. To do what she had to do.

Deliberately she stepped off the boardwalk, hurriedly crossed the street, and slipped soundlessly up the steps to the saloon.

Between the red lettering on the Last Resort's shining windowpanes, Libby's gaze swept the barroom. The wagon-wheel chandelier had been rehung, and a fog of cigar smoke mingled with the lamplight, filling the room with a hazy, indistinct glow.

Sprinkled about the building at several different tables were a handful of men, most of them glowering into their glasses. One lone woman, even her shortened sapphire gown drooping listlessly, leaned against the bartop chatting with Charlie Thompson.

Libby swallowed anxiously and clutched the rock tighter. A tiny curl of hesitation and dread began to spiral from her stomach, spreading throughout her body.

Then suddenly Bobby's face as she'd tucked him in bed only an hour ago filled her mind. So young, so trusting. Wasn't it up to *her* to see that he grew up free from having to watch his grandfather and uncles and even Travis, whom he admired so much, going into saloons? He'd already lost a father because of whiskey . . . no matter *how* indirectly, she added mentally. As his mother, didn't she *owe* it to him to do everything she could to see him raised well and safely?

But what would he think about his mother being in *jail*?

Stop it, she ordered silently. Stop thinking and rethinking this. She'd made her decision, and now she had to carry it out.

The sounds of a chair scraped against wood, a bootheel stamped on the floor, and glass clinked against glass as Charlie poured a drink drifted out to her. Inhaling sharply, Libby tried to steady her nerves one last time.

Then, before she could talk herself out of it, she marched quickly to the saloon doors and pushed her way inside. For a heartbeat no one seemed to notice her. But, as she stomped across the plank floor, her heels ringing out into the unnatural silence, one by one the men looked up.

Just like the first night she'd entered the bar, she felt their eyes on her. Charlie looked up as she approached. But the smile on his face fell away as she lifted the rock in her hand and hurled it at the mirror hanging behind the bar.

Eyes wide, the bartender yelled, *"Look out!"* and ducked for cover under the bar.

The ornate mirror splintered, and for a brief second Libby saw her own shattered image staring back at her. Then, almost before the last shard of glass hit the floor, Travis came out of nowhere and grabbed her.

"What in the *hell* are you doing?"

"Let me go!" She kicked at him, but he was too quick for her and sidestepped her attack.

"Not bloody damn likely," he snarled. His hands at her waist, he lifted her, then tossed her upper body over his shoulder like a sack of grain.

"Put me down!" she shouted and heard an appreciative laugh from somewhere behind her. Libby pushed against Travis's broad back until she could see around the suddenly lively little crowd.

The customers stood in a half circle around her and Travis, and Libby wasn't surprised to note that most of them looked as if they wanted to strangle her.

"Not a chance, lady!" Travis's arms tightened like iron bands around her legs, pinning her to him. "I've had about all of your nonsense I can stand, Libby! What you need is some coolin'-off time."

"What?" She struggled to see him, but he

shrugged his massive shoulders, and she flopped down again.

"And I'm gonna see that you get it!" He turned sharply after a nod at Charlie and headed for the door.

She jounced hard with his every step, his shoulder digging into her middle. Though her fists pounded repeatedly on his back, he didn't even slow down.

"That's it, Travis!" one man shouted. "Lock her up!"

A couple of the others laughed, and one lone pair of hands applauded.

He stomped through the batwing doors, setting them swinging viciously. She hardly had time to take a breath of the fresh night air before he was carrying her into his office, right next door.

When the jailhouse door slammed shut behind them, Travis turned the key in the lock and dropped her to her feet. Hands on his narrow hips, he glared down at her, and Libby just managed to keep from backing up a step.

"Okay, Libby," he said in a deep, low voice that shook with barely controlled rage, "I'm all done now, settin' around waitin' on you. I've been tiptoein' around you since you got home, waitin' for you to come to your senses."

"My *senses!*"

"That's right," he went on quickly, not giving her a chance to argue. "I didn't say much when you started this whole damn mess over the saloon, and even when you called a sex strike and about tore this town apart"—he threw his arms wide—"I didn't say a damn thing!"

Libby swallowed uneasily. "It was none of your business," she said and felt that knot deep inside her twist and tighten.

Travis yanked off his hat and hurled it across the room. "See there? That's just what I'm talkin' about!"

"What?"

"'Not my business,'" he mimicked. "You just don't get it, do ya, Libby?"

The anger seemed to drain out of him, leaving behind a solemn, altogether *different* emotion.

Warily Libby waited. In the light of a single kerosene lamp hanging alongside the door, Travis's deep brown eyes glittered dangerously.

His arms snaked out, wrapped around her, and pulled her to him. Holding her tightly against the length of him, Travis leaned his head back and looked down into her eyes. The knot in Libby's belly tripled in size.

"Everything *about* you is my business, Libby." His eyes moved over her face with a slow, deliberate longing. He bent his head low, and just before his lips closed over hers, he whispered again, "*Everything.*"

His mouth was hard, demanding. Nothing like his earlier, tender kisses, it was as if he wanted to prove to her just how far she'd pushed him. Travis's desire poured into her, and Libby hesitated only a moment before meeting his hunger with her own.

A groan slipped past her throat as her lips parted under his. His tongue darted inside and moved over hers with the damp, caressing warmth she remembered so well. She moved slightly in his arms, offering herself up to him.

Her hands moved to encircle his neck, her fingers threading eagerly through his hair.

She couldn't get close enough. She couldn't feel enough of him.

As his kiss deepened, she held his head down firmly on hers as if afraid he would move away and end the delicious torment he was causing. She felt his hands move over her back. Warm, insistent, soothing . . . so many feelings crowding together in her brain until she couldn't think anymore. Didn't *want* to think of anything beyond what he was doing to her.

Somewhere deep inside her body, the twisted knot she'd carried for the last few days began to unwind. In its place came a wild, raging need. She didn't care anymore if Travis was right or wrong for her. She didn't care what tomorrow might bring. She only knew that she wanted him more than her next breath.

Libby pressed her breasts against him and leaned into his strength. When his hands moved to cup her behind and pull her firmly against his hips, she moaned and broke the kiss, struggling for air.

An overwhelming tide of damp heat flooded her. She'd never known anything like it. His mouth moved to slide down the length of her throat. His teeth and tongue traced gentle patterns over her flesh, and she turned her head eagerly, seeking, *demanding* more.

"Libby," he groaned and reluctantly lifted his head from the base of her throat. "I have to say this—if we don't stop now, I don't know if I'll be able to later. . . ."

She forced her eyes open and looked up into

his passion-shadowed gaze. Her tongue moved over suddenly dry lips, and her chest heaved with the effort to draw breath.

Slowly she lifted one hand to trace the line of his cheek. Libby felt him tremble with her touch and felt the muscles in his jaw lock reflexively.

"Don't stop, Travis." Rising to her toes, she brushed her lips against his and said, "Show me everything. Stay with me tonight. Hold me. Love me."

"Libby—" His voice sounded strangled.

"Travis," Libby went on hurriedly, her voice a rush of soft longing, "you were right before. . . ." Her fingers moved lightly down the line of his sun-browned neck.

"What?"

"When you said I . . . *felt* something when you touched me."

God. His blood raced, his heart pounded, and still he couldn't make himself believe what he thought he was hearing. She kissed the hollow of his throat and his heart stopped.

"And," she went on, "I want to feel that again."

A man could only take so much, he told himself as he swung her into his arms. He cradled her close and felt his heart lurch and begin to pound again when she laid her head on his chest. Quickly he crossed the office floor, snatched at the ring of keys hanging on a peg, and unlocked the heavy oak door leading to the cells.

Inside there were two tiny, barred cubicles, separated by a narrow wooden path. He stepped into one of the open cells and unthinkingly closed the iron door behind him.

He moved to the meager cot, snatched its paper-thin mattress off, and threw it to the floor. Carefully then, he set her down and knelt in front of her.

Libby watched him and, with every moment that passed, felt her body stir anxiously. One lock of his brown hair lay tumbled across his forehead, and she reached to push it back. His eyes slid shut at her touch. Slashes of moonlight poked between the bars on the solitary window and lay across his so-familiar features.

She leaned forward to kiss him. Libby's breath on his cheek fanned the flames coursing through him, and the soft sigh from the back of her throat weakened his knees.

His right hand reached hesitantly for the buttons at her throat. One by one he released them, his hunger making his fingers clumsy. And when her shirtwaist lay open, Libby pulled away from him just long enough to shrug out of the fine, white shirt.

He let his eyes touch her firm breasts, hidden from him only by the fragile material of her chemise. The dark buds of her nipples strained against the fabric, and his palms itched to cup them, tease them.

Slowly, reluctantly, he raised his gaze to hers. If he saw a change of heart on her features, Travis knew that even if it killed him, he would walk away. But shining in the green depths of her eyes was a passion as deep and consuming as his own.

Libby licked her lips nervously, then as he

watched, she slowly reached up and slid the straps of her chemise off her shoulders.

A long, slow breath escaped him, and he tenderly reached out to stroke the soft fullness of her breasts. His fingertips grazed over her erect nipples, and the shudder that racked her body shook him to the bone.

Carefully he laid her back on the mattress and bent to kiss the pale flesh he'd waited so long to touch. His lips closed over the bud of her breast, and his tongue moved in a languid circle, fed by her sighs.

Travis's fingers moved to tease her other nipple, and as he pulled and stroked at her, Libby began to twist beneath his hands. His right hand slipped to the backside of the waistband of her skirt, and when he had the buttons free, he began to tug the material from her body.

Libby arched her back, moving closer to his mouth, and at the same time lifted her own hands to help him discard her clothing. In seconds she lay naked before him, and only a moment later Travis's clothes joined hers in the corner of the cell.

He stretched out beside her, drawing her close, relishing the feel of her nude body cradled close to him. Her breasts moved against the fine hair on his chest, and he groaned in response.

Taking her mouth with his, Travis's right hand skimmed over her breasts, along her rib cage, and over her flat abdomen to the triangle of curls between her thighs. She jumped when he cupped her warmth, but relaxed against him quickly as his tongue darted deeper into her mouth.

Slowly, carefully, he moved his fingers to the damp warmth that beckoned him. When he found her most sensitive spot, her thighs parted to give him access, and she sighed into his mouth.

Again, his fingers dipped lower, and this time Libby arched her hips to meet them. Eyes wide with wonder, she bit at her lip when Travis moved to nibble at her breast again.

With a slow, steady pressure he began to suck at her nipple, and Libby knew that she would die. Something inside her began to tighten and grow with each draw of his lips.

Never in her life had she experienced anything like this. She hadn't even guessed that such feelings existed. In a blinding flash, recollections of Robert's inept fumbling in the dark swam before her. The embarrassment, the awkwardness . . . Libby pushed the old memories aside deliberately and gave herself over to Travis completely.

Even if for only one night, she wanted to feel everything he could give her. She wanted to give the pleasure he'd awakened in her back to him a hundredfold.

Libby raised one hand to his shoulder and let her fingers slide over the hard strength of his back. She felt his body jerk with her touch, and a soft smile curved her lips. Then his thumb brushed over the core of her, and her body shuddered with delight. Her short nails dug into his flesh, and when his fingers slipped inside her body, Libby groaned aloud at the marvelous invasion.

It was as though he'd climbed inside her soul.

He seemed to be everywhere. She gasped for air and writhed beneath him, eager for something she knew waited for her just out of reach. Her body tightened again, and she lifted her hips against his hand, silently begging for more.

He raised up on one elbow to stare down into her face, and Libby saw her own need reflected in his eyes. She raised her head for his kiss, but he smiled and pulled away.

Travis shifted suddenly then and knelt down between her parted thighs. While his thumb and fingers did magical things to her, she watched him as he prepared to enter her.

And for the first time since she'd lost her virginity, Libby was eager for the joining. Her head back, she licked her lips and stared at him, trying to tell him without words just how badly she wanted him. Her hips moved again in welcome, and she lifted her arms toward him.

Travis smiled down at her, and Libby knew completion. Even with the raging need still coursing through her, one look in his eyes filled her with more peace than she'd ever known. When his hands slipped beneath her to lift her hips, she returned his smile, found her voice, and whispered, "Come inside me, Travis. Be a part of me."

She saw his breath catch, then watched his face as he slowly pushed himself into her. His eyes closed, he sighed as his body slid inside her warmth. He filled her completely, finally banishing all the dark, lonely places in her soul. With his slow, deliberate movements Libby felt his presence deep within her and knew that nothing in her life had ever been so right.

And then his rhythm began to change, his hips urging hers to join him in the ancient dance. His hard strength rubbed against her, plunging in and out with the promise of release. Her arms reached out for him, but he shook his head and slipped one hand between them at their joining, stroking her sensitive flesh. Her fingers curled into the spare mattress beneath her, and when her body convulsed around his, she cried out his name with the beauty of it.

Travis leaned close, kissed her until she couldn't breathe, then moved again, harder, faster until his own body shattered, and he collapsed in her arms.

She cradled him close, loving the feel of his warm breath on the curve of her neck. And she smiled when she heard him whisper, "Welcome home, Libby."

Chapter Eighteen

"THIS IS OUTRAGEOUS!" LILLIE LIFTED her hem and stepped down off the boardwalk in front of the mercantile.

"Calm down, dear," James countered uselessly.

"Calm down?" She threw him a quick glare and looked away again just as quickly. "Calm down, he says! His own daughter . . . his *flesh* and *blood* . . . rotting in a *prison*, and he tells me to calm down!"

A tired sigh sounded from behind her, but she refused to acknowledge it.

"Hardly a prison, Lil," her husband stated flatly. "And how much rotting could she do overnight?"

"That's hardly the point," she snapped, "though I shouldn't expect *you* to understand." Lillie kicked the hem of her skirt out of her way and started walking hurriedly toward the jail at the other end of the street. "After all, what does it matter to a *man* when a woman's delicate sensibilities have been stretched to their breaking point?"

"Only thing that's been stretched around here is Travis's temper! And," James added when he caught up with his wife, "I got to say, Liberty's about used up my *own* patience these last few days!"

She snorted, looked at him along the line of her nose, and sniffed. "I shouldn't be surprised. *You* have never appreciated Liberty's delicacy!"

"Delicate?" A harsh laugh shot from his throat. *"Our* Libby? Delicate?"

Lillie's mouth thinned into a mutinous line.

"Are we talkin' about the same girl who talked the foolish women of Harmony into denyin' their husbands—"

"That will do, James Taylor!" Lillie stopped dead in the middle of the still-deserted street. "I will *not* discuss such—*matters* in the middle of Main Street in broad daylight!"

"Yeah," he grumbled, "and you won't discuss 'em in the dead of night, either."

"James!"

He cocked his head at the woman he'd married so many years before. They'd had their share of stormy weather over the years, Lord knew . . . but, he told himself suddenly, to save his life, he wouldn't have changed a thing.

Images of the days and nights he'd spent loving Lillie raced through his brain. He saw again the young girl she'd been—the new mother, her first baby at her breast—but mostly, he saw her as she lay beside him in the darkness. Always turned toward him, her hand reaching out for his in her sleep.

A brief smile curved his lips as he stepped close. "Ah, Lil, don't get all stiff and starchy on me. . . ."

She didn't move away and he went on.

"Do you know, Lillie Taylor"—he leaned in

and gave her a quick peck on the cheek—"that you're as beautiful as you were the day we got married?"

A slow flush of pleasure crept up her neck and blossomed in her cheeks. "Don't be foolish, James," she muttered thickly. "I'm the mother of seven and know that I look it. I *do* have a mirror, y'know."

"You're usin' the wrong looking glass, Lil," he said. "Use my eyes, instead. Because there, you will always look as you did the first day I laid eyes on you."

Her breath caught.

"You were wearing a soft bluish-green dress, sittin' on the front porch swing of your papa's house. . . ."

"Oh, my," she whispered, her gaze distant, as if seeing the memory he described.

"I walked past and you smiled at me." His fingers tucked a stray lock of her graying hair behind her right ear. "I didn't know a soul in town . . . feelin' kinda lonesome, I guess. But when you smiled . . ."

She turned her head slightly to look at him through wide, teary eyes.

"I *knew* I'd come home."

Lillie sniffed frantically and blinked back the water in her eyes. "James Taylor," she said, hooking her arm through the crook of his, "I believe that is the *dearest* thing you have ever said to me."

"Then I apologize, Lillie Taylor."

"For what?"

"For not telling you all that before. *And*"—he

shrugged sheepishly—"for a lot of things here lately."

Lillie looked up at him and shook her head. "There's no need, James. Lately, we've *all* been . . . difficult."

"I've missed you, Lillie."

"I've missed you, too."

He leaned down to kiss her, but suddenly she remembered exactly where they were and jerked her head back. "Not here, James. I can just imagine all the noses stuck into the front curtains watching us right now."

Her husband grinned, and Lillie chastised herself mentally for not noticing recently just what a well set-up man he was.

"Well, then"—he winked—"let's us go get that daughter of ours out of jail and head on home for a little . . . 'talk.'"

She smiled, suddenly eager to get back home. Then, just as quickly, she frowned again. "But what about the strike, James? I promised!"

"I won't tell if you won't."

"Travis!" Libby squirmed, trying to get out from under the heavy weight of his legs, pinning her to the mattress. "Travis! Wake up!"

"Huh?" He stirred slightly and she gave him a push.

"Wake up, I said!"

His eyes opened, settled on her, and a slow grin curved his full lips as he reached for her.

Libby batted his hands away. "Stop that! Oh, good heavens, it's morning!"

Sunlight streamed through the bars of her cell, spilling over their naked bodies, still entwined on the too small pad. Immediately Libby raised her gaze to the dusty, wood-beamed ceiling.

Somehow, naked seemed much more . . . *naked* in daylight.

Unbidden, scenes of the night before flashed through her mind. She squeezed her eyes shut as if wiping away the images, but it didn't work. She doubted that she would *ever* be able to forget a single minute of her time with Travis.

She couldn't help wondering, though, if most women experienced what she had last night. If they did, it was no wonder everyone was so against that sex strike.

Her body ached, reminding her that she'd done things she'd never dreamed of doing. After that first, hurried, impassioned mating, Travis had shown Libby just how many ways there were for two people to find pleasure together.

She bit back a groan. How in the world would she be able to look him in the eye again? How could she look *anyone* in the eye? Surely, the whole town would know. They'd be able to see it on her face.

"Mmm, morning, Libby," he said softly and leaned over her.

She pushed at him. "Don't, Travis."

"What's the matter?" He propped himself up on one elbow and stared down into her face.

"What's the *matter*?"

"Yeah." His right hand smoothed over her abdomen, up her ribs to cup her breast. Idly his thumb and forefinger caressed her nipple until it hardened.

Oh, God, she groaned silently and fought down the surge of delight sparkling through her body. Deliberately then, she inched farther away from him, lay one arm across her breasts, and lay her free hand over the juncture of her thighs.

"Libby, what are you doing?"

"For heaven's sake, Travis! We're *naked*! And it's *morning*!"

"Yeah? It happens every day about this time. What's it got to do with anything?"

"Everything!" she snapped, fighting to keep her eyes on his face and not on . . . the *rest* of him. Pulling in a deep breath, she asked quietly, "Could you *please* fetch me my clothes?"

He glanced at their clothing, still jumbled up in a corner, then looked back at her. He grinned. "Nope."

"Why not?" A hot flood of color filled her cheeks.

"Not till you tell me what's got you so het up! Last night you—"

"Don't talk about last night!" Libby closed her eyes. If he said anything else, she'd shrivel up and blow away, she just knew it.

When his lips covered hers gently, though, she couldn't stop the swell of desire that shot through her. Almost against her will, Libby's body rose up to meet him and her arm fell away from her breasts. His hand quickly moved to take its place, and she sighed into his mouth when his fingers teased at her still-rigid nipple.

He pulled away from her and began to nibble at her neck. Of its own volition her right arm moved to encircle him, and she stroked his smooth, muscled back. "Oh, Travis, we have to stop this . . . we have to . . . *oh*!"

His teeth nipped at her breast, sending shivers of pleasure racing across her flesh.

"You really want me to stop, Libby?" he breathed, and his warm breath caressed her nipple with a feather touch.

"No . . . yes . . . no," she groaned helplessly and moved into him when his palm followed the curve of her hip. "Lord, I don't know anything anymore. . . ."

"Good," he said softly, "and don't think anymore, either. Just be with me, Libby. Just feel."

His mouth moved on its torturous path, and she held her breath, praying he wouldn't stop.

As if from far away, a sound reached her, but Libby ignored it. Nothing mattered. Only Travis's touch. His tongue flicked against her navel, and she smiled.

Another noise, a little louder than the first, and Libby frowned, trying to place it. But then Travis's hand slid to the inside of her thigh, and she moved to accommodate him, parting her thighs just enough to allow him entry.

Metal turning against metal screamed out into the early morning stillness.

Libby froze.

Travis leaped for the blanket lying on the nearby cot.

Lillie pushed the oak door open.

James caught her as she staggered back, her hand at her throat.

The brown wool blanket floated down to cover Libby's nudity, but not before she saw the shocked expressions on her parents' faces.

"God in heaven!" Lillie's shout rattled the eaves.

"Mother?"

"Lillie?"

"Mrs. Taylor?"

"You," the older woman said, staring at her daughter. "And *you!*" She turned on Travis, who held his clothes in front of him like a too-flimsy shield. Spinning around, she poked James's chest. "This is *your* fault!"

"*My* fault?"

"I gave you too free a hand in the raising of that girl, and now see what you've done!" Her left hand swept out, indicating the young woman huddled under a blanket and the near naked man in the corner. "All of you men!" Lillie shook one finger at Travis and narrowed her eyes. "All the same, the lot of you! And as for you, *SHERIFF*, there'll be no playing fast and loose with *my* daughter, Travis Miller! Law or no law . . . in two weeks' time you will be a married man!"

"Yes'm."

Libby wondered if a person could *will* themselves to die.

"Mother, if you'll just let me explain—"

"I don't want to *speak* to you until you've"— Lillie shuddered—"*dressed.*"

Libby pulled the blanket over her head.

Spinning about on her heel, Lillie marched into the adjoining office. "We'll wait for you out here." A long pause, then, "James!"

James looked from his daughter, a huddled lump under the blanket, to the naked sheriff.

Travis sucked in a gulp of air, dropped his clothes, and hands at his hips, faced his future father-in-law. "Hell."

James strangled a grin. "Not yet, son, but it's comin'—and closin' fast!"

"I will not hear a word from you, young woman!"

Libby bit her lip and lowered her gaze. Her mother'd been going at her for over an hour and showed no signs of letting up.

Ever since recovering from the shock of finding her and Travis together, Lillie hadn't stopped talking. Silently Libby acknowledged that she could hardly blame her. Once more that hideous moment rose up in her brain. If she lived to be a hundred years old, she would never forget the look on her mother's face.

Lord! She wasn't even sure how she'd managed to get dressed. She only knew that Travis had been singularly quiet. Libby ground her teeth together and told herself that she was overreacting. After all, it couldn't have been easy for him, standing in front of his would be mother-in-law stark naked! But, a small voice in the back of her mind whispered, he could have said *something*.

"How *dare* you act in such a precipitate manner? What were you thinking?" Lillie's voice reached new heights and scattered Libby's thoughts. "Did you learn *nothing* from that hotel episode?" The woman waved one hand and began to pace the length of her daughter's hotel room again. "Never mind. You *weren't* thinking. That's *quite* obvious."

"Mother, could we please stop talking about this now?"

"No, we cannot. Not until you've agreed to the wedding."

"I've told you," Libby said for the fiftieth time. "I don't *want* to get married."

"What you *want* is what caused this mess in the first place." Lillie took three quick steps and came to a stop directly in front of her daughter. Glaring down at her, she added, "It's high time you started thinking about what you *should* do. Not what you *want* to do."

Libby groaned, slammed her elbow on the small bedside table, and propped her head in her hand.

"And what about the sex strike, eh?"

Libby ducked her head. It *had* been her idea. And here she was, the first woman to break the strike, and she wasn't even married! Good heavens!

"As well you *should* look shamefaced, my girl!" Lillie glared at her, and Libby didn't even have to look up to feel that stare. "Let me tell you something, Liberty Taylor Wilder. Either you marry Travis . . . or I tell every female in hearing distance just *who* broke that strike!"

"Mother!"

Lillie jerked her a nod. "And don't think I won't, either."

Libby didn't doubt it for a minute.

Easing down beside her on the bed, Lillie spoke again, softer this time. "Liberty, let me ask you something."

"What?" Wary eyes watched the older woman.

"Do you intend to remain in Harmony?"

"Well . . . *yes*. Of course I do. It's my home. Bobby's home now, too."

"Precisely."

"I don't understand."

Lillie sighed heavily, tugged at the lay of her skirt, and said patiently, "Then I shall try to make it clear. In a small town certain *behavior* is expected. One cannot simply do whatever one wants to do without its affecting someone else."

"You mean you and papa?"

"Yes." One sharp nod. "And your brothers. And sisters. And your son."

Libby's eyes closed.

"As an adult, you are expected to accept responsibility for your actions, Liberty. You *know* that."

Yes, she knew it. And if she hadn't, Libby had only to remember hearing this very same speech from Travis only a few short days ago.

"Loose behavior isn't tolerated and can hardly be missed in a small town like Harmony, Libby."

Her mother's voice gentled and became almost singsong.

"Therefore, for the good of *everyone* including yourself, you and Travis *will* be married as soon as the house is finished."

"But, Mother," she started, uncertain just what she could say to change anything.

"No." Lillie stood up. "That's all there is to it, Libby. Unless you want to . . . move away, that is."

Libby's head snapped up, and she met her mother's troubled gaze. No, she didn't want to move away, and one look at the green eyes looking back at her told Libby that Lillie didn't want that, either.

"No, Mother. I don't want to move."

"Good. Then it's all settled."

Helplessly, Libby nodded.

"Fine. I'll place the announcement in the paper this very day."

"If you think that's best."

"Libby, dear . . ." Lillie turned for the door. "Don't sound so disheartened. Things are not altogether black, you know. Cord isn't pressing charges against you for the broken mirror . . . you'll be married soon . . . and, thank *heaven*, no one else knows about your escapade in the jail." Shaking her head, she muttered thickly, "On the floor in a *cell*, of all places! We had much better sense . . ."

The unfinished statement died away as Lillie stepped through the door and into the hall.

"Oh!" Lillie poked her head back into the room. "One more thing. There will be no more shenanigans with Travis until *after* the wedding, do you understand?"

Libby nodded and lay back on her bed when her mother closed the door behind her.

No more shenanigans. That shouldn't be a problem. She still had no idea how she would ever be able to face Travis again.

Chapter Nineteen

HER MOTHER WAS RIGHT. SHE HAD NO choice but to get married.

Libby groaned softly. She'd have been willing to fight the marriage over that ridiculous hotel scene. Because no matter what anyone thought, nothing had happened between her and Travis. But now she *had* slept with him.

Her hand flew to her abdomen. What if she was pregnant? Heaven knew, it hadn't taken her any time at all to conceive Bobby! She might very well be carrying a child already. And then what? Without a husband she would be scandalized.

And Bobby. Not only would *her* life be ruined . . . but her son's would be destroyed as well. She couldn't risk that.

Of course, from what she could see, Travis was pleased as punch about the whole thing. After the initial embarrassment of having his future mother-in-law see him naked as the day he was born, he'd dived wholeheartedly into the wedding preparations.

It seemed that Libby was the only one with any reservations. And even *she* wasn't sure why. She couldn't even blame her doubts on her disastrous marriage to Robert anymore.

Libby'd finally realized that Travis had been

right there, too. Whiskey hadn't stolen her husband. It was Robert himself. He'd chosen to have an empty marriage. He'd chosen to ignore his wife and child. And whether he'd had liquor or not . . . he would have been no different.

With or without whiskey, Robert had been a weak man.

There had been something lacking deep inside him. Looking back, Libby wasn't sure if he'd ever known how to love. How to care for someone other than himself.

Not like Travis. A small smile curved her lips. He'd shown her what it was to be really loved. No matter what she did, his feelings didn't change. Even when he was mad, he didn't stop loving her. Sudden warmth flooded her, and Libby's stomach flopped unsteadily.

Good Lord, she thought with a surge of panic . . . she was in *love* with Travis. When did it happen? How? And most of all . . . *why*?

"Libby?" Maisie's voice shattered her thoughts. "What's the matter with you, girl? You look like you seen a ghost!"

"Speakin' of ghosts," Minnie said quickly, "did I ever tell you all about the time I—"

"Yes," Maisie snapped.

Libby tried to concentrate on the tiny group of women clustered in Maisie and Minnie's front parlor. The twins, Lillie, Faith, Jane, and Samantha. The little party they'd insisted on giving her was the last in a series of celebrations she'd been to in the last week.

She and Travis had been to dinners, suppers, barn dances, and sat together at church. And not once in all that time had they been alone together. Thanks to Lillie. To make sure that nothing else happened before the wedding, Libby's mother had insisted that Mary stay with her sister at the hotel until the ceremony.

"Come on, ladies," Maisie ordered, "have some more of that punch! Lord knows, we made enough to float a buckboard."

"It's very good, Maisie," Jane said as she leaned toward the crystal punch bowl and poured herself another glassful. "Whatever did you put in it?"

"A little of this," the older woman said, "a little of that."

"Oh, Sister," Minnie countered, "what's the harm in telling?"

"You hush, Min!"

"For heaven's sake!" Minnie's features twisted into a frown. Then she turned to the other ladies. "Well, we use a good deal of fruit juice, to make it sweet, y'know. But we also put in a little peach brandy . . . just for flavoring, of course."

"Brandy?"

"*Peach* brandy, Lil," Maisie snapped. "Think of it as just fruit."

Libby chuckled and the others turned to look at her.

"What's so funny?" Samantha asked.

"Nothing. It's just that, here we are, the Temperance League . . . drinking brandy punch."

"Oh, that." Maisie snorted and poured more punch for everyone. "That's all finished now, ain't it? I mean, you ain't still gonna be goin' on about that after you get married, are ya?"

"No." Libby shook her head. There was no point in carrying on a losing battle, she thought.

Cord would never close that saloon. She would just have to trust that Travis meant what he said about not being a drinking man.

Her heart staggered a bit. If he changed like Robert had . . . it would kill her.

"Well, good!" Minnie smiled, chewed on a cookie, and took another long drink of punch. "Now that the sex strike is over, too, this town can get back to normal."

"Hmmph! Whatever *that* is!" Maisie snorted.

"Do you know," Lillie said, draining her cup and reaching to fill it again, "it's very warm in here . . . don't you think?"

"Now that you mention it . . ." Jane waved one hand in front of her face, "it *is* a bit warm. . . ."

"Then have some more punch! It's nice and cool. And I got more on ice in the kitchen." Maisie stood up, staggered slightly, and turned for the back of the house.

"Are you all right, Sister?" Minnie asked.

"Fine, fine. Just got dizzy for a minute. Must be that heat."

Samantha undid the top two buttons of her shirt and walked to the nearest window. "Maybe some air would help."

Libby helped herself to more punch.

"I don't recall it ever bein' this warm in here before," Lillie told Minnie.

"True, true . . . but it *is* August."

Maisie carried in a fresh batch of punch and only spilled a bit of it when she set it down with a crash on the table. "Whew! Pour me another, will ya, Sister?"

"Certainly. In fact, I do believe it is the finest batch of punch I've ever made."

"*You* made?" Maisie brought the glass to her mouth and sipped thirstily at the liquid. "*I* made this punch, Sister."

"Maisie, you're gettin' older by the minute." Minnie shook her head. "I dishtinkly . . . distinctly remember adding just the proper amount of brandy myself." She winked at Lillie, and the woman grinned broadly in return. "And just a *touch* more for flavor, don'cha know."

"Now I *know* you're crazy, Sister. *I* put the brandy in the punch only this morning. Put in extra, too, since we was havin' guests."

"Well"—Lillie hiccuped and delicately raised her hand to her mouth—"whoever made it, I commend them. It's quite wonderful!"

"May I have some more?" Jane asked and leaned toward the table. She caught herself unsteadily as she began to tip from her perch. "Excuse me," she said and curled her fingers tightly around the arm of the chair.

Samantha handed Libby another glass, and they toasted each other before draining them.

"What is that noise?" Travis asked as he walked up to the barbershop.

Zeke grinned, crooked one finger, and led the sheriff through his shop to the back. As they slipped along the rear wall of the building toward the boardinghouse, Zeke began to chuckle under his breath.

"What're you up to, Zeke?"

"Shhh!" The older man spun about, his index finger to his lips. "Quiet, now."

The babble of voices and sharp barks of laughter came louder, the closer they got to Maisie and Minnie's back door. Travis shook his head, but kept pace with the shorter, rounder man ahead of him. All he'd wanted was a haircut!

"C'mon, Travis," Zeke said in what was supposed to pass for a whisper. "You got to get close enough to hear 'em good."

"Hear who?"

More laughter followed by the sound of something crashing to the floor.

"The women." Zeke grinned and stepped up onto the back porch of the boardinghouse. Easing open the screened door, he led the way into Maisie's kitchen.

Hell. Travis stared after the man. Even though he lived at the boardinghouse, he didn't relish the idea of sneaking up on *anybody*. Least of all a bunch of women.

The door opened again, and Zeke frowned at him. "You're *missin'* it. C'mon!"

Someone inside started singing, and despite his best intentions Travis's curiosity won out. Carefully he stepped into the kitchen behind Zeke.

They sidled cautiously down the long hallway. Zeke raised a hand for silence, but it wasn't necessary. Travis was too intent on listening to do any talking.

From the parlor Maisie's voice rang out. "Lord, Min! Quit your catterwaulin'!"

Minnie's song died abruptly. "I was jusht shingin' a purty love shong for Libby"—she hiccuped—"and Travish."

"Thanks, Min," Libby spoke up, and Travis cocked his head. "That was real nice."

"Ain't love a grand thing?" Lillie said.

"It is, it is," Jane answered softly. "Could you hand my me cup of punch?"

Travis snorted and Zeke waved frantically at him.

"Miss Maisie," Samantha called out much too loudly, "would you give me the receep . . . recepipe . . ."—she took a deep breath—"tell me how you made this *wonderful* punch?"

"'S a ol' family shecret," Maisie said.

"Ain't a wedding grand?" Lillie crooned.

"My, oh, my, won't Libby have fun on the weddin' night?" Minnie countered.

Maisie snorted. "She already *had* her weddin' night. At the hotel. 'Member?"

"Did not," Libby said quickly. "Did not. At the hotel did not."

Travis moved in closer to peek around the open doorway. Libby sat sprawled across the armchair nearest the window, her mother across from her. Lillie's hat hung down over one eye, and she kept batting at a feather dancing just over her nose. Samantha and Jane were on the floor, Minnie was perched uneasily on the edge of the table, and Maisie was sitting on a footstool, pointing at Libby with a knitting needle.

He smothered a laugh and listened.

"We *heard* ya, girl," Maisie pointed out, "and danged if it didn't sound like ol' Travis knew what he was about."

Libby shook her head violently, spilling her punch. Immediately she reached for more.

Travis glanced at Zeke, saw the older man's grin, and turned back to the women.

"Ah, I 'member my hushban', Mr. Parker?" Minnie sighed heavily. "The thingsh that man knew . . ."

Maisie chortled. "Practiced enough."

"You was jealoush," her sister shot back.

"I should shmile . . . *smile*," Maisie retorted. "My Mr. Hashtingsh . . . Hashti . . . my hushban' din' leave no cause for the jealousies . . . he always was a handy man!"

"But, Cord," Samantha tossed in with a wink and a grin, "is better than all of yer mens put together." She wagged her empty glass at Maisie. "He jus' touches me, and I go all buttery inside."

Jane shook her head slowly. "I know jus' wha'choo mean." She hiccuped. "'Scuse me. Alex is so pretty to look at, he jus' steals my breath away."

"Father?" Samantha looked at her stepmother, amazed.

"Uh-huh."

"James, though," Lillie shouted, "give me seven chilren, chilrens . . . *kids*, and that ain't even countin' all the times we jus' did it to do it 'cause it fel' so durn good!"

"Mother!" Libby cried and leaned toward her. "You like it, too?"

"Course I do." Lillie pushed her hat out of her eyes and squinted at her daughter. "*Ever'body* likes it! Right, ladies?"

The others nodded vigorously.

"Hell, yes," Maisie said on a laugh. "Why you think I keep on feedin' that Zeke?"

Travis glanced at the barber and saw him pale.

"'Cause I reckon that ol' coot's got somethin' special in there, waitin' to get out, tha's why."

Minnie sighed. "Mr. Parker's was special."

"Wha'd he have that other men don't?"

"Oh, Sister, you should have *seen* it!"

Travis swallowed heavily. Maybe, he told himself, it was time to leave.

"Hell," Maisie countered, "sheen one . . . sheen 'em all!"

Lillie laughed hysterically and slipped a notch lower in her chair.

"No, Sister." Minnie stood up, wobbling unsteadily. "Mr. Parker's was the biggesh thin' I ever saw. . . ."

"The only one you ever shaw, Min . . ."

"True, but—"

"No *buts*," Maisie interrupted. Waving that needle again, she declared, "Tha' firs' night with Mr. Hashti . . . Hasteen . . . my hushban' . . ." She shook her head slowly in memory. "Well, I never saw nothin' tha' big since the mule died."

Laughter shot from Lillie's throat, Samantha and Jane leaned against each other helplessly, and Libby threw her head back over the arm of the chair.

Minnie sniffed. "It ain't the shize, Sister. It'sh wha'choo *do* with it."

"Yeah," Maisie countered, "and he knew *that*, too."

Travis glanced at Zeke again. All smiles gone, the man was sweating and tugging at his shirt collar frantically. Travis knew how he felt, but he couldn't make himself leave.

"Well," Libby said thoughtfully, and Travis wished he'd gone, "I been married before, y'know . . . and I got to shay, *say* that Travis is some kind of man. . . ."

"Oh, Lord," he groaned.

"Hah!" Maisie laughed. "Got ya! You said nothin' happened at that hotel!"

"Didn't." Libby grinned and leaned close to the others. "At the jail!"

"The jail!"

"Uh-huh! In a cell."

"On the *floor!*" Lillie added.

"My, my!" Maisie sighed. "Ain't that adventurous."

Travis groaned. Kincaid was right. When women were talkin' and laughin' together, it was downright dangerous for a man.

"And *I* caught 'em!" Lillie laughed.

"You did?" Minnie sounded intrigued.

"Yes, ma'am. Saw Travis Miller wearin' nothin' but a smile!"

A snort of laughter from beside him, and Travis knew that Zeke hadn't missed a word. It would be all over town in minutes. His head dropped to his chest.

But Lillie wasn't through.

"A fine figure of a fella, if I do say so."

"Thank you, Mother," Libby said. "And y'know somethin' else?"

"What, dear?" Lillie pulled the dangling feather from her hat.

"You was right about . . ." Libby screwed up her eyes in thought. "*Robert!* That's him! You was . . . were . . . was *right* about him. He wasn't no good, Mama. I shun't have married him."

"Well"—Lillie gave a satisfied sigh—"live

and learn, dearheart. But y'know, I think Travis'll do fine in a few years after you train 'im proper."

"Think so?"

"I do."

"She's right there," Maisie tossed in. "It's all in the trainin'."

Training? What kind of training?

"F'only there wasn't no . . . *saloon*," Libby said softly.

"Don'choo worry 'bout that, hon," Minnie spoke up. "Travish ain't no drinker."

"Hope not." Libby sighed and drained her cup. "But how do I know for sure?"

"Jus' got to take a chance, Liberty." Lillie raised her glass toward her daughter. "I'm thinkin' it'll be all right thish time. . . ."

She was still worried, he told himself. All because of that no-account dead husband of hers. Suddenly he thought of just how to convince her that everything would be fine.

First thing tomorrow, when she was feelin' as bad as poor ol' Robert ever had, would be the perfect time.

Then Travis watched his bride-to-be smile at her mother.

"I love you, Mama."

"I love you, too, sweetheart."

He smiled and followed Zeke out the back door. He'd heard more than enough already.

Chapter Twenty

"MORNING!" TRAVIS SHOUTED AS HE jumped down the last two stairs and stomped down the hall to the kitchen.

"Oooh," Minnie moaned and hung her head over a cup of tea.

"Good gravy, boy!" Maisie shouted, then winced. "Do ya have to sound like a herd of buffalo?"

Travis grinned, ducked his head slightly to hide it, and turned to get himself a cup of coffee. When he was seated at the long table opposite his landladies, he asked, "And how are you two this fine morning?"

Maisie opened one eye and glared at him.

"Not feeling well?"

"Ooooh," Minnie moaned again.

"That's odd. You were both feeling so fit yesterday!"

"Go away, boy," Maisie snarled and propped her forehead on one hand. "Find someone else to bother."

"Yes, ma'am." He swallowed his coffee in a long gulp, then turned for the back door. "Think I'll go callin' on my almost wife. See how *she's* feelin'."

When the door slammed after him, he heard Maisie say, "Do it quiet."

At the hotel Kincaid was ushering Amanda outside to play. "Not right near the hotel, honey. Mama's not feeling very well today."

"Yes, Papa," the girl answered and shot out the front door followed by her puppy.

"Faith under the weather?"

"Oh. Hello, Travis." Kincaid straightened up and glanced at the top of the stairs before saying, "Yes, she is. Came on her real suddenly this morning. I was just thinking about going for the doctor."

"Uh-huh." Travis kept his mouth shut. It wasn't his business to tell the man that his wife had a hangover. "Have you seen Libby today?"

"Now that you mention it, no, I haven't. Guess she and Mary are still upstairs."

"Thanks." He took the steps two at a time, crossed the landing, and pounded on Libby's door. In seconds it flew open.

"Travis!" Mary's eyes were wide with concern. "I'm so glad you're here. Libby's terrible sick. I'm going home to get Mama. Will you stay here with her for a while?"

"Sure. Be happy to." He patted the younger woman on the shoulder. She'd find out soon enough that Lillie, too, was suffering from the same mysterious illness. "You go on and see your mother now."

He closed the door after her and looked at the bed. Libby lay completely dressed, in the gown she'd worn the day before, across the middle of the bed. Her fingers were curled into the coverlet as if hanging on for fear of falling off. Even from across the room, Travis saw the pallor of her cheeks and the slightly green tinge around her lips.

Well, he told himself, whatever he'd felt about being the part of such a *discussion* the day before, Libby was surely suffering more than he was!

"Morning, Lib," he said and walked to her side.

"Oh, Travis," she whispered miserably.

He plopped down onto the mattress and ignored her groan. "What's wrong, darlin'?"

"Travis . . ." Her hand moved slightly to cover his. She patted him quickly, then curled her fingers back into the bedspread. "I'm sorry . . . I can't marry you."

"*What?*" It figured that Libby would be able to surprise him just when he'd finally found the way to straighten things out.

"Don't shout," she breathed heavily. "Please."

"Sorry." But he wasn't. "What do you mean you can't marry me?"

She winced, swallowed, and bit her lips before saying softly, "I'm dying."

Travis laughed. A loud, booming laughter that shook the room and had Libby groaning for quiet.

"Travis . . . oh, Lord . . ."

"You're not dyin', Lib."

"Yes, I am." She pried one eye open to glare at him malevolently. "Don't tell me how sick I am."

He swallowed his smile. "Your head pounding?"

"Mmmm . . . like a hammer on Jake's anvil."

"Stomach rollin'?"

"Ooooh . . ."

"The room seem to be spinnin' some?"

"Can't open my eyes to check."

Travis shook his head. "Maybe some food would help," he offered, quirking his lips slightly. "How 'bout I go fry you up some bacon and eggs?"

"Ooooh . . ."

"Or maybe some biscuits and red-eye gravy made out of ham drippings?"

She swallowed and her lips turned a shade greener.

"I know just the thing!"

"Travis, please . . ."

"Maisie's got these pickled eggs at home and—"

She lurched off the bed, out the door, and down the hall to the water closet. Travis was right behind her. He held her head and whispered meaningless phrases until the worst of it had passed, and then he carried her back to bed.

He should be ashamed of himself, he knew. But, dammit, she deserved a *little* of her own back. . . . Imagine, telling all those females about their private time together!

Once he had her stretched out across the bed again, he went for a cloth, dipped it into the cool water in the washbowl, and began to wipe her face slowly.

"Travis, I don't know what's wrong with me," she whined.

He ran the cloth over her forehead, down her cheeks, and along her throat. A soft smile on his face, he said, "If it makes you feel any better,

Maisie, Minnie, and Faith are all feelin' poorly this morning, too."

"Oh, no," she breathed, "maybe it's an epidemic. You'd better go before you catch it, Travis."

"I'm safe, Lib." The chuckle in his throat died as he realized that even feeling as badly as she did, she was trying to protect him.

"You don't know that for sure."

"Yeah. I do."

Her eyes opened, and she looked at him through a haze of misery. "Do you know what's wrong with me, then?"

"Uh-huh." He leaned down and kissed her forehead. Straightening back up, he asked quietly, "Do you remember what Robert used to be like on the mornings after he'd been in a saloon all night?"

Libby's brows drew together, and she frowned thoughtfully. "You mean . . ."

"That's right, Libby. You and your friends have got hangovers."

"Hangovers?"

"Uh-huh. A bad case of the morning-afters."

"Oh, my, and to think of all the nasty things I used to do to poor Robert," she said, "making noise and such. And he was suffering so dreadfully."

"Maybe next time you won't be so thirsty around peach brandy."

"How did you . . . ?" She looked at him, suddenly horrified. "Were you . . . but how could you have . . . oh, God."

"Yeah, I heard. Most of it, at least." Travis bent down over her and kissed her lips gently. "I'm pleased to know you thought so highly of me, Lib."

"Oh, great heavens!" She sighed and tried to turn from him. But he pulled her back and held her steady.

"So, you're still a little worried about me and that saloon, huh?"

She looked at him from the corner of her eye. "Well, Travis. It's only that—"

"Oh, I know." He patted her hand companionably. "I finally know just what you mean."

"What?"

"Your worries over being married to a drinker."

"But—"

"No, Lib. I can see where that would concern you." He looked her up and down carefully. Waving one hand over her rumpled, stained clothing, he added, "I surely don't care to be married to a secret drinker myself."

"I'm not!"

"I'd like to point out here, Lib, that it's *you* has the hangover. Not me."

"Oh, dear."

"Like I was sayin'." Travis scooted back on the mattress until his back was up against the bedpost. Lifting his legs to the bed top, he crossed his feet at the ankles and went on. "A secret drinker would be a real worrisome thing to a man in my position, Libby. After all, a sheriff's got to watch himself."

She struggled to sit up, then surrendered to the spinning room and lay flat on her back again. "I will *never* drink again."

"Now," Travis said softly, "I'd like to believe ya, Libby. I surely would."

"You'd *like* to?"

"Well, course. But how can I be sure?" He was enjoying this. For the first time since she'd come home, Travis felt as though he had the upper hand.

"I've given you my word!"

"And that should be enough, I admit." He paused another moment or two, then said, "But as long as there's a saloon in town, how will I know that you can control yourself?"

"Travis . . ."

"Now, Lib, hear me out." He glanced down at her and saw her still-cloudy eyes watching him. "How am I to know that you wouldn't be sneakin' into that saloon every time I'm not watchin' you close?"

"That's not funny, Travis."

"It surely isn't, Libby. Imagine me and Bobby, tryin' to take care of a drunk." He shook his head and sighed. "No, it makes a man think, all right. Why, I don't know if I'd ever be able to trust you around a bottle of whiskey . . . or brandy"— she moaned—"again."

"All right, Travis," she said through gritted teeth. "I admit it. You were right. About the saloon. About Robert. About everything."

He grinned.

"Are you happy now? You won."

"Nah, Libby." He leaned down, scooped her up in his arms, and cradled her close against his chest. "We *both* won."

"Now will you let me die in peace?"

A chuckle rumbled through his chest, but

when she groaned, he choked it off immediately.
"You ain't gonna die, Lib. Leastwise, not till we
get married Saturday next."

She snuggled in close. "Travis?"

"Yes, darlin'?"

"I love you."

"I love you, too."

Everyone for miles around came to the wedding.

Bobby wore Travis's hat and his deputy badge
proudly to stand in front of the church as his new
father's best man. The citizens of Harmony
crowded into the church, waiting for the bride to
make her entrance on James's arm.

Outside, Libby checked her dress one last
time. Jane Evans had outdone herself this time.
Ivory lace touched Libby's throat and lay lightly
over a pale peach silk gown. Gathered tightly
around the waist, the fabric pooled around her
feet and swept the ground behind her in an
elegant train.

A pleased sigh escaped her as Libby realized
that she was ready. More than ready to become
Mrs. Travis Miller. Though she never would have
believed it only a few weeks ago, she loved
Harmony's sheriff more than life itself.

From inside, the strains of organ music drifted
out to them on the summer breeze. It was time.

She glanced toward her mother as the woman
started for the church door. Quickly Libby left
her father's side for a moment and went to the
other woman. It had taken growing up, getting
married, and becoming a mother herself to real-

ize just how much her own mother had given to her over the years.

And now, through all the fights and arguments they'd had, one truth came shining through. Taking Lillie's hands in hers, she said softly, "I love you, Mama. Thank you for everything."

Lillie's eyes welled up. She pulled her hands free and straightened her daughter's flower-studded hat. Her fingers gently trailing down Libby's cheeks, Lillie smiled. "I love you, too, honey. This time, be happy."

Still sniffing, the older woman climbed the steps to the church and disappeared inside.

Taking her father's arm, Liberty Taylor Wilder walked to meet her future.

"I now pronounce you man and wife." The preacher leaned in close and winked at Travis. "You can kiss your bride now, Sheriff."

"Yes, sir."

Turning to his wife, Travis pulled her close and smiled down at her.

Libby stared up at him and saw the answer to every question she'd ever had, shining in his eyes. As his head bent low, she raised up to meet him, anxious. Eager.

Travis's lips touched hers, and Libby leaned into him. Her arms wrapped themselves around his neck, and she felt his grip on her tighten.

Then a little hand began to pat them both in turn. They broke apart and looked down to see Bobby staring up at them.

"Is that 'nough kissin' now, Papa? I want some cake!"

Travis grinned, bent down, and lifted the boy

to eye level. He wrapped his free arm around Libby, and the three of them left the church to the sounds of laughter and applause.

And Libby knew she'd finally come home.

Come take a walk down Harmony's Main Street in 1874, and meet a different resident of this colorful Kansas town each month.

A TOWN CALLED
✤HARMONY✤

__**KEEPING FAITH**   0-7865-0016-6/$4.99
    by Kathleen Kane

__**TAKING CHANCES**   0-7865-0022-2/$4.99
    by Rebecca Hagan Lee

__**CHASING RAINBOWS** 0-7865-0041-7/$4.99
    by Linda Shertzer

__**PASSING FANCY**   0-7865-0046-8/$4.99
    by Lydia Browne

__**PLAYING CUPID**   0-7865-0056-5/$4.99
    by Donna Fletcher

__**COMING HOME**   0-7865-0060-3/$4.99
    by Kathleen Kane

__**GETTING HITCHED** 0-7865-0067-0/$4.99
    by Ann Justice (Coming in January)